We all saw the video of the Chicago cop who shot the kid sixteen time while his colleagues stood and watched. What would happen if Detectives Paul Turner and Buck Fenwick in a similar scenario showed up ten seconds before the firing started. In Mark Zubro's twelfth book in his Paul Turner, gay police detective series, they'd do the right thing and put a stop to it. But that would only be the beginning of the intrigue, danger, and death that surrounds them in a ring of silence as they try to solve a mystery and do the right thing for themselves, their families, their colleagues, the community, and the rule of law.

Ring of Silence

A Paul Turner Mystery

Mark Zubro

Published by
MLR Press, LLC
3052 Gaines Waterport Rd.
Albion, NY 14411

Visit ManLoveRomance Press, LLC on the Internet:
www.mlrpress.com

Cover Art by Melody Pond
Editing by Neil Plakcy

Print format: ISBN# 978-1-64122-015-6
eBook format available

Issued 2017

Trademarks Acknowledgment

The author acknowledges the trademark status and trademark owners of the following wordmarks mentioned in this work of fiction:

Animal Planet: Discovery Communications, LLC
Chicago Bulls: Chicago Professional Sports Limited Partnership
Chicago Tribune: Tribune Media Company
Chicago White Sox: Chicago White Sox, Ltd.
Facebook: Facebook
Google: Google Inc.
Hyatt: Hyatt Corporation
Instagram: Instagram, Inc.
Kool-Aid: Kraft Foods Company
LinkedIn: LinkedIn Corporation
NRA: National Rifle Association of America
Pinterest: Pinterest
Snapchat: Snap Inc.
Sun Times: Sun-Times Media Group
Taser: Taser International, Inc.
Twitter: Twitter, Inc.
YouTube: YouTube

For Barb and Jeanne. That old gang of mine. Thanks.

Thursday 3:15 P.M.

"This goddamn Taser isn't working." Fenwick shook it, then banged it against the brick wall they were walking next to. He glared at the electronic device. "God damn technology bullshit." He shook it again, pressed the on button. Nothing.

"Let me see it," Paul Turner said to his partner. He was aware that Buck Fenwick's technique of smashing at electronics seldom had the effect his partner desired.

Fenwick and anything more technical than a manual typewriter had an iffy relationship at the best of times. Once, he ran over a recalcitrant phone with the tires of his car. Six times. Fenwick most often thought violence to an inanimate object would cause it to behave in ways he thought efficacious. Turner seldom intervened when Fenwick was at war with electronics. Today, he thought he'd give it a try.

Fenwick handed him the Taser.

They were at the beginning of a 3 p.m. to 11 p.m. shift on a hot June afternoon. They'd gotten a call of pursuit in progress. They'd been on foot only about a block or so away near the corner of Harrison and Canal. They chose to hurry over instead of trying to dash back to their car, parked a block in the other direction.

They hustled forward. Outright running was precluded by Fenwick's hefty bulk. They could hear sirens ahead of them and to their left. The wind of a predicted line of thunderstorms gusted in their faces.

They rounded the corner of the building.

Twenty feet in front of them, Turner saw Detective Randy Carruthers, feet spread wide, gun held in both hands, pointing it directly at them.

Carruthers had recently betrayed Turner and Fenwick by providing information on a murder case to the Catholic Church. Turner had been waiting for the perfect moment to confront the squad's most inept detective and now notorious traitor. Carruthers had been on vacation for a week after the events in question. It had only been a few hours since he'd been back on the job.

Between Carruthers and them was a young African-American male who was standing still, facing Turner and Fenwick. Maybe seven feet from them.

Carruthers screamed, "Halt, mother fucker."

In the seconds Turner had been on the scene, the kid hadn't moved. His hands were up. The wind carried the boy's screams of, "Don't shoot. Don't kill me."

Carruthers's bellows mingled with the kid's. Like an LP album stuck in a 'stupid' groove, Carruthers kept repeating, "Stop, motherfucker!"

In between screams for his life, the kid began to blubber and cry, then started to choke.

Turner saw Carruthers's gun wobble then swing wildly. For a second or so, the man's body gave a mighty twitch, but then he renewed his stance and gripped the gun more firmly.

The kid's body began to convulse from his own choking while trying to hold himself rigidly still so as not to be shot.

In the few seconds that passed, Turner wondered where Harold Rodriguez was. He was Carruthers's long-suffering partner.

Carruthers started firing.

Instead of standing around like police officers in other situations when a moronic and incompetent cop was firing pointlessly and murderously, Turner and Fenwick acted. They were not about to do an imitation of inert morons while someone committed murder. Not while they could do something about it. Pope or president, gang banger or fool, it did not matter who was firing. They had to be stopped.

Fenwick rushed to the kid and tackled him, attempting to get him out of range of the wildly firing Carruthers. On his knees, Fenwick tried to yank the kid behind the nearest vehicle. In his mad haste to get the kid out of the line of fire, he managed to bang the kid's head against the fender of a car. With his last shove, he yanked so hard that part of the kid's shirt ripped. Fenwick lost his grip, and the detective's momentum caused his own head to bash into the car's headlight, shattering it.

Simultaneous to Fenwick's actions, Turner aimed the Taser at Carruthers and jammed at the on button. The thing functioned and the wires flew straight for the idiot detective. The thin, electrified cables caught him on his left shoulder.

The dumb son of a bitch fell to his knees but kept firing. His gun swayed in great arcs up and down and side to side, which meant even more people could be at risk.

Turner heard Fenwick grunt and begin cursing.

Then Turner saw Harold Rodriguez running up from the far end of an unmarked police car about thirty feet away. Rodriguez tackled Carruthers, whose gun skittered away.

Turner noted that Rodriguez had Carruthers face down and was handcuffing the dumb shit's hands behind his back.

Turner made sure no one was near the cop's gun which was eight feet from his left foot.

Then he dropped the Taser and rushed to his partner.

Thursday 3:18 P.M.

In seconds, he crossed the few feet to Fenwick and the kid who was half under Fenwick.

The kid was crying, blubbering, and repeating. "I didn't do anything. Don't kill me. I didn't do anything. Don't kill me."

Fenwick was holding his own left bicep with his right hand. He raged his unhappiness. "Dumb, mother-fucking son of a bitch. If he's not dead, I'm going to kill him."

Turner saw red dampness spreading on the cloth of Fenwick's shirt and dripping down to the pavement.

Fenwick applied pressure to the spot the blood oozed from. Turner could see no visible wounds on the kid. He got out his phone, called in, identified himself, and then said, "Shots fired. Officer down. Ambulance needed Harrison and Des Plaines Avenue."

He knelt next to the kid and Fenwick. He placed a gentle hand on the boy's shoulder. Up close, he thought the kid might be all of fourteen, short and scrawny. Several times Turner repeated "You're safe now." Until he saw the kid's eyes stop fluttering back and forth. Turner asked, "Have you been shot? Hurt?"

The kid caught his eyes. His panicky wailing and weeping became reduced to moans and hiccups. Perhaps it was Turner's words or his calm demeanor that eased the kid's fear.

The boy whispered, "No. I think I'm okay." He grunted and tried to wriggle out from under Fenwick. "Except this guy is kind of huge." He gave up attempting to squirm from under the heavy-set cop and gave an abrupt shove to the part of Fenwick's bulk that was holding the left side of his own body flush against the pavement.

Fenwick bellowed. Turner was reminded of a water buffalo in pain. The kid's movement had caused Fenwick's wounded arm to mush against the pavement.

Turner said to the boy, "Hang on for a second. My partner's been shot. He probably saved your life."

Fenwick ceased roaring. Turner saw that his partner was trying to ease off his own shirt to examine his wound.

Turner shifted so he was closer to his friend. Their eyes met. Fenwick asked, "Is Carruthers dead yet?"

Turner looked over. Rodriguez and his prone partner were being surrounded by cops. Others were rushing towards them, guns still out. As Turner watched, he saw Carruthers struggle against his bonds.

Rodriguez yanked on the cuffs and said, "Move again, dumb shit, and I'll shoot you myself." Rodriguez looked up at the assembling beat cops and said, "Make a god damn perimeter around the scene." He pointed to Mike Sanchez and Alex Deveneaux, beat cops they'd all worked with many times. "Make sure no one touches any of the dash cams on any of the cars. Get as many guys to help you as you need. Anybody touches a dash cam, shoot them."

Sanchez and Deveneaux hustled away to comply. Others began ushering the crowd away. Turner heard one man in the crowd whose voiced carried to him. "That cop saved that boy. He's a hero. So is his partner. I've got it all." The guy held up his cell phone in one hand while pointing at the prone threesome with the other. Turner saw a forest of cell phones aimed at the scene from, it seemed, everyone nearby.

He turned back to the kid. He asked, "What's your name?"

"DeShawn." He put his hands on either side of his head and said, "And my head kind of hurts." In another few seconds, he was puking softly. Turner cradled his head. He saw shards of headlight where Fenwick must have hit and a dent in the fender lower down where the kid's head must have banged into the car. Turner couldn't remember the sequence of how soon after a head wound one was likely to puke, and if said vomiting was a sure sign of concussion. What he knew for sure was that it wasn't a good sign.

Thursday 4:27 P.M.

Fenwick grumbled. "The next person who says 'fucking hero' to me is going to get shot."

Turner said, "They don't say 'fucking' hero. They just call you a plain old hero."

"Either one is going to die." Fenwick shifted his arm and grimaced. "It's bullshit. I was diving out of the way to save my ass. The kid came as kind of a bonus."

Turner said, "I don't care what they label any of us. None of us died, for which I am grateful."

Turner and Fenwick were in a bay in the emergency room of City Center Hospital in Chicago. Fenwick was sitting in his T-shirt. He had a small bandage on his head where he bashed into the headlight. He had been seen to by a young intern who, after examining him, said Fenwick didn't have a concussion. The intern had cleaned the head wound and placed a small bandage on it. He also said that Fenwick's arm wound, although it had bled a lot, needed just a few stitches and was little more than a scratch.

Fenwick had said to him, "I knew that."

The intern left to get antibiotics to prevent an infection.

When he was gone, Fenwick went into full grumble. "You got to Tase Carruthers. That is so not fair."

"You saved a guy."

Fenwick shifted his weight on the examination table. It groaned in disapproval. Fenwick said, "If somebody tries to hand me a fucking medal, I'll..."

The intern bustled back in, needle and syringe in hand. He said, "This won't hurt a bit," and jabbed it into Fenwick's unwounded arm.

"No needles." Fenwick gasped, swatting a big paw toward the injection, but it was far too late. Even those two words sounded weak to Turner. In seconds, Fenwick's face turned stark white, his eyelids fluttered. He began to topple off the examination table.

Turner, already next to him, caught his partner's bulk and eased him onto his back.

The intern looked from the syringe to Fenwick and back to the syringe. "It's just antibiotics."

Turner said, "Maybe he's allergic."

The intern shook his head. "I called up his chart from the records on the computer. It says he's not allergic to anything."

Turner said, "Maybe he's afraid of needles. You didn't think to ask?"

The intern gulped. "I guess I figured he was so big, and he kept talking tough, that it wouldn't be a problem. I'm so sorry."

Fenwick pulled in several short, raspy breaths, opened his eyes, and with Turner and the intern's help, struggled back to a sitting position. "What?"

The intern blubbered apologies.

Fenwick's voice rumbled. "Go away." The intern did. Fenwick looked at Turner. "You're not going to let me forget this."

Turner said, "I shall wait a dignified amount of time and then, if it becomes appropriate, I may feel a need to mention your odd aversion to needles and injections. The problem is, you have such a host of oddities, this one isn't all that outstanding."

Commander Drew Molton strolled in. "Where's the fucking hero?"

Fenwick asked, "You heard me?"

Molton said, "I know you."

Turner knew that Molton was one of the few people Fenwick would tolerate such bold humor from. And really, did he have a choice? Molton was their boss and as far as they were concerned, the best Area Commander in the city. In the past, just being part of the Chicago Police department's top brass had not saved many a fool from Fenwick's acerbic wrath.

The other person who Fenwick tolerated such humor from was his wife Madge. Much as he liked his partner and as well as he knew him, Turner didn't take a lot of risks in trying to get away with such humor.

As Fenwick often put it, "I'm the humor guy in this relationship."

The last time he said it, Turner had replied, "Would that it were so."

Fenwick had smiled.

Right now, Fenwick stopped grousing.

"You guys okay?" Molton asked.

Fenwick said, "Flesh wounds. Nothing."

Turner said, "I'm fine. How's the kid?"

Molton consulted his phone. "The kid you saved is DeShawn Jackson. Report is he's a trifle squashed from being underneath a bulky cop. They're a little worried about his head wound." He glanced at Fenwick's bandaged head. "Seems it's touch and go on which of you bashed harder into the car. He may have a concussion. They're going to keep him for observation. There were several bullet holes next to the headlight. You were lucky."

Molton moved the curtain around them and said to the beat cop standing guard, "Would you drag a chair over for me, please?"

In less than a minute, the beat cop pulled a chair into the bay and Molton sat down. He got himself comfortable and said, "I know you've given a statement to Wilson and Roosevelt. I'd like to hear what happened directly from you."

Judy Wilson and Joe Roosevelt were two other detectives on their squad. They'd taken initial reports. First from Turner and Fenwick separately and then with them together.

Molton made no comments as they spoke. When they finished, he said, "You realize you're involved in the biggest thing so far this year."

Fenwick asked, "Compared to what?"

Molton ignored him. "Unlike other cops who stood by while one of their own gunned down an innocent kid, you saved his life."

"That doesn't make us special," Fenwick said,

Molton raised an eyebrow. "You cannot possibly be that naïve."

Fenwick said, "I guess I knew that."

Molton said, "Need I remind you that in no video from any dash cam I know of anywhere on the planet, or any video from a member of the public, not one has shown a cop, much less two cops saving a kid from one of their own. Even as we speak, your moments of fame are amassing hits on the Internet."

"Hooray for us?" Fenwick turned the statement into a question.

At the moment, Turner was a little tired of Fenwick's complaints and protests. He wanted to find out details of what the hell was going on. He knew they could be in a precarious position. While Carruthers was universally regarded as an idiot of the first order, nonetheless, Turner knew far too many cops would rush to his defense, and concomitantly look askance at the other detectives involved in taking him down. He also wondered about Rodriguez, who was their friend. Handcuffing your partner could be a big deal.

The newspapers and television reporters in town often reported on the Chicago Police Department Code of Silence. Turner wondered now, whose side would the code come down on? Fenwick, Rodriguez, and him? Or Carruthers? Or would it be a combination which Turner thought would complicate their lives the most.

Turner asked, "What the hell was Carruthers thinking?"

Fenwick asked, "He thinks?"

Turner corrected, "What was he doing or trying to do?"

Molton said, "He and his union rep will sort out who he's going to talk to. Certainly not me." He shifted himself in his chair, "The key is every video that has emerged shows Carruthers had no reason to begin firing. The kid was unarmed. What you guys and Rodriguez did was justified and right. Plus, Buck, you were wounded in the line of duty, so I think you'll be in the clear with your colleagues and with the brass."

"Where's Rodriguez?" Turner asked. "Is he okay?"

"Safe."

Turner said, "I thought he was going to pound Carruthers's head into the ground."

Molton said, "Only after he found out that Fenwick had been wounded."

Turner asked, "What happens next?"

"Independent Police Review Authority will be around, along with a few other investigative agencies. The usual."

Turner expected that. The Review Authority was the new version of the old Internal Affairs department, which itself had not been totally disbanded. Rumor had the renamed and revamped group as incompetent as the earlier iteration.

Molton continued, "There'll be less time spent with them since you guys didn't fire any shots."

Fenwick asked, "Is Carruthers going to get fired?"

Molton said, "Yes."

Fenwick raised an eyebrow. "It's that simple?"

Molton said, "It will be. It better be. The local media, the Internet, hell, half the planet has seen what happened from numerous angles." He stood up. "You guys are stuck. Heroes now and forever." He pointed at Fenwick. "You sure you don't want to go home?"

Fenwick shook his head. "Not unless the doctor says I have to." He nodded toward Turner. "I'm not going to let him take all the heat."

"Or get more interviews than you?"

Fenwick said, "No fucking interviews."

A female voice from the other side of the curtain said, "How about regular interviews?"

The curtain opened. Madge Fenwick swept in. Turner's husband, Ben Vargas, followed in her wake.

Madge strode to her husband, pecked him on the cheek, and asked, "Are you okay?"

"Just a flesh wound and a bump on the head."

Madge eyed both bandaged areas. "You just have so much flesh to wound."

Madge was one of Turner's favorite people. She had long since been able to demolish the fortress of Fenwick's gruffness.

Fenwick asked, "Are you saying that's a good thing or a bad thing?"

Madge said, "Kinda depends."

Ben and Paul hugged. Still in their clinch, his husband asked, "You okay?"

"Yeah." Ben still had on his work clothes from the car repair shop he owned. He hadn't taken time to change. They smelled of grease, and sweat, and Ben. Paul breathed deeply and held on for a few extra seconds. The smell brought a flash of good memories, good feelings. They were a relief after the mad rush of danger.

When they parted Ben said, "I stopped at home. The boys are glued to the Internet and television. Everybody knew something happened. From the part of the video I saw, it seemed it was all over in seconds."

Paul nodded. "Just kind of a whirl."

When they were on their way to the hospital, Turner had called to let them know he was all right. He didn't want them to worry.

Turner said, "We gotta go back to the station and write all this up. Our shift isn't even half over."

Madge asked, "Are you sure you're okay to stay?"

Fenwick grumbled, "Yeah."

Final bandaging done, a prescription for pain pills obtained, hugs given to spouses, and they were on their way.

In the car, Fenwick said, "You could have inserted a fat-guy-needle comment back there."

"No need. More appropriate coming from you. And with luck, there will come a perfect time."

"We needed something to break the seriousness. I'll work on it."

But Paul sensed that at the moment, Fenwick wasn't in the mood for finding something humorous, a sure sign his partner was more upset than he was letting on. He himself wasn't in much of a mood for such, either.

Thursday 5:37 P.M.

It was still hours before sunset on the June late afternoon when they got back to Area Ten headquarters. The breeze bringing humidity and storms from the Gulf of Mexico had continued to rise.

Area Ten's boundaries were Belmont Avenue on the north and Ashland Avenue on the west, and all along the lakefront south to Fifty-Ninth Street. The building itself was south of the River City complex on Wells Street on the southwest rim of Chicago's Loop.

The structure was as old and crumbling as River City was new and gleaming. Years ago, the department purchased a four-story warehouse scheduled for demolition and decreed it would be a new headquarters. To this day, rehabbers put in appearances in fits and starts. The building had changed from an empty hulking wreck to a people-filled hulking wreck. None of the so-called improvements, departmental or structural, had caused crime to increase or decrease. In all that time, the number of new personnel hired to fight crime hadn't increased.

In the Chicago police department, the Areas still took care of homicides and other violent crimes. The Districts took care of all the minor incidents and gave out traffic tickets. There hadn't been Precincts in Chicago since O.W. Wilson was in charge of the department in the 1960s.

Barb Dams, Commander Molton's secretary as well as being a friend, caught Turner and Fenwick as they were on the stairs on their way up to their desks on the second floor. "You guys okay?"

"Yeah," they both murmured.

Dams's eyes twinkled, "What I do not understand is why neither of you simply pulled out a gun and shot Carruthers. Seems that would have been the simplest thing."

Fenwick said, "More paperwork if we'd shot the bastard."

Dams nodded. "Kind of makes sense. Commander needs to see you."

"Now?" Fenwick asked.

"Or sooner. You can both go, but I think he only wants Paul."

Turner asked, "What's up?"

"He'll tell you." Even if she knew what it was about, he knew she'd keep her boss's secrets.

They trooped into Molton's office.

"You guys okay?" he asked.

More mumbled, "Yeahs."

Molton shook his head. "Home for you both would probably be good." He sighed, "But we've got to get all the paperwork done on this now. It's got to be written up while it's fresh."

Nods from both detectives.

Molton added, "Carruthers is being held in an interrogation room here."

"Why not headquarters?" Fenwick asked.

"This whole thing will be done carefully, and it will be done right. Every god damn "t" will be crossed and "i" dotted. I can finally get him out of my command and off this department. No clout in this city is powerful enough to save him now. You guys will be in the clear, although there might be some diehards who think you should be loyal to Carruthers."

Fenwick slammed a ham-handed fist down on Molton's desk. He blurted out, "The dumb fuck was shooting at us."

Molton let Fenwick calm down for a few moments then said, "You know how it is."

Turner and Fenwick nodded. They knew.

Molton sighed then pointed at Turner. "The new, strangest thing from the last ten minutes is Carruthers wants to talk to you."

"What for?" Turner asked.

"He wouldn't say."

"Is that wise?" Turner asked. "Hasn't he been advised to keep silent?"

"Yep."

"Will it be recorded?" Turner asked.

"Do you want it to be?"

Turner thought for a second. "Whatever you work out with Carruthers, and whatever you think is right, is fine with me. Do you think I should talk to him?"

"Whatever you do is okay with me. I think we're going to forgo recording or having witnesses for this one."

Turner nodded. "Let's get this over with."

Thursday 5:52 P.M.

Carruthers sat with his shoulders hunched and his head bowed. He was no longer handcuffed. He looked up when Turner entered the gray, cinderblock, featureless room. It was one of the rare spots in the building in which the air-conditioning worked. Turner had been told the oddity occurred at this point because of a fortuitous confluence of pipe from some inept new rehabbing being incorrectly placed near a century old conduit. Instead of making the temperature comfortable and pleasant, it made the room cold and clammy.

Carruthers gave him a tentative smile then stopped when he saw the neutral expression on Turner's face.

Carruthers said, "Thanks for agreeing to see me."

Turner said, "You shouldn't be talking to me. You should keep silent. Your union rep should be here at the least."

"I know you'll be fair. You'll listen. Probably the only one who would."

Turner sat across from him on a cold, metallic chair. "What can I do for you?" he asked.

Carruthers launched into a tirade about kids today having no morals, and rioters and protesters flooding the city, and people hating cops. Turner let him foam, froth, and foment. When white bits of spittle appeared around the corners of his lips, Carruthers wiped at them with a hand encrusted with red, scaly blotches.

Turner had heard avalanches of wild justifications from any number of suspects over the years. Carruthers as detective didn't sound much different.

Carruthers finished with, "It's just like 1968 in this town. Nobody respects the law."

Turner spoke in his softest voice. "Nobody is rioting in the streets. Not the public. Not the police. All the cops in the city so far have been calm. Except for you." He paused for a moment then asked, "Why did you want to see me?"

"You're the one they're going to talk to."

"They have eighty-seven million or so feet of video footage of what happened."

"But you're one of us."

Turner said, "I'm not one of you. I'm nothing like you."

"The kid had a gun."

Turner just gaped at him. Finally he managed to say, "We saw no gun."

"He threw it away."

"If you knew that, you knew he was unarmed, so why did you shoot? He was standing still, with his hands up, and his back to you."

That stopped Carruthers for only a second. "I thought he might have had another gun."

"Which you didn't see, couldn't have seen because it didn't exist." For that matter, Turner doubted if the first gun existed except in Carruthers's fevered brain.

"Traitor," Carruthers snarled.

Turner said, "Traitor? Really?" In another second, he thought he might get up and leave. The fascination of watching the wreck that was Carruthers kept him seated, and Turner himself had a few things he wanted to say to the vile betrayer sitting across from him.

Carruthers said, "We gotta stick together."

Turner drew a deep breath. He wondered if Carruthers was truly that far from connecting with reality. Turner said, "Randy, who was feeding the Catholic Church information about the police investigation on the bishop's murder case?"

"Wasn't me."

Turner spoke in clipped tones. "You will not deny reality to me, not now or ever, you stupid son of a bitch."

"How can you know I gave them information?"

"They talked about you. We heard them."

Carruthers switched tacks. "You've got to help me."

"Why?"

"I already told you, I…"

Turner cut him off. "Why did you think I would? Did you think we wouldn't find out about you betraying us?"

"They'll fire me."

"If you get near Fenwick, he may execute you himself. You shot a cop, you numbnuts-dumbfuck." Turner thought Fenwick's usual description of Carruthers fit perfectly at this moment. He was a little torn about throwing it in the guy's face at a time like this. Calling names wasn't his style, but his fury at the long-time squad joke was deeper than he'd expected. Actually confronting him was drawing forth reserves of anger he hadn't been aware of.

Carruthers was likely to lose his job, career, and maybe even his pension. If for no other reason, Turner thought, post-cop work, Carruthers would be hard to employ because he was a jerk. That was if he didn't go to jail, and civil lawsuits against him, the department, and the city didn't drain his resources.

Turner asked, "Why was betraying us so important to you?"

"I didn't do it."

"We have it on video. They said it was you. They said your name."

"It wasn't me."

Turner asked, "Is the sky blue?"

"Huh?"

"I was wondering if you're connecting with reality." Turner took out his phone. He turned the screen toward Carruthers and played the damning clip.

When it finished, Carruthers didn't look at him. He mumbled, "Someone doctored the tape, edited it to make me look bad."

Turner said, "I feel sorry for you."

The beaten-down detective again had his shoulders slumped, head down. He didn't look up. Turner wondered if the poor guy had a friend in the world. If the man didn't have any, Turner understood why. While he did feel a little sorry for Carruthers, it wasn't enough to move him to help the guy. Even if he wanted to, as far as he could see, there was no help available to Carruthers. Not from himself or anyone. He got up and left the incompetent creep.

Thursday 6:34 P.M.

Turner trudged up the stairs to his desk. Fenwick looked up as he crossed the room. All the windows were open to catch the breeze. Storms could blow up at any moment. They'd have to remember to close the windows before their shift was over or make sure maintenance was paying attention.

They'd invested in fans smaller but more powerful than the ones the department had kept probably since the building was wired for electricity soon after the Great Chicago fire. Those had been on their way to clanking, sputtering death. At least the ones Turner and Fenwick purchased offered real relief. The amount of un-fanned sweat that fountained off Fenwick no longer threatened to cause rivulets of rust to seep through the ceiling to the squad room below.

Their desks abutted each other, front to front.

As Turner sat, Fenwick raised an eyebrow.

Turner shrugged. "He wanted sympathy and help."

"So he's not dead?"

Turner shook his head.

"Pity."

After they'd done paperwork for thirty minutes, Rodriguez stomped into the room. He pulled a chair over to their desks and sat. "You guys okay?" he asked.

Turner and Fenwick nodded.

"How about you?" Turner asked.

Rodriguez had soft brown eyes and a mustache that trailed down to his chin in a modified Van Dyke. It gave him a perennially sad expression. Rodriguez sighed, "I hope I will be. It's already started."

Turner and Fenwick raised eyebrows.

Rodriguez shrugged. "I guess I was supposed to let the dumb fuck shoot you guys, the kid, and half the planet."

"What's happened?" Turner asked.

"I stopped at my car earlier. Both sides have been keyed front to back. Wasn't a member of the public. It's on our parking lot. It was one of us. You guys should be careful as well."

Turner and Fenwick nodded.

Fenwick asked, "What the hell was happening on that street before we got there?"

Rodriguez said, "I was doing mostly nothing. Talking to some twenty-somethings who were on their way to one of the protest conference meetings farther down the street. Carruthers was nuts since I saw him even before the shift started."

"He's always nuts," Fenwick said.

"Nuttier than usual. He came in real early. He had enough new electronic equipment on him to open a store. He was talking on them, checking on them. When we got to that spot on the street, we saw clots of people and beat cops. We stopped to see if we could help. At first, Carruthers stayed in the car. That was good. He's awful with people. Then I heard some kind of noise, altercation, or teenagers being stupid, something. I turned to look. Carruthers was out of the car and talking a mile a minute on some electronic device. Then he was yelling at the group of kids. One of them took off and started running."

"That was DeShawn," Turner said.

Rodriguez nodded. "So there's Carruthers screaming at the kid, running after him, listening to this electronic device, and pulling his gun."

Fenwick said, "I didn't think he could chew gum and walk at the same time."

Turner said, "Maybe he took lessons while he was off."

Rodriguez said, "The kid stopped. That's when you guys came around the building and shit hit the fan from every direction. I don't know how many people Carruthers might have hit if I hadn't tackled him."

After fifteen minutes further rehashing didn't get them any more insight, Rodriguez got up. He said, "I have eight million more people to talk to tonight. I'll see you later."

More promises of having the other's back followed and then Rodriguez slumped away.

Fenwick said, "He's a hero to me."

"Got that right."

A few minutes later, Joe Roosevelt and Judy Wilson appeared at the top of the stairs. They strode over to Turner and Fenwick's work station. They pulled over another chair and plunked it and the one Rodriguez had been sitting on, in front of the fans to try and get some relief. Wilson got back up and grabbed a third fan from nearby to add to the desperate wish for respite.

Roosevelt and Wilson had been detectives since the year one. Joe, red-nosed, with short, brush-cut gray hair and crooked teeth, and Judy, an African-American woman with a pleasant smile, had a well-deserved reputation as one of the most successful pairs of detectives on the force. Despite this, they averaged a major squabble about a senseless issue at least once a week. It usually started with something minor and stupid and ended with them in pouty silence. As soon as they started a new case, they shrugged off the problem. Anyone observing that stage of their relationship would have thought they were best friends, which in fact they were.

Roosevelt asked, "How are you guys?"

Mumbles of, "Fine," and "Okay."

Turner said, "I talked to Carruthers."

Wilson said, "You had another chance to shoot him. Great."

Roosevelt said, "You are way too kind. Do you realize with him dead, the IQ level in the whole country would go up an average of two to three points?"

Turner asked, "Does he know he has no friends, that the world is laughing at him? He has a wife and kids. Does he love them? Do they love him?"

Wilson said, "He is an asshole traitor to the job."

Roosevelt said, "Guy deserves every road bump in his life."

Wilson asked, "Is today's event in the competition for stupidest thing he's done this year?"

"Why wouldn't it be? He's been number one in the stupidest male on the planet competition award for years."

"Lots of fierce rivalry for that these past few years."

Roosevelt cleared his throat. "There is something else."

Wilson said, "This is not an official investigation question, although I was dying to ask earlier."

Roosevelt burst out laughing.

Wilson continued, "Why didn't you just shoot him out there on the street?"

Fenwick said, "Adds too much paperwork."

Turner sat back and for a moment let the almost adequate breeze cool him, then he said, "It happened too fast. I had the Taser in my hand. I didn't choose or decide or think. I just acted. My actual thought process must have been, 'taking out your gun would waste precious seconds, you've got a Taser in your hand, use it.' I wasn't conscious of thinking all that."

Fenwick said, "That too. Except I didn't have the Taser, and I was only a few feet from the kid."

Roosevelt and Wilson nodded. They understood, as all good cops did, that instant decisions they made too often had life and death consequences.

Turner said, "I've been wondering, what if we were five or ten seconds earlier." He hesitated then added, "Or later."

Wilson leaned toward him, tapped her finger on his arm, and said, "Bullshit. All bullshit. Self-doubt is pointless. You did right in the milliseconds you did have. We are trained for those seconds. For those instants of life or death. But we never know where or when they're going to happen. Yes, I know we are all aware of that and even with all the training in the world, who you are and what you are takes over, and what you did was right. Whether you like it or not, you're both heroes because you did right."

Roosevelt added, "Nobody died. You guys are both still with us. And Carruthers won't be."

"How's Rodriguez?" Wilson asked.

"He left a few minutes ago." They told them about their colleague's car being keyed.

"Motherfuckers," Wilson said. "We better be watching each other's backs more than usual."

Everybody nodded.

Roosevelt and Wilson moved to their own desks and lugged out their laptops and began working on paperwork of their own.

After a few minutes, Wilson looked up at Turner and Fenwick. She asked, "You guys seen that Taser?"

Each piece of equipment they used had to be accounted for. Losing something like your badge or your gun was a huge problem. The Taser, while not in the same category as those two, if missing, it would be a problem. It would have a serial number and could be identified.

Turner said, "I must have dropped it at the scene. I remember rushing to Fenwick and the kid, looking at Rodriguez and Carruthers." He shook his head. "I wasn't thinking about the damn thing. I saw Carruthers moving then being restrained so I knew he wasn't hurt from the Taser. Then I was worried about Fenwick and the kid. Sorry."

No one teased him about his concern for his friend. It was all too easy to lose a partner, or a friend, an acquaintance, or a coworker, or a fellow member of the department, for anyone to feel a need to make a joke. Even Fenwick was muted.

Wilson said, "We'll go back over the scene with some uniforms. It probably got kicked under something as people rushed madly about. Or even maybe a member of the crowd took it as a souvenir."

Fenwick nodded toward the stairs. "Commander Molton." Turner looked over his shoulder and saw their approaching boss.

Thursday 7:09 P.M.

Molton arrived and perched on the edge of Turner's desk. He was frowning. Turner sensed something was amiss. Molton said, "We have a bit of a media problem and some community issues and a sort of mundane situation."

The detectives waited.

Molton continued, "The press wants interviews. Every local and national news outlet from coast to coast. They're all calling, including from overseas." He sighed. "And they want you to do a press conference."

"They who?" Fenwick asked.

"The mayor, the police superintendent, the press office, everybody."

"Have they met me?" Fenwick asked. "They want me to do a press conference? I can see the headline, Fenwick Unchained, film at eleven."

Molton said, "The chief should know better, but I know the spokesperson for the department is new." Molton smiled. "They want both of you."

"Paul can."

"No way," Turner said. "Both of us or nobody. Besides, you're the hero. You got shot."

Molton said to Turner. "Don't sell yourself short."

Fenwick snorted. "Do they really have a notion of how I behave?

Of my ability to shoot my mouth off and be an asshole? They really want that on television?"

Turner said, "Maybe they could just do a profile, a side view, so to speak."

"Of all my fat?"

"Getting all your fat into a picture might be a problem," Wilson said.

Fenwick gave another snort. "Tell them I won't appear without every ounce of my heft."

Wilson said, "You could do the interview naked."

"The world is not ready…"

Molton interrupted. "I'll stall them."

Fenwick stirred and began an objection.

Molton held up a hand. "There's more. The community wants to give you medals. You saved a kid instead of letting him get killed. I agree with the medal-giving aspect of this. Downtown has been tight-lipped on that so far, but I think they'll cave."

Fenwick said, "I'm going to do paperwork then take your advice and go home."

Molton shook his head.

Turner's sense that there was another shoe to drop increased. The Commander looked tired. Molton said, "Unfortunately that which is mundane for our jobs has also occurred."

Turner knew when Molton's language turned formal and close to convoluted, he was frustrated.

The Commander said, "We just got a call. There's been murder done." He pointed at Turner and Fenwick. "I know you're not up for the next case, but unfortunately you are."

All the detectives gave him confused looks.

Molton said, "With all the activists in town for the big protests and meetings, everybody has been hyper alert."

Nods. For weeks, the department and the city had been preparing for thousands of activists who had descended for meetings, talks, and a convention.

"One of the leaders of the activists, Henry Bettencourt, is dead."

"Who?" Fenwick asked.

Turner said, "You've heard of him. Guy from the south suburbs who's been leading an anti-gun violence crusade."

Molton nodded. "That's him. I've had a call from downtown. The other leaders of the activists are already putting huge pressure on anybody they can get hold of to have you two take the case. They say they trust you."

"Hold on," Fenwick said. "When did this happen?"

"A little over an hour ago now."

"And that was enough time for activists to get through to downtown, apply pressure, have the pressure succeed, and get back to us?"

Molton said, "As far as I know, it went to the moon and back. I suggested I have many excellent detectives. They mentioned Carruthers name as an example of incompetence among my detectives. I was not about to get in a pissing match with top brass about whose clout it was that saved Carruthers's ass time after time. This is directly from the mayor's office and the superintendent's office. If it will help keep the city calm, and/or the activists mollified, and an excellent job done on the case, it's you guys."

Fenwick said, "So we're being punished for our competence."

Molton said, "A special circle in hell for those who do their jobs."

"And the paperwork on the Carruthers mess?" Fenwick asked.

"Will get done. Give Barb what you've got so far. We'll work it out."

Fenwick said, "We were mostly done."

Many of the forms for the paperwork had been computerized. Fenwick worked from an iPad at his desk. Turner from a PC on his.

Turner asked, "Who has the kind of pull and power to call the mayor and or the police superintendent to get us assigned to this?"

Molton said, "I'm afraid you guys will find out as you investigate. I have no idea. I'll try to sniff around on that as well."

Fenwick asked, "And the corpse has been just lying there?"

"Patiently waiting for you," Molton said. "Crime Scene people are there. Beat cops are keeping it secure for you. There is one other little thing."

A collective raising of eyebrows ensued.

"When I said 'murder done,' I meant two of them. You have a second corpse, Preston Shaitan."

Fenwick, Roosevelt, and Wilson looked mystified.

Turner said, "Fuck."

Fenwick said, "That's my line."

Turner said, "You are referring to the notorious idiot?"

Fenwick said, "Shaitan is a notorious idiot?"

Turner said, "Yep."

Molton ignored them. "The bodies are on the roof of a building on Harrison about a hundred feet west from the intersection with Racine. The bodies on the roof are ten feet apart from each other."

"What were they doing up on the roof?" Fenwick asked.

Molton mused for a second. "Unless you've got a perfect place for a murder, and victims were all coincidentally queuing up to be killed or become corpses at that one spot, who knows? Perhaps the universe contrived it."

"Lot of that going around these days," Fenwick said.

Molton said, "Some of the activists have heard rumors about the murder."

"How?" Fenwick said.

Molton held up his phone and showed the anchor of a local cable news show on CLTV reading about the rumors of deaths.

Turner and Fenwick peered at it for a few seconds and listened. It was mostly rumors but gave the site as the Racine Street bridge over the Eisenhower Expressway.

Fenwick said, "They've got the place wrong."

Molton said, "Yeah, by about a hundred feet. Traffic around there is probably a mess, but if you happen to pass the bridge on your way to the scene, if you think the cops on duty need help, lend a hand. The corpses aren't going anywhere, and we can't have protestors on the bridge starting a riot."

Molton texted them the details and left.

Wilson said, "You do know video of you guys saving the kid has already been posted to YouTube?" She checked her phone. "It's had over a million hits already."

They looked at her phone. The crawl underneath the scene of them saving the kid said, "Cops Save DeShawn."

Turner said to Fenwick, "You're a star."

Roosevelt said, "I'm surprised it's a sensation so soon."

Wilson sneered, "Do you live in the modern age? Do you listen to the news? It happened over four hours ago now. Half the planet has probably seen it, and listened to the broadcast of subsequent rumors."

When the Commander had disappeared down the stairs, and Wilson and Roosevelt were out of hearing, Fenwick said, "Double, triple, and quadruple fuck."

Turner said, "Once again, you've come up with the correct medical term."

Fenwick asked, "Who's Preston Shaitan?"

"A supposedly gay, professional asshole. I'll explain in the car on the way."

Thursday 7:21 P.M.

On their way, Turner noted ominous clouds looming over the city to the west. Violent weather was predicted. Huge gusts of wind shook the car at random intervals.

Unlike the ordinary course of events, Turner was driving. As they left, with his newly bandaged arm in a sling, Fenwick found it awkward to reach, grab, and pick up his laptop case. Turner had raised an eyebrow. Fenwick had said, "Stiffening up a little. You better drive."

As they pulled out of the parking lot, Fenwick said, "I want a new one."

"New one what?"

"Unmarked car. I want the kind with those little blue lights on the sides of the windshield that flicker off and on instead of those stupid rotating Mars lights that we have to pull from under the seat and stick on the roof ourselves."

"I'll order one just for you. Be grateful this one is air-conditioned. It's better than sweating in the not-breezy-enough station." He stopped at the light at Harrison. "Any background on Bettencourt and Preston Shaitan?"

Fenwick Googled on his phone. For years, he'd sworn he was a Luddite, but when he'd seen the ease with which Turner and others were using electronics, especially for forms and paperwork, he'd groused but succumbed. Basic data gathering was also easier. Fenwick liked easy.

A few minutes later, Fenwick read out his results. "Bettencourt is a minister in the south suburbs, with a small congregation in Ford Heights with one of those non-affiliated churches."

Turner knew Ford Heights was one of the poorest south suburbs in the Chicago area.

Fenwick read some more then reported. "He led a coalition of protests groups advocating militant nonviolence." He looked up. "Gandhi strikes again."

"Are you saying that's a good thing or a bad thing?"

Fenwick shrugged. "I think the question is always how do you get things to change? And there isn't just one answer."

"You're more philosophical today because you got shot?"

"If either wound was serious, I suppose I would be. I think it's more likely the weather. When storms are moving in, I reflect more on the whims of the universe. I think I'm one of the universe's larger whims. Change things? I just try to catch bad guys. Some days we have more luck than others."

Turner glanced over at his reflective partner. "Getting shot scared you."

"Yes. I'm alive more because Carruthers is a shit shot. And because of luck. I tried to save a kid and almost got killed. Decisions in an instant." He paused. "Death in a flash. I don't like thinking about how pure random chance is so much part of our lives."

"Sort of what Wilson and Roosevelt said."

"We had a rush of action. Now we've got a rush of investigation. I don't think it's going to be in our next union contract that we get random moments for possible reflection."

They were stopped at an intersection. Turner said, "You want to stop and talk about it?"

Fenwick shook his head. "Talking won't change the rush of adrenalin, the dangers of the world, or the random chance of the universe. We've got work to do. I can immerse myself in reflection later. Or write a poem about it. I didn't really want to talk about it with Wilson and Roosevelt. You I don't mind." Fenwick paused. "You're not upset by all this?"

Turner said, "I'll deal with my emotions when I have time. In bed tonight with Ben, we'll talk, and any residual fear will bubble to the surface. I can let myself be frightened then, and he'll soothe me. Right now, we've got a job. Molton trusted us to handle this. He knows we're going through shit. We always handle tough cases. It's what we do."

"Yeah, I guess."

Turner knew that for all his bombast, Fenwick had a gentle and philosophical soul. He'd cut out his tongue before he let others outside of his inner circle know that. That he was a poet who did occasional readings around the city was also a deep dark secret. Turner was loyal. He went to all the readings. Sometimes Ben joined him. Turner liked those times because then he and Ben could sit in the back and help keep each other awake.

"You sure you're okay?" Turner asked Fenwick.

"Yeah." Fenwick looked at him. "You were there. Carruthers was fucking up, and either one of us could have died."

"But we didn't."

"It'll take me a while to get used to what happened. Probably the same for you."

Turner nodded. He knew it was best not to push his partner. He turned left on Harrison. In the early evening with rush hour traffic still dwindling, Harrison was one of the secret, best ways to go from the south Loop to the near West side.

Turner said, "The crime scene is two and a half blocks from where Carruthers didn't manage to kill somebody. Coincidence?"

"You mean Carruthers could have done the murders as well?"

"We couldn't be so lucky, but neither one of us likes coincidences."

Fenwick muttered, "I guess we'll find out."

"What's the most recent news on Preston Shaitan?"

"You know him?"

"I know of him."

While Fenwick Googled, Turner said, "He's this supposedly gay guy who does right wing shtick."

"A right wing gay person?"

"So he says. He's been written about in the gay press. He also publishes essays in some supposedly high-brow right wing journal, *Thought*."

"Never heard of that either."

"Lucky you. I read one of the essays. He tried to prove that we didn't need any anti-discrimination laws of any kind for any group."

"He's delusional?"

"He also said that states have the right to have any kind of laws they want about any kind of discrimination they want."

"So we can have state-wide discrimination just not nationwide non-discrimination? Discrimination depends on the size of the jurisdiction? That the people of a state have the right to vote for or against discrimination? Is he insane? We'd still have slavery in the South."

"You asked me what the man said, not if what he said was sane."

"Why do you say 'supposedly gay?'"

"Some articles quote him as saying this is all in fun and he only says things to be provocative and that the linear sexual structures of the patriarchy are passé."

"Linear sexual structures of the patriarchy? What does that mean?"

"He'll fuck anything that will let him."

"Animal, vegetable, or mineral?"

"Yes."

"You memorize shit he says?"

"I'm not quoting exactly."

Fenwick looked back at his phone and tapped. He said, "I'm

Googling 'linear sexual structures'." He gazed at the front for a minute then said, "By damn, you're right."

"Happens once in a while."

Fenwick checked his phone some more then reported. "What I've got is a few articles about a tour he was making around the country. He called it "The Back Room is not Your Friend" tour. What does that mean?"

"That he's not as good at marketing as he thinks he is."

"Huh?"

"It's not a very catchy title."

Fenwick gave what was on his screen a quick perusal. "This says he's gay, but only has sex with Latino drag queens. Is that important?"

"Not something I'd feel the need to kill anybody over."

"In eight cities, people stormed the stage, and the promoters and/or the authorities, or both were forced to stop the show."

"Shaitan's people didn't hire security?"

Fenwick read then reported. "Doesn't say why they didn't have enough, or why they didn't increase it after the first time, or the first few times."

"The people were stupid? Or he wanted to be interrupted to increase the publicity factor? Or he was trying to generate headlines with the help of anti-him protesters? Maybe he was trying to generate publicity to sell books. I hear authors can be pretty desperate."

Fenwick shrugged and said, "Feed my ego. Feed my sheep." He read some more. In a minute, he said, "There was one audience, here in Chicago years ago. He doesn't actually draw all that many people these days either. I mean, college Republicans, how many can there really be? Used to be, they usually didn't need much more than a classroom to hold the crowd." He read some more then said, "So Shaitan and his people were expecting the usual small crowd, maybe twenty-five, but people kept streaming in. It wasn't like today when often crowds are screened. And he wasn't a presidential candidate or famous, so nobody checked much. So they had to move to a bigger venue. Turns out the vast majority of the crowd was there to protest."

"What happened?"

"Here, they didn't rush the stage. The protesters all just sat there in complete silence. Nobody held up an anti-idiot banner. Nobody much moved at all. The rest of the audience kind of got intimidated, according to this, and got kind of quiet themselves."

Turner said, "The Gandhi approach. I approve. What did Preston Shaitan do?"

"Halfway through his speech, he stormed off the stage and left the building. Says nobody laughed at his usual laugh lines or applauded at his usual applause lines. People outside texted and sent pictures to the protesters inside showing Shaitan getting into a limo and leaving. Then the protesters all stood up in silence and walked out. After that, they held a candlelight vigil in a park a few blocks away where they sang songs of peace."

"Hell of a thing," Turner said. "What do you do, if you're expecting wild and crazy and all you get is silent? Must have driven him nuts. Let's be sure to talk to whomever organized that."

"You think they had something to do with the murder?"

"I want to pin a medal on them."

Thursday 7:37 P.M.

Uniformed police officers diverted the traffic approaching from all directions for blocks before the intersection of Racine and Harrison. Turner and Fenwick were halted a half a block east of Racine Street. The Racine Street bridge over the Eisenhower Expressway began over fifty feet to the north of the intersection itself.

Traffic from all directions was at a standstill. Honking and cursing filled the air.

Turner gave up trying to get closer and parked in a bus stop on Harrison Street about thirty-five feet east of the intersection. The crime scene van was also on Harrison but another one hundred feet west of the intersection in front of the building where the bodies were on the roof.

The wind was now at a howl out of the south. The trees that lined the streets swayed and creaked in the wind. To the west rays of sunset escaped through rents in the still-building clouds.

The detectives noted clumps of people gathered at various spots. The largest clot was about fifty people near the south end of the bridge. Five cops stood in a line keeping the crowd from proceeding south. Several in the crowd were shouting at the cops. Some people had phones and cameras out.

Fenwick said, "I wish those people were in our way to get to the crime scene."

"Why?"

"Then I could bull through them like a cliché Chicago cop."

"I know being a cliché Chicago cop has been a goal of yours for some time."

Fenwick sighed. "A dream come true, lost again."

Turner said, "I can picture the meeting with Molton after you did that."

"Oh?"

They stood at the intersection amidst the cacophony of the wind.

"Yeah," Turner said. "I can hear him in that soft voice he uses with the first year officers. And he says, Buck, and he would be using your first name the way he does when he's annoyed."

"Yeah."

"'Buck, why did you go out of your way to go north on Racine Street to the bridge and through all those people who were not in the way of you getting to your crime scene.' And you'd say in your gruff voice, something nonsensical about claiming that we had to show those people who was boss."

"He would not be happy."

Turner went on. "And then Molton's voice would get even softer." Turner and Fenwick had seen their boss engaging in this kind of discipline with those just out of the Police Academy. They'd never been victims of it themselves. They knew what good police work was. "And he'd go on, 'And rushing to the crime scene instead of helping on the bridge was important because one or both of the corpses had a hot date that night? That your delay at the bridge would show that you were a rotten cop that didn't know how to do your job?'"

Fenwick gave a gargantuan Fenwickian sigh. "But they aren't between us and the crime scene."

"They never were."

"And Molton did tell us to help out."

"We could go back get the car, and go all the way around to the north, and park up on Racine Street north of the bridge. Then the crowd of about fifty people standing around aimlessly would be between us and the crime scene. Then you could bull through them like a cliché Chicago cop."

"And get bawled out by Molton for being an asshole? Not on my to-do list for the day, now or ever."

To their right on the bridge about fifty-five feet away, they saw a cop and a protestor go at it for several seconds, arms flailing. The cop started to fall, but was righted by another protestor. The violent one the cop scuffled with disappeared into the back of the crowd. Voices began to be raised.

Turner and Fenwick hustled over. In his head, Turner could almost hear Molton's voice, "You madly rushed to the crime scene while avoiding helping out with the confrontation on the bridge? What were you thinking? And the riot that followed that grew to three nights of chaos in the city and cost billions in property damage? And six people dead? But no, you had to get to your crime scene when you could have lent a hand. Why? Did you think the dead bodies would miss you? Get up and leave? Weep because you were late?" Molton could be as sarcastic as Fenwick.

Approaching the bridge on their way north away from the intersection, among the police, Turner saw only the blue uniforms of beat cops. He didn't see any stiffly-ironed and heavily-starched white shirts with gold braiding that indicated someone from the command structure. The detectives clipped their badges on their shirts as they hurried forward.

A beat cop saw them and said, "We need more help."

"Where's your local District Commander?" Turner asked.

The young cop shrugged.

Fenwick snapped at the officer. "Call him." Then Fenwick walked another ten feet north, onto the bridge, and inserted his bulk between the straggly line of cops and the crowd. Turner stood next to him. For a few seconds, silence reigned.

Then one of people in the crowd pointed and said, "He's the one who saved the kid over four hours ago."

Another guy said, "Yeah, yeah, it's on the Internet." By now, half the people had their phones out replaying the video of Turner and Fenwick saving DeShawn. Turner could see on the face of several of the phones the same YouTube video he'd seen on Wilson's phone back at the station over a half hour ago.

More people pointed.

"The other guy Tased the shooter."

Sporadic applause broke out. Phones and cameras emerged. The crowd surged toward them.

Fenwick smiled, held up his hands, and said, "No autographs, please. Is there something we can do to help?"

Many in the milling group looked confused.

Turner knew exactly what Fenwick was doing. In all the most modern police training, the goal was to defuse tension, not create it. That hundreds of police forces hadn't gotten the memo or the training didn't lessen its effectiveness as a sane thing to do. Salt Lake City was the most recent place he'd read about with the new training. The article had appeared in the *Chicago Tribune* in May. Molton had drummed it into the heads of all the people who worked at Area Ten, that the most important thing was to calm and/or neutralize a situation if they could. The Commander had repeated it at roll call after roll call and had made special training sessions mandatory.

Molton was definitely in the camp that was against police departments buying tanks, and bazookas, or tactical nuclear weapons to control crowds in cities. To go bulling into a situation like cliché Chicago cops from the '68 convention was stupid. Making illogical demands of people and insisting they obey was pointless, such as making demands that people 'move along' for no apparent logical reason.

All making such demands ever did was show that it was important for you, the official person, to make people obey you. It might come to that, but this situation wasn't near that point. The key to crowd control isn't showing that you can bully them into submission by making them obey random demands. The key, in all modern training, was to see if you could find a way to calm the situation. Asking if they could help was a far better ploy for crowd control than demanding that they comply with some pointless directive.

The Racine St. Bridge over the Eisenhower wasn't some main, vital artery, but just another two lane bridge, one of many, on the long march the Expressway took to the western suburbs. Clearing it would be good but wasn't vital to the commerce of the city or of ambulances getting to any nearby hospitals. A few people might be home late for dinner. This was nowhere near a crisis situation. Yet. They needed to help prevent that if they could.

The woman nearest to them wore a clerical collar and a black tunic. She stepped forward and held out her hand, "I'm Marjorie Zelvin." She pointed behind her. "Several members of my congregation are here. We keep hearing rumors. That attendees of the conference are dead, perhaps even Mr. Bettencourt, one of the organizers. We need to be heard. Attention needs to be paid."

Fenwick asked, "How did you know there might be a murder here and who it might be?"

Again people held up phones which now showed the same anchor on the local television news that Molton had shown them back at the station. Turner sighed to himself. Half the city was probably rife with impossible rumors. He realized it would be absolutely moronic to start in on any of these people much less accuse them of something or treat them as suspects. Anyone with a phone with access to the Internet could have heard any number or rumors. If they were going to treat everyone who heard the rumors as a suspect, they'd have to go back and start their interrogations with Molton, Wilson, and Roosevelt.

Fenwick said, "Perhaps you could help us out."

Marjorie Zelvin looked like a modern spokesperson, trying hard to look young, with long blonde hair that was probably dyed, more makeup than a fashion model in high season. She had a shrill voice.

Turner knew you didn't start situations with the public with people you chose. You dealt with those you had. He said, "Let's talk over here."

Turner, Fenwick, and the cleric shuffled a few feet away from the crowd.

Fenwick lowered his voice. "It will help us if you and these officers can work something out. We need to get to a crime scene. After that, maybe we can do more talking."

Zelvin said, "We won't be silenced. We need to know what's going on. It isn't only the police who want peace."

Fenwick gritted his teeth. "Have you talked with the Commander of the local District?"

"He's been less than helpful."

Fenwick said, "Let see if we can't get a few people from the local District over here. They're in charge of local crowd control. They'd be able to help you most."

"We can't just deal with you?"

"We have jobs to do," Fenwick said.

"So there has been murder done! Ha! You can't conceal it."

"We know that," Turner said. "Right now, we want to do what's best for your people. Find out what will help the most and see how we can accommodate you."

Fenwick brought two of the local beat cops forward and introduced them to Zelvin and the others nearby. They began to talk. Fenwick turned his bulk and began to trundle away. Turner saw more cell phones out for video and pictures. He followed his partner.

Turner no longer marveled at his gruff partner's ability to calm tough situations. He'd seen it numerous times. Maybe it was his bulk, or air of command. Certainly here, it was his, or both their, status of newly-minted hero-dom that calmed everything.

A man in a tie and sport coat rushed up to them. Even though he was on this side of the police line, the detectives were wary. The guy said, "I'm Adam Edberg from the mayor's office. We can't have violence." He pointed to the crowd. "Any such gathering would be a disaster, a disaster waiting to happen, rife with possibilities of violence and civil disorder."

Fenwick let out his deepest rumble. "What's your official role here?"

"I'm representing the mayor."

"Has he committed a crime?" Fenwick asked.

Edberg looked confused.

"Is the mayor here to calm things?"

"Uh, no."

"Are you?"

"Uh, no. Uh, yes."

"You have no place here. Get your ass out from behind the police lines."

"You can't talk to me that way."

Fenwick faced the man, spread his legs, and said, "Yet I just did."

A florid faced man dressed in full command uniform rushed toward them. Turner recognized him as the local District Commander, Gerald Palakowski. The man paused to listen to several of the beat cops then hurried forward.

"What's going on?" Palakowski demanded.

Edberg began to explain. Palakowski brushed him aside with an abrupt wave of his hand. "I want to hear from the detectives."

Turner and Fenwick summarized what little they knew about the situation on the bridge from the short time they'd been here.

Palakowski rubbed his hands together. "What the hell am I supposed to do?"

Turner was pissed. They must train them for moments like this. The entire force had had seminars in recent years that included refreshers, reminders, and information about new tactics for defusing situations, helping the community, and causing just such moments to de-escalate from violence. What was wrong with this idiot? Maybe he was afraid that if he screwed up, he'd be blamed for violence and death.

Edberg butted in, "Get every cop you can and get them here. Move these people!"

Fenwick inserted his bulk between Palakowski and Edberg. Fenwick said, "Simplicity itself. The woman in the clerical collar talking to the beat cops seems to be the leader, or one of the leaders. Try her. Send them on a march to someplace that's significant but a long way away. Make sure they're protected, find their leaders. At their destination, someone can make a statement. They'll be exhausted. With luck it will pour rain."

A few moments later the Commander along with several members of the group, including Zelvin, huddled together with several other beat cops and Edberg, whose presence Turner thought was useless.

Turner and Fenwick stood to the side. After five minutes, Turner could feel Fenwick's impatience nearing the boiling point. They had a crime scene to get to.

Edberg, Zelvin, and Palakowski began walking away from the others. All three were talking at a great rate of speed. Then they began shouting at each other.

The protesters looked confused and began to shuffle and mill toward the arguers.

Fenwick marched to the three of them. Turner followed.

Palakowski began waving his arms. "We can't just let you march anywhere. You've got to be controlled and follow the rules."

Edberg said, "You've got to control your people."

Zelvin's voice was shrill. She pointed to Edberg, "Are you saying he should control his people, or I should control mine? Who has more dead people in their history, my peaceful protesters or your violent officers?"

Fenwick stepped between them. They glared at him. Fenwick said, "The next one who says a word, I will sit on and crush." He held up one hand and with the other pointed at Zelvin, "Why don't you get ready to march to the local alderman's office and to Daley Plaza?" He pointed to the police contingent. "And you get ready to provide logistics and support." He turned to Edberg. "And you get on the phone to the local alderman and make sure he's there to greet them with a smile and a neutral statement."

Growling, stammering, and shrugging broke out among the small aggregation.

Fenwick looked over to where the crowd on the bridge had grown to several hundred. He moved to Palakowski and pulled him away from the group. Turner joined them.

Fenwick said, "We've got a crime scene to get to. Why not let them march to somewhere?"

"What if your plan doesn't work?"

"If it doesn't, then do your damn job, think of something."

Fenwick marched away. Turner followed. They trundled south down Racine Street and came to the intersection with Harrison. They turned west and began walking to the building with the bodies on the roof. A few minutes later, still several feet from their destination, they looked back. Zelvin was explaining to demonstrators, Palakowski to his officers, and Edberg was on his phone.

Turner and Fenwick moved to get to work.

Fenwick muttered, "Numbnuts assholes."

"Which one?" Turner asked.

"All of them."

Thursday 7:58 P.M.

A few steps outside the entrance to the building where the bodies were, a man, who looked like he was still in high school, met them at the front bumper of the Crime Scene van. He asked, "You guys okay?"

"Who are you?" Fenwick demanded.

"I'm Kent Duffy. The Chief Medical Examiner assigned me to this case."

"Where's Bernie?" Fenwick asked. "He's been around forever."

"He retired."

Fenwick asked, "You graduated high school?"

Duffy gave him an extended look then said, "I heard you're some kind of an asshole."

Fenwick snorted. "I'm not 'some kind' of asshole. I am *the* asshole. And I tell the jokes. Get over it now."

"All of them?"

"All."

Duffy said, "Yeah, rumor is you have a funnier-than-thou attitude."

"Bullshit," Fenwick said. "It's not a rumor. It's true."

Duffy raised an eyebrow, but then he grinned. "Is it important that I laugh at all your jokes?" His eyes met Turner's. "Or maybe you'll let me know when to laugh?"

"You're on your own," Turner said, "but I can safely ignore them. I suggest you do the same."

Fenwick glared at Turner. "Fine. Be unappreciative. You're teaching these new kids bad habits."

Turner said, "Nothing you're not used to."

Silence for a few moments, then Duffy said, "Let me try this again. You guys okay?"

Grunted yeahs from the detectives.

Duffy asked, "Is Carruthers really going to be gone?"

Fenwick said, "We can hope."

Duffy said, "Party at my place."

"You know about Carruthers?"

"This isn't my first case. It's the first time I'm connected to you guys. Everybody knows Carruthers."

"Pity," Fenwick said.

"What do we have?" Turner asked.

"We've got a lot done already but with more hours to go. What took you guys so long?"

Fenwick said, "Bullshit."

They walked into the building.

The bodies were on the roof of a mixed use classrooms and conference center at Little Village Community College. Turner judged the building to have been built in the forties. Lots of faded red brick, pollution begrimed from over half a century in the city. Windows that might let in gray light, that probably used to open, but now most had air-conditioners crammed in their lower half.

They took the elevator up the four flights.

Fenwick said, "We gotta have somebody check all the stairways."

Turner nodded.

The ME said, "We already processed the elevator."

The door opened on the fourth floor. A uniformed cop led them to a doorway. He banged the door-opening-bar.

"No emergency alarm," Turner said.

Fenwick's turn to nod.

As he walked onto the roof, as any good cop would, Turner made a careful examination of his surroundings. He saw skinny chimneys, a few more modern heating and air-conditioning units still in their wrappings, a brick balustrade on all the edges of the roof. In the center, he saw a few pockets with patio furniture around rusted tables. Their tattered umbrellas flapped in the wind. Turner figured this wasn't so much an emergency exit, although it could be such, but a place for people to relax on a summer evening.

A few streaks of lighter blue shone in the west between billowing clouds. To the east, he could see the lights of the Loop buildings.

Across the street to the south was a block-long building several stories higher than this. He saw bright lights on its roof. He walked to the balustrade and looked over the edge to the street below. The tops of trees swayed in the stiffening wind. He heard traffic, a distant siren, the usual from a big city. Two-and three-story houses filled the neighborhood in the other three directions.

Duffy pointed to the center of an area well-lit by crime scene arc lights, which were anchored with heavy weights to keep them from flying off in the rising gale. Duffy said, "Two dead bodies. Both shot twice, once in the head, once in the torso. The blood spatter tells me the head shots came first. The two torso shots came when they were on the ground. Victims probably never knew what hit them. Or if they did, there wasn't time to react. They were facing each other when the shots started, a few feet apart. The shots came in rapid succession, from a distance." He pointed to the lights on the roof to the south. "I've got people up there already."

Turner asked, "They were talking, fighting, embracing?"

"I've got no evidence of offensive or defensive wounds from a fight they might have been having with each other. I got no indication of what they were doing. They could have been two random guys who happened to be walking on the roof in the same direction at the same time and got murdered."

All three raised an eyebrow. None of them believed in anywhere near that level of coincidence.

Fenwick said, "Had to be an expert shot."

Turner nodded. "Nobody is that lucky."

The ME said, "Or one murder could have been deliberate and the other random chance or collateral damage or blind luck. For both or either of them."

Fenwick raised an eyebrow. "They must be teaching you guys good stuff these days."

"Maybe I can be the smart one in the bunch."

Turner said, "As long as you don't start telling jokes." The ME had voiced possibilities that a good cop would be aware of. He liked that.

People from the Crime Scene unit had blocked off the roof into squares. They used bright lights on their cameras to film each square. When they finished, each square had been dusted and any debris picked up, no matter how obscure a connection it might have to the murder.

Turner and Fenwick donned their blue booties and gloves then approached the corpses.

The detectives stood at the edge of bright light and scanned the area. Even though the scene was being videotaped, they still took out their notebooks and made sketches and anecdotal notes. Both detectives preferred to have hand-written reminders. Moving forward, they walked in their delicate ballet between bits of pulverized brain and gore, the remnants of life. At the moment, it wasn't hard to forget almost being shot. Human bone, blood, and gristle could certainly focus the mind.

Turner wondered when all cops had body cams, if people would want to see such details. More real than Hollywood could make it, but he didn't doubt that there would be some reveling in the remnants of life and once-living flesh.

Duffy pointed. "The one closest to the west is Preston Shaitan. The one a few feet to the east of him is Henry Bettencourt. Half of

Shaitan's brain wound up over there. Basically, his head exploded." He turned slightly. "We got most of Bettencourt's brain over here."

Shaitan wore a black and white floral shirt with a cutaway collar, tight fitting retro shorts in camo, and black sandals. His toenails needed cutting. Bettencourt wore a gray polo shirt, white slim Chinos, and black deck shoes. They both looked to be in their late thirties or early forties.

Fenwick said, "We've got a sniper with a high-powered rifle. Four shots. First two fatal. Second two just for meanness or maybe to be certain. Does anyone think this was random chance?"

Head shakes.

"Why here?" Fenwick asked.

"What were they doing up here?" Turner asked.

They were used to mulling out loud in rhetorical excess. Helped them think as they investigated.

The ME said they could examine the bodies. They approached closer. With a Crime Scene person, they took each item from the pockets, catalogued them, preserved them. Nothing leaped out at them as clues.

Turner took out his cell phone and called Barb Dams at Area Ten headquarters. Pleasantries exchanged, Turner asked, "Is Fong in?" Fong was Area Ten's tech guy. No one's expertise on the CPD, as far as Turner and Fenwick knew, matched his abilities.

Dams said, "The Commander called in everybody. They've been afraid of violence since this started, so it's been all hands on deck for two days. You know Fong. He practically lives down there anyway."

"Could you have him do credit card checks on the two victims? That will give us some sense of their movements and, with luck, where they were staying."

She already had the names from earlier. He gave her the numbers they'd found on credit cards in the wallets. She promised to get on to Fong immediately. The detectives said they'd deliver the cell phones of the deceased when they returned to headquarters.

Thursday 8:28 P.M.

They'd learned all they could from the scene and the body. Finished with their examination, they approached a uniformed cop near the door that led back downstairs.

"Anybody report hearing gunshots?" Fenwick asked.

He was an older man whose gut hung out over his belt. He said, "You expecting someone on the roof of a building to jump in front of the bullets?"

Turner always figured it was the sneer in the beat cop's voice that caused what happened next.

For a moment, a light shone on the guy's name tag: Blawn. Turner didn't remember working with him before.

The area around the door was in shadow. Fenwick made no threat. In one swift move he had his good arm pressed against the guy's throat and was using his own bulk to move the guy deeper into shadow.

Turner eased after them.

The beat cop flailed against the pressure of Fenwick's arm. Seconds later, the cop halted as his head thudded against the wall. Fenwick pulled him forward an inch or so then rammed him back against the bricks. Fenwick's growl was at its deepest and most menacing. "You got a problem, motherfucker?"

The beat cop attempted to swat at his captor.

Fenwick snarled, "Go ahead, mother fucker hit me. I've got one wounded arm, and I'll still beat the shit out of you.'"'

The man struggled for breath. Between gurgles, he gasped out, "You made shit choices."

Fenwick asked, "What did you want us to do? Make decisions based on what the situation calls for? Or pick and choose our behavior based on the ethnic identity, social connections, or job qualifications of the people the situation contains?"

Turner knew when pissed, Fenwick could talk very fast and very loud with no trace of his own Chicago origins. Once Turner had asked Fenwick about the penchant for the professorial when he was pissed. Fenwick had said, "It's a gift."

Right now, Blawn, the beat cop, managed to gasp out, "Huh?"

"We faced death, you shit. We made instantaneous decisions that might have cost us our lives, others their lives. You want to second guess that?"

The guy managed to shake his head and then gasped, "I give. I give."

Fenwick kept his arm on the man's throat, but eased back a fraction of an inch.

Turner asked, "You know Carruthers?"

The guy nodded.

"He a friend?"

The guy shook his head.

"Are we your friends?"

More head shaking.

Fenwick snarled. "You and any of your buddies try to fuck up our investigation, I will personally cut off your balls and feed them to you. Do you understand?"

The guy nodded.

"If you try to fuck with us, I will find out where you live and I will come over with a baseball bat in one hand and a machine gun in the other. Do you understand?"

Between gurgles, the guy nodded.

Fenwick eased up on Blawn's throat. The guy bent over, retched for a moment, then pulled in great gulps of air.

"Let's try it again. Anyone report hearing gunshots?"

The answer came between heavy pants. "No one has come forward."

Fenwick ordered the guy to organize and begin the canvass of the building.

Blawn tottered away.

Fenwick gasped for a few moments and rubbed his wounded shoulder.

Turner asked, "You feel better?" He knew behind his often snarly exterior, his partner was a gentle soul, but it did not do to piss him off.

"Not as much as I'd like." Fenwick shook his head. "We're going to have to put up with far too much of that."

"Maybe this guy will relay the message. Or report you."

Fenwick glanced around. "No witnesses." He peered at the eaves and corners nearby. "Even if there are cameras, they can't see anything in the dark back here." He drew another deep breath. "Almost getting killed and then harassed by an idiot who is one of our own takes it out of me."

"Pisses me off, too. Remember Rodriguez's car already got keyed. All kinds of shit could happen."

Fenwick nodded.

Turner said, "We can't count on Blawn to do his job."

They hunted for Sanchez. The beat cop appeared at the top of the stairs. "You heard any rumbles about us?" Fenwick asked.

Sanchez said, "That an idiot detective might be fired and you guys saved an innocent kid? Other than that, not much. Feelings aren't running strong because Carruthers was so hated. Although there are a few morons around. They aren't likely to talk to me or Deveneaux.

They know we've worked together a long time. If we hear anything, we'll tell you."

They asked him to follow up on the canvass. Sanchez nodded.

Turner asked him, "Who found the body?"

"Guy named Ian Hume. One of the old guys says he used to be one of us. I never heard of him."

Turner said, "What the hell?"

Fenwick raised an eyebrow.

Turner knew Ian. He was the star reporter for the city's major gay newspaper, the *Gay Tribune*. Years ago, he'd won the Pulitzer Prize for investigative journalism for his exposé of the medical establishment's price-fixing of AIDS drugs.

Turner and Hume had gone through the police academy together and had been assigned the same district as beat cops. They'd come to respect and like each other. But Ian had gotten fed up with the system, and in addition, made the decision to come out. He'd gone back to school for his journalism degree and begun writing newspaper articles. Then he'd quit the department to work full-time as a reporter for the local gay newspaper. Ian had been a great help to Paul in the emotionally difficult time after his wife's death, when Jeff was born. They had been lovers for three years and close friends since their breakup. Occasionally they had been of some help to each other on cases or stories.

Although this was the first time Ian was the finder of the body, or in this instance bodies, on one of their cases.

Sanchez said, "He let the ME swab his fingers for gunshot residue. The ME said he looked clean, but he'd know more when we get lab test results back."

Turner knew Ian would have the knowledge that he'd have needed to scrub his hands and change clothes to hide any possible gunshot residue. Would he have had the time?

"Where is he?"

"Sitting in a classroom on the fourth floor."

They thanked him. He left.

Thursday 8:48 P.M.

Ian wore his usual slouch fedora, even indoors. He was six-foot-six, kept his blond beard short and scraggily with the hair on top of his head at businessman's length.

"Hell of a thing," Ian said.

"Great shot," Fenwick said. "Brains all over."

Ian said, "According to what I heard and from what I saw, Preston Shaitan losing that much brain wouldn't have made him any stupider. I never read anything that said something good about him."

"Why were you here?" Turner asked.

"I had meetings with both of them. I didn't think they'd be here together. I certainly hadn't planned on it. First, it was supposed to be Shaitan, then Bettencourt."

Fenwick asked, "You were meeting with the evil gay guy."

"You know about him?"

"My level of knowledge is not the issue," Fenwick said. "Why meet him?"

"I wanted to find out for myself if he was as phony as I thought he was. He struck me as a charlatan. I wanted to talk to him face to face."

Turner asked, "Why were you supposed to meet Bettencourt?"

"It was his turn to be interviewed."

"For what?"

"An article I'm doing on the conference."

Fenwick asked, "What exactly is this conference?"

Ian took out his phone and tapped at the front and then showed it to Fenwick. Turner leaned close so he could see. The screen showed a home page with all kinds of print in a wide variety of colors and fonts urging people to attend the 'ALL EARTH BE-IN, AND HAPPENING, CONFERENCE AND CONVENTION OF THE GOOD PEOPLE, CONCERNED PEOPLE OF THE EARTH LEFT, RIGHT, AND CENTER TO MAKE THE WORLD A BETTER PLACE, A CONFLUENCE OF GOOD TO MAKE CHANGE A REALITY.'"

Fenwick asked, "Huh?"

Turner said, "Title must have been put together by a committee trying to be inclusive."

Ian said, "Or a bunch of idiots."

Fenwick said, "So which the fuck is it? A conference or a convention?"

Ian looked exasperated. "Who gives a fuck what they precisely called it? And what earthly difference does it make? All these do-gooders and protesters were here in town at the same time. They called it a confluence. Maybe they were all confluing at the same time."

Turner said, "Confluing is a word?"

Ian said, "Can be if I want it to be." He pointed at Fenwick. "If you're desperate, you could name it. You could call it 'Bob?' Or a 'Bob Confluence.' Would that make you happy?"

"It's gotta be called something."

Ian sighed. "It means a lot of well-meaning people were trying to organize the disaffected to be more effective. If the name they gave it is any indication, they weren't very good at organizing. I do know a lot of activists on the Left and Right had a hand in bringing huge crowds of people together to Chicago at this time. They were planning to meet, hold lectures, roundtables, brainstorm, have blue sky sessions, panel discussions, teach-ins, thinking outside of the box, and any other cliché that's used for meetings of people these days. Why the fuck do you care what they called it?"

Fenwick muttered, "It's important."

Ian's eyes lit up. "I can hear the attendees now, 'My dear, are you here for the bob?' Or maybe something like this, 'Honey, remember that bob we went to in Chicago? Best bob we were ever at.' I like it."

Fenwick grumbled. "I care."

Ian said, "Congratulations. No one else does."

Turner patted Fenwick's shoulder. "If it will make you feel better, we'll call it a conference. Or Bob. Or whatever you want. Up to you. Whatever makes you feel better, that's what we'll do."

Fenwick said, "Fuck it."

Turner got back to business. He said to Ian, "Had you met either of them before?"

"I'd exchanged emails with both of them to set this up." Ian held up his hands. "Hold it a second. I gotta ask you guys this. Did you really save some kid?"

"You must have seen the video," Fenwick said. "What do you think happened?"

Ian said, "I think it's great. Instead of standing around and letting a psycho-cop kill another African-American kid, you did something."

Again Turner returned to the issue at hand. "You work for a gay newspaper. Was there a gay angle to both of these guys?"

"You know how things are getting thinner and thinner at newspapers?"

"I thought things were fine at the *Gay Tribune*."

"They are and they aren't."

"Huh?"

"They keep reassuring us, but I'm expanding my freelance work. I want to cover my bases. My boss at the paper approves. We all know newspaper reporters who moved out on their own and went broke. I'm working on a book on the history of gay activism. Some of the old timers gathering here have been involved for years in lots of different organizations. These two were among the new and with it, in the modern wave of Facebook, Twitter, Pinterest, Snapchat, Google Plus, LinkedIn, and Instagram, and all the other relevant perils in the electronic age."

"You use all those?" Fenwick asked.

Ian grinned at him. "Doesn't everyone?"

Turner intervened before a possibly pointless round of repartee and asked, "Bettencourt was gay?"

"As far as I know, no. He's married to a woman and has two kids, but he's part of the world of young activists for which being pro-gay is a good thing."

"So what perils did these guys face?"

"One thing, some bloggers were laughing at Bettencourt about how he made claims for the efficacy of protests."

Fenwick asked, "What's an efficacy protest?"

Ian ignored the pathetic attempt at humor. He said, "Because a protest occurred in close proximity to some change, therefore it was the protest that caused the change. The old killing-turkeys-causes-winter fallacy. To some degree they were both being laughed at. They hated it. I believe Shaitan had set a record by being banned from all social networks."

"All?" Fenwick asked.

"Yep, all. And before you ask, the reason was, he was the most consummate asshole on the planet."

"Good to know who's the worst," Fenwick said.

Turner asked, "Other than stand-up comedians, is there anyone who does enjoy being laughed at?"

Ian smiled. "Not the point here. Bettencourt was also being laughed at for being old fashioned. He turned everything into a reference to the Bible, no matter how obscure. He was liberal but Biblical, and don't give me any shit about that being contradictory. I'm just reporting. He was losing respect. He was pissed."

Fenwick asked, "The Bible is 'out?' I thought thousands still waved them around."

Ian said, "It's 'out' to those he wanted to influence the most."

"Do you know the blogger or bloggers?" Turner asked.

"No."

Fenwick said, "I wonder if he, she, or they are at the conference."

Turner said, "We'll have to work on finding anybody else in particular who hated either of them and who is also in town. Shaitan's had a storm of criticism for being right wing and gay. There was even a rumor he attended a traditional Latin Catholic mass every day."

"How?" Fenwick asked. "If he travelled a lot, he managed to find one in each city? If they even have one in each city."

Ian said, "An online broadcast would be easiest."

"Why?" Fenwick asked.

"Why attend?" Ian shrugged then suggested, "Catholic guilt?"

Fenwick shook his head. "How famous can they be if I didn't know one of them existed, and I was only vaguely aware of the other?"

"The unkindest cuts of all. They all think they're famous. They all have an outsized view of their power and influence. As Neil Steinberg put it in his column in the *Sun Times*, they have 'illusions of significance.' All too sadly true."

Fenwick shook his head. "Unless their grip on reality or lack of grip on reality had something to do with the murder, I'm not sure I care."

Turner pointed upward. "Why meet on the roof here?"

"It was the spot for all the secret meetings with the open and transparent activists at the conference."

"All the activists had secret meetings here?" Fenwick asked. "So they could have all decided to meet here secretly? They could have had their own secret mini-convention. How secret was it?"

Ian had the grace to smile. "Turns out this space could have been busier than a Starbucks at high noon."

"Only two of them were here tonight," Fenwick pointed out.

Ian said, "Three with me. If he'd waited to shoot another minute or two." His voice trailed off.

Turner said, "So the location was known. What was so great about this spot?"

"No one could overhear us."

Fenwick asked, "Why be afraid someone was going to overhear you?"

Ian said, "Secrets."

Fenwick shook his head. "What kind of secrets? Bullshit secrets of people caught up in how important they think they are to the universe? Or embarrassing secrets?"

Ian held up a hand. "Secrets that if their true believer followers knew, would condemn them to perdition, or irrelevance and insignificance, which are the same thing as perdition to these people. They had to be important, but real people who wanted to get real things done know you have to be able to talk to other people."

"About what?" Fenwick asked.

"Tactics, who was willing to compromise, philosophy, who caused the problems in your organization and what to do about them, who were the ones willing to listen. You know the drill. In any organization, there are true believers that will never compromise and wind up so far out on the limb of their ideology that no one could ever rescue them. Some of those bring down whole organizations. And some think people like that are infiltrators designed to keep organizations in chaos. If you keep them arguing about the third semi-colon from the left in the third paragraph, nothing will ever get done."

"These two guys were willing to listen, compromise?" Turner asked.

"That's one of the things I was here to find out."

Fenwick asked, "Who'd want them both dead?"

Ian shrugged. "That's what I was trying to figure out while I was waiting for you guys."

"It's a mildly public spot," Turner said. "There's chairs and tables up there. Anybody could have walked in. Or the killer didn't care who he killed. These two guys were just unlucky?"

Ian shrugged. "That's possible. Most of the convention goers are radicals answerable only to their own organizations, if then." He called up the home page again on his phone and showed them the section with the list of sponsoring or participating organizations.

Turner glanced through the lists of groups. He said, "I haven't heard of any of these."

"The main line protest groups mostly weren't here. Not officially, although a few sent representatives."

"Why not officially?" Turner asked.

"Deniability."

Turner said, "I can understand Shaitan having enemies."

Ian gave a snort. "He was a professional enemies collector, but Bettencourt had them too. Hell, they all had enemies. Sometimes, their worst enemies were in their own heads. Or within their groups, although they often fought with other groups."

"Can you be a little more specific on enemies who might be in town?"

"Specifically? I have no idea. The notion I got from researching Bettencourt was that he was the compromiser type. The one who thought by being united, one, some, or all of these groups would get more accomplished."

"United with him as the supreme leader?" Fenwick asked.

"Not from what I heard," Ian said. "The guy may have been the real deal, someone who cared about people and did his best to make their lives better."

"How about Shaitan?"

"From articles I read, he was one of those cliché type guys. Everybody he met hated him. Except if you were of some use to him. Then Preston sucked up to you. Quite willing to suck your dick, if it would get him something. For example, if you published his writing, he was quite nice to you."

Fenwick asked, "He was sucking off all the guys who worked on right wing sites?"

"According to rumors, just the ones who were of use to him."

"How about friends and family?"

"Bettencourt's wife, as far as I know, has been making day trips to the conference. Shaitan, I have no reports of close relationships."

Fenwick checked his notes. "Any specifics among these blogger people?"

"There'd been a stink today among the attendees about bloggers from all sides being out of control."

"Wait a second," Fenwick said. "How many sides are there here?"

"Count the number of people. They don't really have sides as much as opinions. It's not really all of us over here, all of you over there. More like, I'm here with all the rest of you against whatever, but just for the moment. That's not a rigid categorization. More like an attempted descriptor."

Turner said, "Somebody had to want to get something done. They couldn't have all been ineffective, ego-maniacal morons."

"Bets?" Ian asked. He paused, then leaned forward, and resumed. "But see, that's the thing. They cared very, very much. Blogs, and postings, and who got added to editorial boards on obscure web sites. Maybe six people read the web site or blog or Instagram message, or Twitter posting. But they're all waiting for their Susan Boyle moment. When their few phrases of deathless prose get them a huge audience on television or any other handy medium. They want to be stars. There's as many of them as the Internet, infinite."

"What were they fighting about?" Fenwick asked.

"Who had the bigger ego?" Ian said.

"How does that work?" Fenwick asked.

"Selfies at two paces?"

"Do you wish you were one of them?" Fenwick asked.

"You don't want to touch that raw nerve," Ian said.

Turner asked, "Who organized this conference?"

Ian said, "It was kind of amorphous."

"Someone must have started the ball rolling."

Ian shrugged. "I'm not sure."

"How did you hear about it?"

"Internet chatter. There's no one national umbrella group everybody pays dues to. It started out as an intellectual, philosophical debate to be held on the Little Village Community College campus. Then it got out of control."

Turner knew Little Village Community College had been established five years ago and had taken over this series of old buildings.

Ian was continuing. "Later on tonight, I was going to what was supposed to be a meeting of the three biggest rival groups. They were supposed to work out their disagreements."

"Why didn't they do that beforehand?"

"I don't know. There was some hope that meeting face to face would somehow cause them to be more amenable to compromise."

Turner asked, "How'd it wind up being at Little Village Community College?"

"There were a lot of useless university professors, assistant professors, random hangers on, who were bored to tears with academic life and wanted a little action."

Fenwick asked, "They all came looking for a fight?"

Ian said, "More like they were ready for a fight at the drop of an ego. And remember this was all kinds of activists from around the country. Not just gay activists, but everybody. Some people wanted it to be reminiscent of Port Huron."

Turner knew this was a reference to the meeting of the Students for Democratic Society that wrote the eponymously named document.

Ian was continuing. "They fought back then over communitarianism and individualism. Hasn't changed much since then."

"Why do I care?" Fenwick asked.

"Because people were killed over it?"

"You sure about that?" Fenwick asked.

"Bettencourt was getting a following among the conventioneers. He'd sit at the endless meetings and be silent, until they'd all been arguing for hours. Then he'd stand up. He was kind of tall and good looking. He had these riveting blue eyes and this deep voice. He knew the trick of waiting until they were all exhausted, then he'd propose what was, in fact, a fairly reasonable compromise. He also had sense enough to have friends in the audience who would then immediately speak up for what he proposed."

"He had plants? He planned that far ahead?"

"He was one of the few who knew how to work a group."

"What about Shaitan?" Turner asked.

"He preferred verbal assaults."

"Who'd he piss off?"

"Everybody?"

Turner called up the conference brochure on his own phone, turned to the page with the list of attendees, then handed it to Ian. Turner said, "Try to be specific."

Ian perused the names for half a minute. He looked up at Turner. "It's kind of an amalgam of anarchic groups. What you've got here is hate groups facing off with no-hate groups, but both sides armed to the teeth.

"The left-wing hate groups were armed?" Fenwick asked.

"Can be if they want I suppose. I sort of care about which side these groups are on and then sort of don't."

"How's that?"

"As long as I get an article someone's willing to buy, I don't care."

Fenwick paused a moment then mused. "Why not wait for you and get three of you? Or the killer didn't know who he was shooting at or care? I refuse to believe a random sniper showed up on just this afternoon and these two people just happened to be here."

Turner shook his head. "I think it's a possibility we've got to consider."

Fenwick pointed at Ian. "Are we getting all the truth from you?"

Ian said, "I'm your helpful inside information reporter."

Turner realized it wasn't a real answer to the question. For the moment, he swallowed his suspicion. Ian might have something to say he didn't want Fenwick to hear. He'd wait, but not long. He wasn't going to let any past relationship with Ian get in the way of the investigation.

Ian asked, "Am I a suspect?"

"You know how this works," Turner said. "We check everything."

"I'm not asking you to cover up. There's nothing to cover up. I didn't do it."

Fenwick said, "Good to know."

Turner asked, "Have you interviewed a lot of conference attendees?"

"I was just getting started."

Fenwick said, "If these are all nobodies and their small groups aren't going to influence the outcome of much of anything, why bother to fight? If you drag someone else down, maybe your influence grows. You diminish the size of his fish, maybe, but the pond is still minuscule."

Ian looked at Turner. "Is that metaphorical or metaphysical?"

Turner shrugged, "He's been in a mood since he got shot."

"Worse luck."

Fenwick said, "It's poetic."

Thursday 8:59 P.M.

Once the reporter was gone, Fenwick asked, "Is he a suspect?"

"Mostly not." Turner sighed. "We can't dismiss him, but I trust him. We both know him, and he's helped us before. He understands how this works. He knows we're going to do our jobs."

He checked his phone. He had a text from Fong with the names and addresses of the hotels where the victims were staying. Fong included a brief message that he'd found this information from their credit cards.

It was now almost full dark. The wind was still up, but for the moment, it had forborne to rain. Turner checked his phone for the local weather radar. The nearest storms had dissipated a great deal in the last hour.

They trudged across the street. The wind whipped the clothes they wore. The last remnants of sunset didn't manage to break the gloom.

They entered another renovated building that was now part of the campus. Half was a floor of dorm rooms, other floors offices and classrooms, the other half parking garage. A beat cop led them to the stairs.

On the roof, they circled outside the light from the crime scene people. Turner and Fenwick used their flashlights to illumine shadows. The crime scene people were good, but Turner and Fenwick didn't like to leave the slightest thing to chance.

Duffy appeared in the light nearest them. He led them to the side of the building facing the one with the dead bodies on top. "Okay, your killer stood about here. We've got disturbed movement of roofing tar and small bits of debris all over, but concentrated here. We'll try to get footprints, but I don't hold out much hope. Nothing we've found yet indicates who it might have been. The manager says the tenants were never given keys to get up here, and nobody ever used it."

No buildings in the neighborhood looked down on this rooftop. It was the tallest structure until you got closer to the Loop.

Fenwick glanced to the street below. "Too far from the edge to be seen from the street."

Turner asked, "Was the door to the roof locked?"

"The building manager says any junior high kid could have picked it. He has no idea where the lock went to. We found no lock or debris from one. Beat cops are canvassing the tenants. So far, nobody saw or heard anything. It's a quiet building."

One of the techs called Duffy over. He left them.

Turner said, "It would have been full daylight when he shot them, but it's been off and on overcast all day. Could he have known for sure who he was killing?"

Fenwick said, "If he was stalking them, and he knew people met up there. With a reasonably good sight on his gun, he could see them as if they were standing right next to him."

"But he couldn't be sure they would be the only ones up there."

"Maybe he didn't care."

"And risk someone running over here?"

They gazed across the way.

Fenwick said, "Maybe he waited for a particularly cloudy moment?"

"Or he took a chance."

Fenwick said, "Or he didn't care who he shot."

"Does that make sense?"

Fenwick asked, "How many murders do we have where everything makes perfect sense?"

"You want a guess or accurate statistics down to each and every bullet hole and stab wound?"

Fenwick shrugged. "I'm not picky."

Duffy returned to them. "We just found something a little odd. Sally Bentine has the boxes of evidence from here and the roof across the street." They walked over to a young tech who was taping a box shut.

The woman looked up, pointed to a second box, and said, "It's in there."

With gloves still on, Duffy reached into the box and pulled out a Taser.

Turner and Fenwick bent over and aimed their flashlights at it.

Fenwick said, "It looks like department-issue."

Duffy turned to Bentine. "We get a check back on the serial number?"

She was a woman in her mid-twenties. She looked at the display on her phone. "Just came in. It's been checked out to one Buck Fenwick, and is presumably the one used earlier today on the stupidest man on the planet." She pointed at Turner, "Used by you on Carruthers."

Fenwick said, "How the fuck did it get up here?"

Turner felt a chill down his back the humid air could not ease.

Thursday 9:16 P.M.

Duffy and Bentine had the good sense to keep quiet.

After a few moments, Turner asked, “Where was the damn thing?”

Bentine said, “Way in the back, kind of hidden.” Using her phone she showed them the video and pictures they’d taken earlier then led the aggregation to the far end of the roof, more than a half block away.

Fenwick said, “‘Kind of hidden’ means what?”

“It was in a plastic bag.” She pointed with her flashlight. “The bag with the Taser in it was wedged in that spot where the roof tar is coming undone.” She waggled her flashlight over the spot then moved it about six inches to the left, “And that vent.”

Turner said, “Why hide it at all? Or put it up here at all, and then sort of hide it?”

Nobody had answers to any of that.

They returned to where the marksman had stood. Fenwick asked, “We know any expert marksmen in the city?”

Turner said, “I don’t.”

Duffy shook his head.

They examined the distance. Fenwick said, “I think you’d have to be good, but not that good.”

Turner nodded agreement.

Thursday 9:43 P.M.

Turner and Fenwick sat on the edge of the balustrade on the roof of the building from which the shots had been fired. Their feet dangled over the street five stories below. They'd gotten sandwiches from a sub shop on the first floor of the same building.

Fenwick gnawed at his avocado, turkey, bacon, and garlic concoction, slurped on his diet soda then asked, "What the fuck?"

Turner finished chewing a bite of his salad, swallowed, said, "This is nuts."

"Adds a lot of spooky and eerie to the case. Hate when that happens."

Turner said, "Either the killer just randomly picked it up, and he or she just happened to be at the Carruthers's idiocy scene, or someone at the crime scene randomly picked it up, and gave it to the killer, or a series of someones deliberately handed it off to the next someone until it got to the killer. Hell of a lot of planning."

"Not a lot of time between that scene and the dead bodies."

Turner said, "Well, a couple of hours."

"But if it was random finder or finders then at least one other person knows who the killer is. Or is in league with the killer."

Turner riffed on a bit of the old Joe McCarthy bombast. "A conspiracy so immense, as it were."

"And a little unnerving."

Turner added, "Or a lot unnerving."

"But there were a million cops at that scene." Fenwick paused. "The killer then knows one of us, both of us, is one of us."

"All possible. It can't be random chance."

Fenwick said, "Or one of ours did it as a joke."

"Even you don't have a sense of humor that sick."

Fenwick sighed. "I guess I do have limits."

"For which I am thankful."

"I'm having a hard time with it being one of ours who did it deliberately."

Turner nodded. "Remember, Rodriguez got his car keyed, and it is possible that one of ours is the killer and did all this deliberately." The breeze helped control the sweat that wanted to escape from his every pore.

Fenwick asked, "Can we fight our own and the bad guys?"

"I guess we do what we have to. We just have to remember, convoluted as it may be, our own could be the bad guys in both cases. Or the same guys in both cases."

Fenwick said, "Why?"

Turner said, "I have no idea, but I think as we follow the threads of our murder case, we have to keep in mind, odd as it seems, that the threads could overlap with the Carruthers bullshit."

Just as they finished eating, they heard steps behind them and turned to the noise. Molton was silhouetted against the crime scene lights. He took a seat next to them and looked down on the street below. The three of them watched a bus just miss a pedestrian and an SUV as it pulled away from the curb.

The detectives had called Molton instantly with the news of the Taser being up here and then decided to grab a quick dinner while they waited for him. It didn't do to keep Fenwick from regular provender.

Molton gazed at the lights of the city for a moment. He said, "My guess is they will find no fingerprints on the Taser."

Fenwick and Turner nodded.

Fenwick said, "If the killer wanted to implicate me, us, he'd have had to be planning far enough ahead to bring gloves to the Carruthers scene. He couldn't have known it would be there for the taking."

Molton said, "We can all imagine scenarios about why the killer would bring it with."

Turner said, "It also means, has to mean, he was a witness to the Carruthers fiasco, and that somehow, the two events are connected."

Molton said, "We got how and why issues, timing."

Fenwick said, "Have to try and get every bit of security cam footage between here and there."

"That's presuming he or she took a direct route. I'm guessing we've got a smart killer. He could go any number of ways around."

Fenwick said, "And then the killer just strolled up here to randomly kill some activists? Why bring the Taser? And why not just dump it from where he took shots?"

Turner said, "All to screw up the investigation?"

Molton said, "To implicate you in this?"

"But how would this do that? He couldn't know we'd be assigned to the case."

Turner said, "Maybe he didn't care if we were assigned to the case. Maybe it was just to implicate us."

Fenwick said, "And to make any case against Carruthers suspect. He can scream about chain of evidence."

Molton said, "I'm not sure that holds much water. Taser here, and the lock from here missing. Strange." He shook his head, swung his legs, then gripped the balustrade with his hands, and looked at them. "Maybe it was to scare you guys."

"Take more than that to frighten me," Fenwick said.

"No, not scare in terms of make you frightened. Sure some of that, I suppose, but to make you uncertain, to make sure you're nervous. With all the police shootings, maybe somebody is targeting you specifically."

Fenwick said, "So why not just shoot at us? Why kill two activists?"

"Makes the investigation more complicated," Turner suggested.

"It does that," Fenwick said.

Molton said, "Or it could have been one of ours."

The detectives nodded. Turner said, "We discussed it. Didn't get us closer to the killer."

Fenwick said, "Made us more determined to get the son of a bitch."

Molton nodded.

They sat silent for a few moments. Then Molton said, "You guys want off the case?" He'd never made such an offer before.

"Should we?" Turner asked.

"I'm leaving this up to you."

Fenwick said, "Bullshit. We're not in danger because of this case. The Taser was left here as a message about us, not about solving the murder."

"I think you're right," Molton said.

Turner nodded.

Fenwick said, "I'm in."

Turner said, "Me too."

Molton said, "For now, treat your murder and the Carruthers incident as one thing. If they're connected, that means deep shit is going on. If not, fine, we've done extra work, but we need to be thorough. Until it's proven they aren't connected, we assume they are. We can't take a chance they are and we missed it. It might be a long shot, but we have no choice. That Taser at least is a cause for a suspicious and even deadly connection." He took a deep breath. "What's next?"

Turner said, "We go to where each of the dead guys were staying."

Molton turned to Fenwick, "How are your wounds?"

Fenwick grumbled. "Arm and head are still attached."

Molton said, "Good thing it was your arm and your head and not your wrist. You don't need more excuses to tell that stupid 'wrist joke.'"

Fenwick said, "You begged me to tell."

"And I'm still sorry."

The three of them stood. Molton said, "Good luck. Be safe." He left.

Turner and Fenwick sat in the air-conditioned car and each phoned home. They reassured respective spouses and children that all was well. Neither went into details.

Turner said to his older son Brian, "You don't have to cancel your plans and sit in a chair waiting for me."

"I already did. It's what you'd do for me."

"Ben can handle it."

"Dad, I made my choice."

"Thanks."

Thursday 10:21 P.M.

They walked into the Hotel Stevenson on Blue Island Avenue just south of Roosevelt Road.

Fenwick took one glance and said, "Hôtel Modière."

Turner knew Fenwick was making reference to the hotel where Melissa McCarthy stayed in Paris in the movie *Spy*. Turner knew Fenwick had a collection of all of Melissa McCarthy's movie work. Fenwick claimed to the unwary that *Spy* was one of the top three comic movies of all time.

Turner thought the movie was funny, too. He also glanced at their surroundings: woodpanel wallpaper wainscoting with paisley wallpaper above. Both upper and lower deeply faded with gray tints from not enough or excessive cleaning. Turner thought the tile on the floor might originally have been bright yellow festooned with masses of daises. Now it looked like amorphous dirty flowers surrounded by swaths of mud.

Turner said, "We never see the lobby of the hotel in the movie."

Fenwick was undaunted. "This is what it should have looked like."

The clerk behind the thermal glass at the counter didn't meet their eyes or deign to look at the IDs they held out. He snapped, "We're full."

Fenwick said, "We're cops."

Still ignoring them, the clerk picked up his phone, and said, "Arnie, you need to get out here now."

Turned out Arnie was the manager, thin, sharp faced, with hair dyed bright blond. On a teenager it might look trendy. On this guy, well into his fifties, it just looked odd.

Arnie spoke with a nasal twang. "We're full."

Fenwick repeated, "We're cops." Once again they held out their IDs.

Arnie glared at the clerk. "Why didn't you say so?"

Fenwick asked, "You're full?"

"Is that a crime?"

Fenwick said, "I'm not much in the mood to harass managers of seedy motels, but I can be convinced."

Arnie answered the original question, "Yes."

Turner said, "With all the activists for this week's meetings?"

Arnie said, "I guess."

Extracting a tooth from an angry rhino might have been easier than getting answers from him.

Fenwick said, "Double the rates to make a profit?"

"Being in business isn't a crime." Arnie glanced at the lobby. "They're in here all hours arguing about individual communities creating angst. I don't know what half the shit they say means."

"You listen?" Fenwick asked.

"They're loud."

"You know Henry Bettencourt or Preston Shaitan?"

"No."

Turner said, "We need to see Henry Bettencourt's room."

"You got a warrant?"

Fenwick said, "He's dead. His room is considered part of a crime scene."

"There's another person staying in that room."

"Who's that?"

Arnie nudged the clerk out of the way and tapped at the computer. He looked up and said, "Guy named David Westerman."

They phoned the room. There was no answer.

Arnie gave them the key.

No amount of industrial strength steam-cleaning could rescue the maroon roses in the tattered carpet in the second floor hall. A window at the end of the hall showed a bare dim bulb over a bricked-up window across the alley.

Hands near their guns, they knocked on the door. No answer. Turner unlocked it and eased it open. He flipped on the light. They entered. The dull-maroon carpeting continued from the hall into the room.

Fenwick made a quick check of the bathroom. Coming back out, he shook his head. It was empty.

Two full-sized beds were made. One suitcase sat on a table next to a television. Another suitcase was on the bed nearest the door. Both were closed and locked. From the keys they'd retrieved from Bettencourt's pocket, they were able to open the one on the table.

Years of work as detectives made their search quick, efficient, and thorough. Arnie had told them the maid had listed in her work chart that she'd finished the room at 2:36 that afternoon.

Finished, they stood together in the center of the room. Fenwick said, "Two different suitcases, two different names. Confirms good old Arnie's information."

They found nothing of value inside Bettencourt's suitcase. Turner had the key for the room's safe. He opened it. "We've got guns here and ammo."

"We'll have to see which of them owned them and if they had permits."

Near the door, they turned back to give the room a final once-over.

Fenwick said, "Looks like they checked in, but then maybe rushed right out again."

Turner pointed. "That table's been moved." The dresser had a television on top. Next to it was a chair and a table with a lamp.

"Huh?"

"You can see the faded part. See." He pointed to where inch-wide squares of non-faded carpet shown on the rug.

Fenwick said, "So somebody moved the table. It's an old motel. Probably gets cleaned, but it's not like the Ritz."

"Why?"

"Why move it? The maids in this hotel are crazed table movers? Moving tables was decreed from on high by great flaming dragons? Stop me when I get to something you like."

"What I like is when you stop."

Fenwick huffed.

Turner said, "We should question the maid." He moved the table back to fit the faded groves. It coincided perfectly. He moved it back to where it had been when they entered. He squatted down and looked underneath. He glanced over his shoulder at Fenwick. When he caught his partner's eye, Turner put his finger over his lips in a hush motion then beckoned him over.

Fenwick raised an eyebrow but had the sense to keep his mouth shut. He trundled his bulk over to Turner and attempted to squat, but after much huffing and puffing, he knelt next to his partner and peered where Turner pointed under the table. They gazed for several seconds then looked at each other, stood up, walked to the door, and took a few steps down the hall.

Turner asked, "You think all these motels bug their guests' rooms?"

"Who would do it? Why would they bother?"

"Somebody who is really paranoid, really pissed?"

"You think it's one of ours?"

"We're going to find out."

Turner called the crime scene unit. The oddity of a dead guy and a listening device made it a necessary step.

Coming down the hall was a beat cop walking alongside a tall African-American man in his mid-thirties.

The civilian asked, "What's going on in my room?"

"You David Westerman?" Turner asked.

"Yeah."

The beat cop left.

They talked in the hall.

Westerman asked, "What's going on? You can't go into my room without a warrant."

Turner asked, "You sharing this room with Henry Bettencourt?"

"I'm not answering any questions until you tell me what you're doing here. I'm calling my lawyer." He reached in his pocket and pulled out a phone.

Fenwick said, "Mr. Bettencourt is dead."

Westerman's hands stopped moving. He looked from one to the other of them then glanced toward the room.

"There's a body in my room?"

"No. He's not here."

"What happened?"

"He was murdered."

Westerman slumped against the wall and leaned his head back. After several deep breaths, he said, "I don't understand."

"Where have you been?" Fenwick asked.

"Out organizing. What happened?"

Fenwick said, "He was shot. Got his brains splattered all over a roof top."

"Oh, my!" Westerman shut his eyes and breathed deeply. After several moments passed, he looked at them.

Turner asked, "How well did you know him?"

"We were sharing this room. We'd emailed for a few months, but we'd just met here today."

"You didn't know him well?"

"By reputation, of course."

"How'd you wind up sharing a room?"

"The convention had a room-sharing service. Cheaper that way. Or for people like Bettencourt, who lived in the suburbs, but didn't want the hassle of driving through rush hour every day to get to meetings. There was lots to do and people to talk to. You don't want to be stuck in traffic."

Fenwick asked, "Why were you here with the other protest groups?"

"I'm the head of the organization Guns for Gangs. White people have the NRA. Black people should have the same right to be armed."

"Doesn't that kind of go against the cliché?"

"I don't care. Wendell Pierce said, 'If every black male 18-35 applied for a conceal & carry permit, and then joined the NRA in one day; there would be gun control laws in a second.' I agree with that."

Turner thought that sentiment was quite likely true.

Westerman continued, "Did you see the movie *Mississippi Burning*? How the white power structure was terrorizing the African American community? Too often, that's the way it's been and continues to be. What those people in that movie—in that community—should have had were their own guns, so that when the white folks showed up, they could have answered by blasting away with their own shotguns. We should be answering with guns now. We're just following the NRA, arming ourselves to protect ourselves. If it works for whites, it works for blacks."

Fenwick asked, "You making a profit from selling guns to people?"

"I'm raising awareness and making a profit, it is not a crime."

"You sell any guns while here?"

"No."

"Are you armed?"

"Not at the moment." He glanced toward the room.

Turner said, "The motel manager gave us the key to the safe."

"That's not right."

"Why not?"

This seemed to take him aback.

"Why are there five guns in the safe?" Fenwick asked.

"Why not? I have permits for all of them. I'm also the liaison with the national gun rights groups."

"They're happy about a group named Guns for Gangs?" Fenwick asked.

"The right wing has been making cash out of frightening white people. I see no reason not to make money out of frightening black people. Works the same way." Westerman gave a snort. "For some reason the biggest and largest of the national gun organizations won't have anything to do with us. Can you say racist pigs?"

"Did Bettencourt have guns?"

"I have no idea."

"Where were you from five to seven today?"

"I told you, organizing."

"We're going to need specific names."

"I'll need my lawyer."

"We're not arresting you."

"Then I'm free to leave."

Fenwick said, "No one ever said you had to stay."

Westerman moved toward the room.

Fenwick held up his hand and said, "For now, it's part of a crime scene."

"When can I get my things?"

"When we're done with the room."

"Are you confiscating my guns?"

Turner switched topics. "Were you aware there was a listening and recording device in the room?"

"What? That's an outrage!"

"Any idea who put it there?"

"Enemies of all that is free and good. Perhaps the Chicago police." He paused. "Was it a video recorder or just voice recorder?"

"Something you didn't want video of?" Fenwick asked.

"Without my consent, I want nothing videotaped or my voice recorded. Doesn't matter what's on it. What matters is my lack of consent."

Fenwick said, "If you had the guns for protection, who were you afraid of?"

"Any random cop."

"You were planning to have shootouts with cops?"

"We need good men with guns."

Fenwick burst out laughing. Turner was more circumspect. They both knew the fallacy of that myth.

Westerman knew nothing more. He retired grumbling.

When Westerman was gone, Fenwick asked, "Guns for Gangs?"

Turner said, "I've never heard of them, but it's one way for the gun culture to infest more of society."

Fenwick said, "No matter what Westerman said, the name is redundant in the specific. I thought that's what defined gangs, guns and violence."

"Are you positing there are left wing or right wing pacifist gangs armed or unarmed?"

Fenwick said, "Either of them if it helps solve the case."

"Problem is once you add 'gang' to a group, in this day and age, it assumes violence."

"Yeah, but I bet the NRA is behind Westerman too."

"Why?" Turner asked.

"It's all about sales not safety or the Second Amendment."

Thursday 10:58 P.M.

They walked to the address Fong had provided for where Shaitan was staying, a block from Bettencourt's hotel. Fenwick called Sanchez. The beat cop said they'd managed to get in touch with Mrs. Bettencourt. She had her kids to take care of and wouldn't be available for an interview until the morning.

Shaitan was staying at a bed and breakfast hotel. Oscar's Endeavour was three old homes, one on a corner, renovated into one Victorian gingerbread confection. The shutters were freshly painted royal purple on bright white clapboard.

The front desk was in the corner house's old parlor. Turner and Fenwick showed ID to Jason Smith, a muscular man in his mid-thirties.

Turner said, "We understand Preston Shaitan was staying here."

Smith said, "If I'd known who he was when he rented the room, I'd have found an excuse not to rent to him. I do not need self-hating morons staying here."

"How come you didn't notice him?"

"One of the hired help took his reservation."

"Who told you about him?"

"The guy who checked him in."

Fenwick said, "Shaitan is dead."

Smith gaped for a moment.

Turner asked, "Was he here alone?"

"As far as I know. He's in the cupola room, the gazebo at the top, the meeting of the L. We just finished renovating it last month."

"Can you give us a key?"

He presented them with a plastic key card.

They took the short elevator ride to the top. There was only one door on this floor. It opened into a six hundred-square-foot room that had a nearly 360° view of the city outside. Turner could see distant lightning to their south.

Fenwick gazed around. "This is kind of nice." A circular bed in the middle of the room was covered in a thick comforter, and strewn with comfy pillows. Their colors matched the two plush couches, one on the north wall, the other opposite it. The air conditioning was on high. The room felt good.

Turner said, "I hear water running, a shower, I think."

Fenwick cocked his head. They looked at the only other door in the room. The bathroom was on the opposite wall from the desk. Fenwick lowered his voice, "Who the hell would be in the shower here at this time?"

They pulled their guns and moved to either side of the bathroom door. The sound of falling water was louder now.

Fenwick tried the door. It was unlocked. He opened it a crack. "Police!" he bellowed in his best menacing baritone.

The water stopped abruptly.

"Who's there?" yelled a female voice.

"Chicago police. We need to talk to you."

"This is absurd. Get out. I'm calling the manager. How did you get in here?"

"We need to talk to you," Turner said.

The door was yanked open. They leveled their guns at Marjorie Zelvin, the protester from the bridge.

"What the hell are you doing here?" Fenwick and Zelvin spoke at the same time. She wore a bathrobe with the logo of a prancing bear on it. In one hand, she held a towel, in the other a phone.

Marjorie Zelvin tried to barge into the room. Fenwick prevented her from moving forward by the simple expedient of standing in the way. There wasn't much room on either side of him for a shadow, much less a person, to get by.

"Let me pass." Marjorie's voice was at shriek level.

"What are you doing up here?" Fenwick asked.

"I've got a key."

"You do?" Fenwick asked.

"Yes."

"The manager didn't tell us Shaitan had someone staying with him. Or you didn't register, but stayed here unofficially to save money. You were staying with Mr. Shaitan?" Turner asked.

"Yes." Her eyes shifted. "No."

Turner and Fenwick waited.

"I knew him," she said.

"Intimately?" Fenwick asked.

"Sort of."

"Please explain," Turner said.

Her voice rose to a shriek. "I don't have to explain to the police. This isn't a police state. I have my rights. And I want to finish drying off and get dressed. I don't want to stand here half naked."

Turner said, "You can leave or answer questions." In the brief time they had to look, he had seen no evidence of a second person staying in the room, but they hadn't opened all the suitcases yet.

She thought for a moment and said, "What do you want?"

Turner said, "We need to know why you're here."

"I'm one of the leaders of the conference. I'm monitoring what's going on."

Fenwick asked, "How'd that protest march go from the bridge?

That break up already?"

"I try to be many places. I just got back. I was tired and sweaty from all the marching. Are Preston and Henry really dead?" She gulped.

"I'm sorry, yes," Turner said.

She turned very white. She said, "I'm going to finish drying off, and then I'll be out."

She shut the bathroom door.

While waiting, they rooted through a suitcase open on the luggage rack. A few skimpy bikini briefs all in faux-tiger patterns, a few wrinkled shirts, and a pair of jeans, and a few toilet articles. They found a small bag of pills and a baggy of marijuana. In the closet they found a navy blue sport coat, a thin red tie, and a wrinkled white shirt. Two more suitcases and a backpack.

Fenwick asked, "They were trying to hide her stuff in case the cleaning staff got suspicious?"

"Possible," Turner said.

Zelvin emerged a few moments later. Her hair was still damp. She wore the clothes they'd seen her in earlier.

She sat on the bed. They sat in chairs.

"You stayed with him to save money."

"Yes, there was a lot of that at this convention."

Fenwick asked, "What was your relationship with the deceased?"

"We've had many meetings and discussions."

"You agreed with his politics?" Fenwick asked.

"What does that have anything to do with it? We talked. We were of use to each other."

"In what way?"

"We wanted to get crowds here. Shaitan drew crowds."

"You were that desperate for attendance?" Fenwick asked.

"We wanted to make the police listen to us. We can't let the police run roughshod over us."

Turner asked, "Did Shaitan have enemies?"

"All of us who are leaders in the group had enemies of some kind."

Turner asked, "Are there any specific threats that you were aware of?"

"Well, no, I guess not. He always talked about being a martyr to a cause. We all did. We were willing to give our all, each for his own cause."

"Did you know where he was going today, this evening?"

"We were all rushing around madly planning, organizing, seeing old friends. What can you tell me about what happened to him?"

Fenwick said, "You know we can't discuss an open investigation with anyone. I'm sure there will be a press conference you can attend."

"How well did you know him?" Turner asked.

"We had some uninspiring sex last night. Ate breakfast together this morning. I haven't seen him since."

Fenwick said, "I thought he was gay."

"I'm not prejudiced. He wasn't very good. He needed lots of help. We were slightly intimate, but we weren't really friends. He didn't confide in me."

Turner asked, "Do you have training in marksmanship?"

"I've never even held a gun."

Fenwick asked, "What's the deal with this guy? We heard one story that it was all fake on his part. He said outrageous things just to make money, so he could get attention from an audience."

She gave a half smile. "He created animosity through melodramatic provocation."

"What does that mean?" Fenwick asked.

"He didn't care what other people thought. He would debate, and I've seen him take several sides on one issue, just as long as the side he took was controversial and likely to get him publicity."

Fenwick said, "He was a blatant hypocrite, but you were staying with him?"

"Being a protester and getting what you want takes time, effort, and commitment. The more protests, the more publicity, the more people attend."

Fenwick said, "Unless they get frightened by the violence and don't show up."

"Fear cannot be what rules our protests. There are a lot of good well-meaning people here. Some have sacrificed their lives to try to make the world a better place. Real people have been shot by real police."

Fenwick interrupted, "And vice-versa."

She shook her head. "You represent the patriarchal power structure so I wouldn't expect you to understand."

Turner interrupted before Fenwick could get into full debate mode with her. He said, "We'll need to seal off this room. We'll let you take a few things. We haven't opened all the suitcases. If you want, we can have a woman officer here to check your things before you take them."

"I don't need much or have much."

"If he didn't confide in you, who did he confide in?"

"Sorry, I don't know. You'll have to talk to some of the other protesters." She rounded on them. "I have some questions for you."

They just looked at her. They had learned to let players in the drama keep talking. They were more likely to trip themselves up. She stared at them each for a few seconds then said, "What are you doing to find out if this was a false flag operation?"

"Beg pardon?" Fenwick asked.

"Killing those two as being part of a plot by the government to switch the focus to protesters."

"How does that work, exactly," Fenwick asked.

"The important part for our conversation," she said, "is my trying to figure out if you're part of covering up the crime, or you may have committed the crime. Or the crime was planned by the government to have another excuse to take out guns."

Fenwick said, "Other than pointless, endless speculation, do you have any evidence for that?"

"Hah! Evidence. Maybe all you're doing is going around making sure the evidence that the government cooked this up is all destroyed."

Fenwick asked, "If there's no evidence for anything that you say, how could there be any proving what you say?" She started to respond, but he held up a hand. "If it's all endless, proofless, speculation, why then aren't we free to speculate that you did it, for whatever reasons we could find, or hell, according to you, don't need to find, or we could plant some evidence, to make it look like you did it? Since we're endlessly speculating, why don't we just arrest you and be done with it?"

"I wouldn't put it past you."

Tuner put his hand on Fenwick's arm to forestall further debate. He said, "We have work to do, Ms. Zelvin, so unless you know something specific, we'll have to ask you to take a few things under our supervision."

She knew nothing else. After she grabbed some basic articles from the smallest suitcase, she shuffled out the door. They made sure she got on the elevator before returning to the room.

Back in the room, they looked at each other. Fenwick pulled in a lungful of air. He said, "False flag?"

"You're not up on your conspiracy theories?"

"I've never actually met anyone who admitted to believing that shit. The government holds a massacre in order to take away your rights, often gun rights? Who believes that shit? And is it supposed to make sense?"

"You expect a working cop to be able to explain the lunacy of the universe? We've both seen too much to even try."

Fenwick sat on the edge of the bed. He said, "What the hell was that all about? She makes no sense to me."

Turner said, "She wanted to make sure she'd be higher on our suspect list?"

"If that was her goal, she has succeeded."

"Or this may have been her room, and she didn't care if the guy she was sharing it with was dead."

"The dead guy wouldn't mind."

"Presumably not."

"She didn't seem broken up about either guy being dead."

"Have we run into anybody who's sad about either one yet?"

"Well, no."

They inspected the room. The computer they bagged for Fong. Turner opened the third suitcase and called Fenwick over. "Half of this is clothes." He pointed. "Then there's all this electronic shit crammed into this other side."

"What the fuck?"

Turner said, "I recognize an iPod, the iPad, and there's all these millions of wires, but I'm not sure what all these other components are or what connects to what."

"Bag it all, and we'll take it to Fong."

Along with the key, the manager had given them the combination to the safe which was on the floor of the closet. Turner opened it and gave a low whistle. Fenwick leaned over. He gave a soft, "Wow."

It was filled with stacks of money.

Turner said, "We need the crime scene people in here. They'll have to count all this."

Without touching anything, Fenwick glanced at the bills visible at the tops of several stacks. "All hundreds." Fenwick stood up straight. "Zelvin didn't seem concerned about the safe."

Turner nodded. "If she knew this money was here, you'd think she'd have tried to get into the closet and the safe in some way."

They shut and locked it.

After their inspection, Turner and Fenwick stood together looking at the distant lights of the Loop.

Fenwick said, "Strikes me as a special kind of stupid to be carrying around that much cash. Why?"

Turner shrugged. "Let's try simpler stuff. Where's he from?"

While Turner checked the wallet the found on the body, Fenwick Googled. Turner said, "This says he's from Newton, Iowa."

Fenwick said, "The Internet claims he lives in a yurt in India. Don't people live in yurts in Mongolia?"

"Jeff was watching one of those Animal Planet wilderness shows." Jeff was his younger son, super smart, and often surprisingly well informed about esoteric bits of out of the way knowledge. Turner continued, "Some guy lived in a yurt far out in the woods in Minnesota. Looked to me more like a luxury yurt condo than a nomad's tent. For several months, Jeff did huge amounts of research on making yurts handicap accessible."

They checked the room for listening devices. Under the swivel chair Turner found two items taped to the bottom. He got Fenwick's attention and motioned him over. Together they turned over the chair.

Turner said, "I'm pretty sure these are CPD dash cams or at least they look like them."

Fenwick said, "What the fuck?"

Turner said, "More stuff to give to Fong. We've got to know if they're new or used, and how the hell they got here, and if it was Shaitan, how the hell he got hold of them in the first place."

Fenwick asked, "Shaitan is in on a conspiracy against us? Against the Chicago police? Just likes to collect souvenirs from crime scenes?"

"If these are from cop cars that were at the earlier scene."

Fenwick said, "Double and triple fuck."

They found no other listening devices. Turner said, "We should have checked for them first."

Fenwick said, "We'll have to check every place we enter for them."

When the crime scene people arrived, they pointed out the safe and its contents.

Thursday 11:31 P.M.

They strolled back to their car. The wind was still up but a glance at the local weather radar on his phone showed Turner that all the local storms had dissipated.

Sounds from the cars whizzing by on the nearby Eisenhower expressway mixed with the rustle of the leaves on the trees.

Turner pressed the unlock button on the car's remote.

Fenwick bellowed, "Gun."

Turner flopped to the ground and yanked out his gun. In seconds Fenwick squat-walked onto Paul's side of the car.

"What?" Turner asked.

"There is a bullet hole in the car door next to the handle. There wasn't one when we parked."

"You sure?" Turner asked.

Fenwick gave one of his most menacing grumbles.

Turner called for backup then said, "You didn't scream 'bullet hole.'"

"Would have taken longer. And wouldn't have been as effective. And I didn't scream."

Turner dropped any discussion of voice level.

Still crouched on the ground, Fenwick eased open the car door. The interior light went on.

Turner said, "If someone had a gun, you just made us targets."

Fenwick pointed to a hole in the headrest of the passenger seat. "And it travelled inside. That wasn't there." He slammed the door shut.

Fenwick was fastidious about his environment. Turner knew his buddy would have noticed.

"Random or deliberate?" Fenwick asked.

"I'm low on extra-coincidence pills right now."

"Who then? And connected to what? The sniper who hit the guys on the roof top was bored and decided to attack us too? The sniper wanted to kill us so he killed those two in hopes we'd be assigned the case, knew where we parked, risked taking a gunshot on the street when we weren't around? We saved the kid and rogue cops are after us? We saved the kid and rogue community members are after us? Stop me when I get to something you think is plausible."

Turner said, "At this point I think a million things are possible. I'm just not sure which one is probable. And there could be several thousand other possibilities. If they were trying to kill us, why not wait until we got back here to the car? Or, hell, shoot us as we walked down the street."

"Maybe they wanted to scare us?"

"To what end?"

That stumped Fenwick for several moments, but then he said, "It could have been a random shot. I suppose."

"That's definitely plausible, but I'm going to keep an open mind. A random shooter killing two guys on a roof top, hits two victims with incredible accuracy, and then sets out to murder a car. Why? What does he gain, accomplish, prove?"

Fenwick says, "I think the correct medical diagnosis for this is 'fucked up.'"

"And who could disagree?" Turner asked.

Fenwick speculated, "Someone knew we'd be going here? Somebody recognized the car? Knew our schedule? We can't be sure this is about us. Some bad guy doesn't just randomly begin going places and come up with us. There's gotta be sense to this."

Turner grinned. "Good luck with that."

They sat in shadows on the pavement and pulled in breaths. Fenwick broke the silence. "As a reaction to this, maybe we could try running around like morons with our hair on fire."

"Dealing with frustration in an immature manner isn't my style."

"Another one of your flaws."

"Are we having a contest?"

"No, I'd win that one."

A squad car squealed to a stop six feet from them. Turner and Fenwick held up badges.

Everybody began doing reports and paperwork. Molton showed up with the bomb squad. He said, "We're going to be certain." An initial check found no explosive device.

The three of them speculated about possible and plausible, but got no further than when Turner and Fenwick discussed it. At the news of the cash in Shaitan's room, Molton raised an eyebrow. "I'll monitor the crime scene folks on that."

As they were leaving, Molton told them, "Be careful. We can't leave out the option that this was a deliberate attack. We're getting random bullshit since Carruthers opened fire. I don't like random. Consider all of it as one. After we get evidence, we'll sort out what goes with what."

Rather than inconvenience some beat cops, they took a cab back to the station. Molton would stay with their unmarked car until the bomb squad was completely finished. He'd also take direct charge of all the forensics at the scene.

Outside their cab, but before they entered headquarters, they stood on the steps. Fenwick said, "How did that beat cop have the nerve to confront us?"

"Huh?"

"The more I think about it, that might be the oddest thing that's occurred today."

"Not the gunshot in the car?"

"I guess they're neck and neck."

"Maybe he was just an asshole."

Fenwick said, "Maybe there's a Friends of Carruthers society."

"If there is, we could join, and maybe get some insight into human nature."

"Insight into stupidity?"

"Far too often these days, kind of the same thing."

"I wonder if that cop we confronted had a camera."

Turner said, "He didn't. I was careful to observe his uniform. He was from Palakowski's district. They aren't using them yet. There were no witnesses."

In Chicago, police body cams were being introduced over a number of years. They were only in one or two districts by this time.

Turner continued, "I'm not sure what we're going to have to put up with from our own."

"You criticizing my actions?"

"No."

"You're not happy with my behavior?"

"That list is too long. Specifically tonight? No. The problem is, I think I would have done the same thing if I'd been the one closest to him, and he'd mouthed off to me. Or maybe worse."

"You? Mister Calm?"

"As a dear, hefty friend of mine is wont to say, it's a curse."

Fenwick said, "What if the Friends of Carruthers Society is also killing random protesters?"

"What'd Molton say? Consider all this as one?"

"Yeah."

"We'll have to just follow the evidence. Like we always do."

Fenwick sighed. “I’m tired, and my arm is beginning to ache.”

“Let’s see if we can’t wrap this up and get the hell out of here at something like a reasonable hour.”

“That’ll be lucky.”

Friday 12:14 A.M.

Inside the station, the first thing they did was find Steve Fong who inhabited an office in the deepest sub-basement of the decrepit old building. Naked pipes clanged and gurgled in the hall. The linoleum on the floor had long since faded to yellowish gray and begun to curl at the edges. Although today, great swaths of the old linoleum were now stacked in a corner. Fong was replacing it with new materials on his own time. The job looked to be over half done.

His office had been part of the coal bin back when someone actually had to stoke coal into a furnace to heat the place. The LED displays from all the electronic equipment added to the dim light from a forest of small lamps. Fong had tried to install stronger lamps, but if he plugged in too many even slightly high-powered electronic devices, all the circuits in the building shorted out. He had the largest computer monitor Turner had ever seen, but it was seldom on, as it used up too much of Fong's limited power. More wattage in the basement had been promised. Like all promises at Area Ten, it never got fulfilled.

Fong was six-foot-three and rail thin. He had a wicked sense of humor.

"You guys okay?" Fong asked.

They mumbled yeah.

"Somebody attacked your car?"

"Word travels fast."

"I got scanners down here that cover the city. You heard what happened to Rodriguez." Fong tapped a speaker.

"What?"

"He got threatened. Some anonymous scammer got into the system, threatened him over the police radio."

"Son of a bitch," Fenwick said.

Turner asked, "How is that even possible?"

"I've heard of it happening in other cities," Fong said. "In one place, someone used a store-bought two-way radio and turned it into a police walkie talkie."

Fenwick rattled the box of electronics they got from Shaitan's room. "Anything in here that might work to cause that?"

Fong glanced. A few seconds later, he took out what looked like a kids communication kit from a toy game.

Fenwick said, "That?"

"I'll go over it. Could be."

"When was the call made?"

"After eight."

Turner said, "Shaitan was dead long before then. Unless someone put this stuff in his room to implicate him."

Fenwick said, "Or he just randomly happened to have duplicates of the exact stuff we're looking for."

They looked at him. "I know," Fenwick said. "Not likely. What the hell is going on here?"

Fong said, "It all sounds kind of inexplicable, eerie, and moving toward frightening."

Fenwick said, "Got that right."

Turner asked, "Was it a male or female caller?"

"I've listened to the tape." He pulled it up on his computer. It only took a few seconds to play. The caller said, "Be true to the blue, or we're going to slit your throat."

"Sounds male," Turner said, "and it doesn't sound like he was trying to disguise his voice. Does the caller want Rodriguez to be true to me and Fenwick as cops who saved a kid, or to be true to Carruthers who almost killed a kid?"

"You want people who threaten to be more specific?" Fong asked.

"Well, yeah. If someone wanted to comply with a threat, it would be great if we knew what compliance was."

Fenwick said, "You're so demanding."

Fong said, "Maybe you should put out a *Threatener's Handbook*."

Turner had the grace to smile and thought a moment. "We have to be careful and take it seriously, although it could be just some random nut."

"Nothing on us?" Fenwick asked Fong.

"I've been expecting something. Nothing so far."

Again Fenwick rattled the box of electronics. "Can you do anything else with all this shit?"

Fong said, "Like always, I'll do my best with all of it. There's more news. You guys know that Carruthers' dashboard cam has been reported as missing and has been reported as not working at the time?"

"So which is it?"

"People are scrambling madly. If I can, I'll get copies of all of what they've got, and/or what there is, and put something together for you."

Fenwick said, "Cover up."

Fong asked, "By whom about what?"

Everybody shrugged.

They gave him their bags of equipment gathered from several scenes. Turner said, "Some of this stuff might answer some of the questions you just asked."

"Or give us new ones," Fong said.

"Maybe," Turner said.

Fong said he'd begin working on all the cameras on the city streets or in any local businesses around the Carruthers scene, the shooting scene, and the bullet-in-the car scene. "It's going to take me a while to look into the phones, listening devices, and dash cams you just gave me."

Friday 12:37 A.M.

At their desks, fans turned to high, Fenwick leaned back in his chair and perused the brochure from the convention. After a few moments, he said, "Every angry cliché is represented here at this event. Why? Was that planned? Or they invited all the angriest groups of protesters here? Or just leaders of the angriest groups? Anti-government officials left and right? Good people trying to help the world? Inarticulate boobs? Screamers? People ready to lose their tempers? Who gains? The right wing? Are we saying they organized all their enemies just so those enemies would come to town and make fools of themselves? Or they'd get all their enemies to town and commit murder? Or both sides had the same goal, death and destruction? Both sides already treat each other with disdain. If you pile cliché upon cliché, what have you gained?"

Turner said, "I'm not sure they care about what they gain. Think about it, whoever you are, say you're in the middle of a huge rally by the opposition. And you stand up and start screaming. There's one of you and ten thousand opponents. What do you expect to gain? If you're that kind of person, are you really capable of that kind of thinking ahead?" He opened his laptop. "Let's get paperwork done and go home."

Fenwick grunted.

Fifteen minutes later, Rodriguez walked in. He clumped over to their desks and plunked himself into a chair. He looked at each of them then said, "I just got done talking to Fong. He told me about the threat. I heard you guys had a hell of a night as well."

They swapped stories.

"All this to protect Carruthers?" Rodriguez said. "I've worked with him for years, and there's always been a certain arrogance in his behavior, but this is nuts. His career, presumably, is over, and the problem that he was, or the problems that he caused, don't go the fuck away? This is nuts."

"Got that right," Fenwick said.

Rodriguez nodded at Turner. "Carruthers wanted to talk to me like he talked to you."

"Did you?"

"No. I figured it was useless."

Turner said, "It pretty much was."

Rodriguez stood up. "I'm going home."

After exchanging 'hang in theres' and 'everything's going to be all rights,' he left.

They finished the essentials of their paperwork in half an hour and left.

In the parking lot, Paul walked around his car to check for any problems. No key marks. Nothing obvious. Too paranoid? Too tired? He started the car and was pleased it didn't blow up. He smiled at himself. Too melodramatic? Not frightened enough? More frightened than he needed to be?

Friday 1:07 A.M.

It was just after one when Paul pulled into his driveway. Ben sat on the front porch. He stood up as Paul strode up the sidewalk. They met on the bottom step. Paul felt the fierce embrace and a feeling of safety washed over him. He could feel Ben's chest and legs solid and firm through their clothes. He took a deep whiff of Ben's after work smell, sweat, grease, the warmth of his skin on the June summer night, and a hint of deodorant. Early in their relationship, Paul had asked Ben if he would not shower after work. The aroma of all of him was a turn on, but it also reminded him of his husband, a scent of intimacy he could carry in his memory for when they were apart. Right now was a thousand times better than the few moments they'd had in the hospital.

In a few moments, Ben leaned back and said, "He's started another textbook."

"What this time?" Their younger son, Jeff, had a habit in times of stress of quantifying things. As a child who had dealt with spina bifida every instant of his existence, Jeff was sensitive to showing any sign of weakness, no matter how often his dads told him how proud they were of him, that physical strength wasn't the only kind of strength, and that there were lots of ways to be strong and brave.

It often didn't matter what Jeff counted. When he was three, it was railroad cars. In kindergarten, he moved on from counting random items to math textbooks. He'd go through a whole book, finishing every problem in every chapter. Checking his answers. These days, when under heavy stress, he worked on calculus textbooks.

Ben said, "More calculus, but this time he's saving articles too, anything to do with police."

"He and I have talked about me being in a dangerous profession."

"I've talked with him too, but with all the recent events, his anxiety has gone up." Ben paused for a moment then said, "So has mine."

They embraced again. This was a discussion they had as often as they needed to help relieve each other's anxieties, as well as those of their kids.

"How's Brian?"

"Probably holding it in like he always does." The older boy tended to hold in his emotions in what he thought was a macho-male mode of reticence.

They entered the house. The air-conditioning hummed below the level of consciousness. Brian was sprawled on the couch. He'd fallen asleep with the first Harry Potter book on his chest and his head resting on Jeff's left thigh. He and Jeff had been reading the books out loud to each other. The whole family had read them when they came out, but the boys had decided reading them out loud again would be a good gift to give to each other before Brian left for college in the fall. Brian wore baggy soccer shorts and a deep purple ASOS sleeveless side-cut T-shirt with extreme dropped armholes. With one arm thrown across his eyes, his damp under-arm hair shone and glistened.

Jeff was wide awake. The boy seemed to relish outré sleep habits during summer vacations. As long as they didn't spill over into the school year, Turner didn't mind. Other than his large, athletic brother, Jeff's wheelchair and every other surface was covered with textbooks and strewn with paper. Jeff liked to switch from computer to textbook to hard copy as he worked the more difficult problems.

He looked up when his dads came in.

"You okay?" he asked.

Paul gave him a brief hug and said, "Yeah."

Brian shook himself awake. "You okay?" he asked.

"Yeah."

Jeff asked, "Were you scared?"

"Yes."

"How did you know what to do?"

"I just acted."

"What were you thinking?"

"I just acted."

The kid could be more persistent than a well-trained reporter.

Jeff held up his iPad. He asked, "Why is everyone so angry?"

Ben said, "It's very late. We're all tired. Why don't we discuss all this in the morning?"

Everybody headed for bedrooms.

Friday 1:27 A.M.

As Turner perched on the side of their bed, he eyed the bulge in Ben's black boxer briefs. He felt a stirring of interest. Ben was placing his well-worn and freshly stained work clothes in their special hamper. Ben took direct interest in fixing the foreign oddities his car, truck, and motorcycle shop specialized in. Paul loved the smell of grease, grime, grit, and sweat.

Ben sat next to him and gazed into his eyes. "You faced bullets today. From one of your own. Are you okay?"

Paul's phone buzzed. Late night calls seldom boded well. He glanced at it then over at Ben. He said, "Ian is on the front porch."

Ben said, "Something must be wrong."

Turner nodded. He threw on a pair of jeans and hurried down stairs.

Even at this hour, the air outside continued humid-sticky. Ian sat on a swing on the far south side of the porch. He wore his slouch fedora low on his forehead, legs stretched out far in front of him, khaki pants winkled after a full day.

Ian said, "Mrs. Talucci let me pass."

"For some reason, she likes you."

"For that, I'm glad."

Paul glanced at his neighbor's house. He heard a faint rocking from the darkened and shadowed front porch. Mrs. Talucci would be there reigning magisterially over her street. She told Paul once that she didn't sleep much anymore. Just lots of naps while knitting in her favorite chair. Late at night when out on her porch, she might have her knitting in her lap and her shotgun propped next to her. She said she did that mostly for effect to keep up her reputation as this was one of the safer neighborhoods in the city. Or at least her part of it was.

Ian stared from under his hat brim at the nearest street light. He said, "I went there to kill Shaitan."

Turner gazed at his old friend and former lover. "What stopped you?"

"He was already dead."

"Why didn't you tell me and Fenwick this earlier?"

"I'm not as perfect as I presume I am."

Paul sat in the empty portion of the swing and gazed at his friend. "Why did you want to kill him?"

"He deserved to die. And don't quote that Tolkien shit to me. Not now. Not again."

Turner knew Ian was referring to Gandalf's words in the *Lord of the Rings,* "Some die that deserve life. Can you give that to them? Then be not too eager to hand out death in the name of justice, even the wise cannot see all ends." Turner believed that, although he could see why Ian was tempted in this case.

Paul said, "How about if you tell me your story, with all of the parts this time, and make sure all the parts are true."

For a moment, Ian lifted his hat brim with one finger on one hand, turned to Paul, caught his eye in the dim light. He said, "You know me too well."

One of the reasons they'd broken up many years ago was Ian's infidelity, and the rigmarole of lies he invented to disguise his perfidy.

Ian said, "I was going to meet Preston Shaitan."

"What was Bettencourt doing there?"

"I really did have a meeting with him but set for much later." Ian shrugged. "Maybe he was just unlucky showing up when he did. I've met Bettencourt. He's worse than you. He thinks if people talk about things, they can resolve their differences. In the past, he's talked about meeting with Preston Shaitan to establish a new paradigm for opposites getting along." Ian hesitated, took off his hat, and placed it on the porch. He rubbed his eyes. "I didn't get there and find them dead. The door to the roof?" He hesitated.

"Yeah."

"I'd just opened it when the shots were fired. I saw the blood. The violence. I saw them die."

Paul watched his old friend. "You couldn't have stopped it."

"I know, and yes, I know I saw violence and the results of it when I was on the job. I know. I know. Maybe I'm no longer used to it. Maybe I never was. It was..." He sighed. "I was frightened."

Paul patted his old friend's shoulder. "You'll be okay."

"I guess." After a few moments of silence, Ian said, "I had sex with them both. Not tonight," he rushed to add at Paul's look.

"You'd met them both before." Now Paul was angry.

"I know. I lied."

"You're still so good at it."

"I'm sorry."

Paul's voice was clipped and short. "Tell me about it. Everything."

"I did preliminary interviews in my hotel room."

"Where?"

"I'm staying at the Park Hyatt. I got a room with a view of the Water Tower. I like to stay there if I'm working on a story, and when I can afford it. It's like a vacation. Preston and I were in my room. It was late at night. For half an hour, he bragged about what a shit he was, and how he loved being a shit to the world, how he loved shitting on everyone and making them miserable. I'd read about him for years. And then he started coming on to me." Ian shook his head. "He bragged and bounced. I couldn't resist making him think I was giving in to him."

"I didn't know you were a celebrity fucker."

"I'm usually not, but I let him think he was seducing me. I needed the story. Things aren't bad at the paper. They're awful. By the end of next week, I think half the staff is going to be let go. I needed this story. I wanted the two of them to meet. I wanted an historic get together."

"Of two unknowns? Who cares about these two except masters of the esoteric protest?"

"Please, let me explain."

Turner subsided.

"I wanted a connection with them. I worked my charm. He seemed to think he was working his charm on me. I let him think so."

Ian was still an attractive man who worked out five days a week.

Ian continued. "The foreplay was disappointing. The actual play was anemic at best." Ian sighed. "I wanted to find out what he was up to. Was he as big a charlatan as I supposed? He certainly was sexually."

"You know he had fifty thousand dollars in his closet in his hotel room?"

"Yeah. He told me about it."

"You didn't think we'd be interested in knowing that?"

"You gonna berate me or let me talk? You used to let me talk."

"You used to not be this big of an asshole. You were willing to sacrifice our friendship to your job?"

Ian hung his head. "I apologize. I'm sorry. I'm sorry. I'm sorry. But I can make it up." He glanced up at Turner and corrected, "Begin to make it up to you. I will apologize for as long and as often as you like." He sighed. "When he told me about the money, it was like he was showing off. Like he was going to bribe the city into a riotous holocaust all by his devious doing. So I met with Bettencourt around four in the morning. He wasn't staying in town until the day of the murder. He was quite friendly. He was quite good sex, actually fun.

He was comfortable enough to sleep there for a few hours after we finished."

He cleared his throat. "So, I told him about all that money, and the bribes, and the chicanery. Bettencourt's people were taking actions of their own. Of course, they both knew about each side trying chicanery, but not how extensive it was. I wanted to get the two of them together as flashpoints of stupidity against each other." He gave a deeper sigh. "So yes, I was a shit, so yes, I should have told you, so yes, I may have ruined the most important friendship in my life for a piece of crap story, no matter how newsworthy it might have been. But see there's more."

"More? They're dead." Paul sighed, "Why bother?"

"Why not? I thought having had sex with either of them was something I could use later."

"How?"

"Who knows? I like to keep things in reserve."

Ian's devious streak had been another problem when they were a couple.

Ian continued, "Shaitan wouldn't kiss. Turned his head away when our lips got close." Ian leaned forward. "He had a three inch dick fully hard. I almost laughed at him. He came as soon as I entered him then just lay there. I did some in and out for about a minute, but he was so unresponsive. I never came."

"What about Bettencourt?"

"It was a friendly, funny interview. He was a lot of fun. We sat on the couch, and I sat a little close, and he didn't back away, and I moved a little closer, then I set my glass of soda down and touched his leg as I put it on the table. And one thing led to another. I think he just liked fun. He was ten inches and a great kisser. When I entered him he said, 'You're big, go slow.' He's married to a woman, so I guess he might be straight, but either way, he was a fun guy."

"How do you run into so many who are willing?"

"I just don't tell you about all the ones who aren't."

"You knew both intimately, and you were on the scene when it happened?"

Ian asked, "Are you going to arrest me?"

"I'm going to be pissed off at you for quite a while. Really pissed off."

"I'm so, so sorry. I know I fucked up."

"And I have no forensic evidence that you killed them. You know that. You knew that before you came here."

"Lecture me about being unprofessional?"

"Would it do any good?"

"No."

"And part of why you came to me is, you know, no matter how pissed I am, it isn't my style to lecture."

"You are kind that way."

"As Fenwick would say, it's a curse."

"I've also gone to a couple of Shatain's talks. I was there at the one where most of the crowd sat there in unmoving silence. I nearly busted out laughing. The guy looked frightened."

"It might have been fun to see."

"Shaitan was a danger to others and himself for that matter. We are justified in our paranoia. He fueled the hatred and was one of our own."

"And you'd sacrifice the rest of your life to kill him?"

"I didn't say I was thinking logically. That closeted guy who tried to shoot up a gay street fair in Chicago a few weeks ago considers this guy a hero. I wrote an article on that guy. I wanted an article on this guy." He pulled in a deep breath. "I didn't want an article. I wanted this guy to realize that he was causing pain and suffering."

"He knew he was. He wanted you to be angry. Did they say anything about each other?"

"I asked. They claimed they only knew superficial stuff. I guessed there was more. That's why I wanted a second meeting with both of them. One after the other on that roof. Maybe even later on at some other venue, or hell the same venue with both of them together. No matter what scenario I can imagine, now I'll never know."

Turner examined the nearly starless city sky above them for several moments.

Ian looked up at the universe and asked. "What real good does an extra dead activist or two make?" After several beats, he answered his own question. "Not much, in the larger scheme of things."

"You know some of these people. Who do you suspect?"

"All the gay people showing up hated Shaitan."

"How were you going to kill him?"

"Push him off the roof."

"Doesn't sound like a really well-thought-out plan. Was it an impulse you'd never have given into, or were you planning to stand and be caught?"

Ian shrugged. "I guess an impulse. I hated him."

"Why'd you come tonight?"

"Guilt and hoping for forgiveness. I figured you'd find out. You find out everything. You always do." He looked his friend in the eye. "Are you going to forgive me?"

"For being yourself? I broke up with you for some of the same reasons. You know who you are and what you're like. My forgiveness or lack of forgiveness isn't going to affect who you are. Am I pissed because you lied? Yes. Am I going to arrest you? No. Fenwick I can't answer for."

Ian got up to leave, "Confessions over. I'll let you get to bed." He stood up, turned to his friend. "Why is there a cop watching your place?"

"I didn't know there was. Where?"

"I guess just shy of Mrs. Talucci's jurisdiction, or he's more careful than most."

Paul gazed out at the street, saw nothing untoward, shrugged, and said, "Molton probably taking a precaution, and I have faith in Mrs. Talucci's connections."

"They've never failed yet."

Paul stood up and put a restraining hand on Ian's arm. "Why isn't your visit here now part of trying to fuck up the investigation?"

"You think I'd do that?"

"Do you possibly think if you came to me, I wouldn't ask all the questions a good cop would? You knew that when you came."

"Yeah. I know. Don't you ever get tired of playing by the rules?"

"Would you like me to stop?"

Ian caught his friend's eyes. He shook his head. "No, I guess not."

"I have my sons and my husband and my conscience to answer to."

"What does your gut say about me being guilty or innocent?"

"My gut says I want forensic evidence before making an arrest."

"I guess I counted on that, too."

They stood in silence. Paul let it drag an uncomfortable length of time. He wanted Ian uncomfortable. He didn't think his friend was a murderer, but he was furious about the omissions.

At last, Paul said, "I'm going to bed." He got to the door.

Ian put his foot on the top porch step. "Aren't you going to tell me not to leave town?"

Paul smiled at his friend's attempt at levity. He shook his head.

After Ian left, Paul took more time to examine the cars parked along both curbs. He saw no benign protectors nor any lurking predators.

In the house, he checked Jeff's first floor room. The boy was fast asleep. Upstairs, Brian's door was ajar with light streaming out.

Paul knocked softly and put his head around the opening. Brian looked up from the book he was reading. He asked, "You okay?"

Paul nodded. He sat on the edge of Brian's bed. The boy had

changed to his summer sleeping outfit, baggy basketball shorts, ankle socks, and a T-shirt taut on his flat abs that also managed to show off the bulging muscles of his arms and shoulders.

His son's eyes searched Paul's. The boy rolled his shoulder muscles, an unconscious sign of his teenage stress. "Been a while since you were shot at."

"I'm okay."

"I meant." The boy pulled in a deep breath. "I'm glad you called earlier. I still worry about you. I guess I always will."

"Just like I worry about you." He paused for a moment as they both thought about their concern then Paul said, "It's okay. I'm fine. We've talked about worry being a part of a cop's family's life."

"Doesn't make it easier. They gonna fire that asshole Carruthers?" Paul didn't talk about his cases with his kids, but they'd all heard stories of the multi-Stupid-Award winning Carruthers. The cops had a betting pool each year on the dumbest criminal who committed the most useless crime. They called it the Stupid-Award. Years ago their inept coworker had been given an honorary entry into the competition. Since being added, with an emphasis on stupid rather than criminal, Carruthers had won multiple times.

"Yeah. He's off the job for now, and they'll go through the process, but he should be gone."

"Good, one less thing to worry about."

When Paul entered their room, Ben put down the book he was reading, *Mr. Mercedes* by Stephen King. Paul got undressed and sat on the edge of their bed in his gray boxer briefs.

Ben raised an eyebrow. "What did Ian want?"

"He misspoke in his statements to us."

"About what?"

Turner told him. He finished, "I'm a bit afraid that he might still be holding something back."

"Why?"

"I don't know. I'm tired."

Ben swung his legs out from under the covers and sat behind Paul with his legs draped on either side of him. He kneaded his husband's shoulders.

Ben murmured, "You're not okay?"

"Not really."

"Ian?"

Paul smiled. He leaned back into his husband's strong hands. "Not Ian." He sighed. "When I get home is when I'm scared, or at least it's when I have the time to let all the emotions of the day catch up with me."

Ben stopped and sat next to him on the edge of the bed. He wore a pair of white, classic fit boxers.

Paul let the turbulent sensations of the day, all that he'd held in while working and in front of the boys, rush over him. Ben put his arm around him. Paul nestled into the warmth and closeness.

After a few minutes, he leaned his head back and said, "I was scared. In the midst of that wildness, what I thought about most was you and the boys. About all the things I'd never do with the three of you." He shuddered.

Paul had more to say. "And I've been wondering, in moments when we weren't madly dashing about, what if we were five or ten seconds earlier." He hesitated then added, "Or later. Now those thoughts are like headlights coming straight at me."

"You did what you could. You had less than seconds to decide."

"I saw that dumb fuck's gun. The huge black muzzle pointing at us, me. It's like he was pointing it at my whole world."

He shut his eyes and felt Ben's warmth soothing him as nothing else could.

After a few minutes, Ben said, "I was wondering."

"Yeah?"

"Maybe Carruthers is suicidal? Maybe he wanted to get shot."

Paul shrugged. "I don't know. He wanted to talk to me at the station." Paul filled him in.

When he finished, Ben shook his head, "When it comes down to it, I don't care what happens to that dumb son of a bitch. I just care about you."

"I know you worry."

"I love you."

Paul said, "If I died this day and left behind the notion, I am loved by you, and I have two beautiful sons, that would be okay. That would be my definition of a good life."

Paul put his head on Ben's shoulder. Ben held him tight and Paul whispered his own, "I love you."

The tired detective let the waves of relief wash over him. He was loved and loved someone in turn. Was that enough? It was for tonight.

They turned out the lights. Paul crawled into bed and they snuggled together. Paul heard his husband's breathing become regular. He lay awake longer than he wished, staring at the ceiling and wondering about friends and murder, his sons, his husband, and death. His fear of the vagaries of the universe most often allayed by the activity of his job, the joyful burden of his sons, and the love of his husband.

Except moments when his fears did more than nibble at his consciousness. He listened to his sleeping husband breathe as he slept.

Paul's mind churned with flashes of blood, gore, and possible death. The longer he brooded the larger the black hole of Carruthers's barrel grew in his imagination.

Finally, he lay with his fingers laced behind his head staring at the ceiling of their room. He could hear the air-conditioning. He saw the shadows of the backyard trees tremble on the walls of their room, back-lit by the distant light in the alley.

Giving up, he eased out of bed to avoid waking Ben. His husband stirred but did not waken.

In his boxer briefs, he padded downstairs, through the kitchen and onto the back porch. The air was warm this June night. In the deepest shadows of the covered, screened-in porch was their old family swing-rocker. He remembered being rocked in it when he was a kid. He remembered rocking his boys when they were babies. Other than being in Ben's arms, this was maybe his most comfortable, safe place on Earth. He rocked only an inch or two. He let his mind wander to love and loss, happiness and despair.

He smelled the basil and sage from Ben's herb garden. The dampness of the earth from the drizzle earlier. The harshness of the humidity still filled with promise of storms to come.

He must have nodded off, because when he woke, Ben was sitting next to him on the swing. Paul found his head on Ben's shoulder. Feeling him come awake, Ben reached over and caressed the stubble on Paul's chin.

Paul whispered, "Couldn't sleep."

Ben also kept his voice low. Paul loved the deep thrum. "I've been here for fifteen minutes. You must be exhausted."

Paul nodded.

Together they made their way upstairs to bed and blessed sleep.

Friday 7:38 A.M.

Paul wanted to get an early start on the day, get into work, and get on with solving problems. He also had an early meeting with a team from the Police Review board. Ben was in the shower. He didn't need to be at work at his auto shop until ten.

Paul joined him in the shower.

Both boys were still in the house. Brian almost certainly asleep at this hour of a summer morning. Jeff downstairs probably plotting how to enervate his parents.

Ben and Paul were careful about lovemaking noises when the boys were around. They preferred long, wild lovemaking sessions. Like all parents, they balanced and danced a delicate privacy ballet. A week in the summer when both boys were at a camp of their choosing was like a blissful, butt-pounding interval.

But in the shower, while the time was short, they could get away with more as long as they didn't become too rambunctious. Paul loved the cascading warm water amid Ben's fierce embraces.

Paul heard Brian's shower running as he trooped down the stairs.

He stopped in Jeff's room. Jeff was in his wheelchair. His torso slumped forward in the chair, his head resting on the computer keyboard. He often wound up so, sleeping after working late at his computer. Or arising early and working away, then not bothering to get back into bed, falling asleep where he sat. Paul moved closer. The boy was fast asleep. No way to tell how early he may have gotten up.

He had a new banner on the wall above his desk, "Free Reid

Fleming." Paul knew this was a reference to his son's newest pop culture obsession, a cartoon milkman.

Paul glanced at the top papers of each of two printed-out stacks. Intrigued, he riffled through a few. Jeff had one stack of reports about rotten cops and one stack of reports about good cops.

Paul looked up at Ben standing in the doorway. Paul beckoned him over and pointed to the stacks. He whispered, "He's got tons of each downloaded from the Internet."

"For what reason?" Ben asked.

"Working out his identity in relation to his cop dad is my guess."

"You could just ask me." Jeff's newly deep voice emerged from the mound of the no-longer-sleeping teen. "You're not the only one who could can go undercover."

Ben left for the kitchen to work on breakfast, less ritualized in the summers than it was in the school year.

Paul sat down on Jeff's bed.

"We've talked about my job."

"I know."

"I understand, you're newly worried."

"I always worry."

"You don't show it."

"You going to change jobs?"

"No."

"Then what good does me showing I'm worried do?"

"If you're unhappy, I'd like to discuss that and see if there's anything to be done."

"Fine," Jeff said, "you know what worries me most about your current mess, there's been tons on the news, and on the Internet, and rumors?"

"What worries you the most?"

"Carruthers."

"What about him?"

"Cover-up," Jeff said. "They're going to cover it up. Shit is going to hit the fan."

With Brian graduating from high school, the rules on language in the house for both boys had been eased.

Jeff was continuing, "And you and Mr. Fenwick are going to be in the middle of it. I know it. Look at all this Code of Silence shit."

"Which we've talked about."

"But not when it's going to be directed at you. And look at the cover-ups of police bad behavior. They're going to lie. I know they're going to lie. They always lie."

Paul said, "I'm going to stick with the truth."

"Will that be enough?"

"I have to hope so."

Paul got up to leave.

Jeff touched his arm.

Paul halted.

"Dad, have you covered up crimes other cops committed? Like on that video tape. I've seen so much of it. You're part of the group."

Paul said, "I have always followed the letter and spirit of the law as best I can. I don't let people get away with murder. I just do the best job I can, as a cop and taking care of my family."

Jeff pointed at the stacks of paper. "But I've read all this stuff." He then pointed at his e-reader. "And I've read all the recent non-fiction cop books. The realistic ones. What I don't get is who has that much power to command all that silence and what are they protecting?"

Paul sat down again and looked in his son's eyes. "Those are good questions. As for why, I'm not sure. Sometimes they're afraid for their jobs, their reputations, their pensions, other stuff too, I suppose."

"Why don't they worry about all those before they lie?"

"That might be your best question so far." He shook his head. "I don't know the answer."

Jeff asked, "How do they have so much power? How can they cover up so much?"

"What do the articles and books say?"

"Contradictory stuff. You know I hate that."

Paul nodded. He knew his younger son had developed a complex, rigid set of rules for the reality he lived. Partly from living with spina bifida every instant of his life and from being so smart, and maybe because he had good parents. Although the rules seemed to be flexible when mischievous or malevolent teenage Jeff wanted them to be, especially when he was attempting new levels of deviousness to get around his parents' dictums.

Jeff said, "What none of these talk about, not the books or the articles, are what the police, men and women, are like when they get home? When the cameras aren't on, are they normal? Carruthers must have a home."

Paul said, "I know he must."

Ben called to them from the kitchen, "Breakfast is ready."

Paul and Jeff left the boy's room and moved down the hall. Brian sat at the table drinking from a glass of his special, homemade health juice. He wore a bright orange ASOS sleeveless side-cut T-shirt with extreme dropped armholes and a pair of white silk boxer-briefs. Ben was placing bowls of cut-up fruit at their places. A mound of toast and a pitcher of fresh squeezed juice sat on the table.

Paul filled them in on the conversation he and Jeff had been having.

Jeff asked, "Do the police officers know what they're doing is wrong?"

"Who?" Ben asked.

"Cops who shoot unarmed people."

Brian said, "It's not that they don't know what they do. They know what they do. They feel entitled to do it."

They ate. Topics ranged from cop morality back to teenagers' needs and schedules. Paul preferred the latter this morning as better than dealing with the philosophical and moral implications of someone being in service to the community.

After breakfast, Ben walked Paul out to the front porch. Ben asked, "Are you worried about the Police Board investigation?"

"My union rep will be there. If it's fair, I don't think I'll have a problem."

"And if it's unfair?"

"We'll deal with that if it happens."

They kissed and hugged goodbye.

Friday 8:18 A.M.

Mrs. Talucci sat on her front porch. Paul went over to share the morning.

Their ninety-something neighbor lived by herself on the ground floor of the house next door. She cared for Jeff every day after school or on weekends depending on the family's schedules. For several years after she started, she refused all offers of payment. Being neighbors, and nearly family, precluded even discussing such things. But one day Mrs. Talucci couldn't fix a broken porch. Paul had offered, and since then he'd done all repairs. He and Ben had even completed several major renovations.

One daughter and several distant nieces still inhabited the second floor. While Mrs. Talucci ruled this brood, her main concern was to keep them out of her way and to stay independent.

She rarely lost to Jeff when they played chess.

Although the temperature and humidity were cloying, Mrs. Talucci wore a summer dress and a white summer shawl she'd knitted herself. The sky was bright blue. The wind an occasional puff. Storms were predicted for the afternoon.

Paul leaned his butt against the porch railing. They exchanged pleasantries. Paul said, "We may finally be rid of Carruthers."

"It's about time." She rocked for a moment then said, "Be careful of him. His kind may be stupid, but they have a native cunning. He's the kind that would try something furtive, but in his case, undoubtedly inept. Unless he's got friends in the department."

"As far as I can tell, he has no friends."

"How as he kept his job?"

"Clout."

"Then someone, somewhere has a connection that involves power, money, friendship, or family or some combination of them. Beware."

"Did you see someone watching, maybe a Chicago cop car, protecting on the street last night?"

"For a while, there was a car that was not from one of the local Districts." She rocked her chair for a moment. "You'd want to think it was a benign reason, but right now, I'd be as suspicious as I suspect you already think you should be."

He nodded.

"Is Buck okay?"

"Some of his fat got disturbed. Little more than a scratch or two."

"Tell him I'm thinking of him."

"I will."

They listened to the noise of the neighborhood for a few moments.

Mrs. Talucci said, "You got the protesters case."

"Yeah. You know any of these people?" He handed her his phone, loaded to a page with a list of convention goers that he'd downloaded from the Internet.

She perused it, shook her head, "I haven't been in a demonstration since the fifties. I'll see if anyone I know has a notion. Back in the day, I used to know all the protesters in town. I can check with the few who are still alive from that time and see if there are any tendrils of information to be found."

"Thanks."

"You think the powers that exist in the city might be involved in the murder itself?"

"We're just starting."

"You guys going to be hassled for saving that boy?"

He told her about the incident between Fenwick and the beat cop.

When he finished, Mrs. Talucci stopped her gentle rocking and met his eyes. "How are you holding up?" she asked.

"It's going to be a little delicate."

"If you need help, let me know."

Paul was never quite sure about Mrs. Talucci's connections. Her "talking to people" could mean anything from being connected to the most powerful mafia don in the country to gossiping with the neighbors. Often, amazing things seemed to get done when Mrs. Talucci talked to people.

Several years ago, a gang of street kids had been harassing older women returning from the neighborhood grocery store on Harrison Street. One of the kids had been found hanging naked upside down from the front of the store the day after Mrs. Talucci had "talked to someone." The problems at the store never recurred. The kid was fine, but never said a word about who attacked him. Turner also knew that the local alderman had Mrs. Talucci on speed dial. Politicians tended to recognize real power when they saw it.

Friday 8:57 A.M.

Turner strode into the station, up the stairs, crossed the room, and plunked himself down at his desk.

Fenwick looked up and said, "Ian did it."

Turner gave a great, gulping Fenwickian sigh. He said, "Maybe." He told him about Ian's visit the night before.

Fenwick's first reaction was, "Our buddy lied to us."

Turner nodded. He said, "He's still lying."

"Why do you think that?"

"He says he went there to kill Shaitan. Fine. Why? I get nothing close to a motive for murder."

"We've never had a case where someone killed the other person because he had a tiny dick."

"Something else is going on. For now, he's back in the asshole category. He's got some making up to do."

Fenwick said, "He was really going to kill Shaitan?"

"I think it was an impulse. Who knows? I don't think he would, but there's been a lot of anger brewing since the election. Ian sees Preston Shaitan as a traitor to not only his cause but to the human race."

"Well, he is."

Turner nodded. "Why did you say he did it before I told the story?"

"The more I thought about it, the odder he sounded to me. Turns out it was odder than either of us knew. Although having sex with both guys who got murdered within twenty-four hours, that moves from odd to beyond weird."

Turner said, "We'll have to talk to him some more, but we've got all kinds of people to get to today, including Bettencourt and Preston's co-workers, friends, enemies, and family."

Friday 9:17 A.M.

A rush of clattering on the stairs caused them to turn. Fong leapt up the last step and rushed over to them. His hands were full with a bundle of electronics, wires, and routers, and chargers, and Turner knew not what-all else. He fumbled with the mass clutched between his folded arms. Fong stopped, juggled the electronics so he could free a hand, then put his finger to his lips in a hush gesture.

Fenwick said, “What the hell?”

Fong banged his hand on Fenwick’s desk and repeated the ‘hush’ gesture.

The detectives gaped at him for an instant. Fong waved his right arm in a gesture that Turner interpreted as ‘follow me.’ He looked at Fenwick. In silence, they stood up and followed.

They trooped down to Fong’s lair in silence. Fong dumped all the electronic gear on his desk and threw himself into his chair. The detectives settled onto four legged stools.

From the left breast pocket of his cargo shirt, Fong took out, then held up, an item the size of a child’s toy brick. Turner thought of the clothing Fong wore as ‘cargo’ everything. Each item tended to have as many pockets as possible, even his socks and sometimes his boots in winter. On a few of these garments, he was known to hand-sew extra pockets. Today, he wore khaki cargo shorts and a Marine green cargo shirt.

“That the device from the hotel room?” Fenwick asked.

Fong shook his head then said. “From under your desk.”

Fenwick said, "Huh?"

Turner asked, "Is it ours?"

"You mean is it Chicago police department issued, no. That does not mean someone from the Chicago police department didn't put this device there, but whoever placed it got it from some other organization."

"How'd you find it?"

"Dumb luck. Earlier, I was bringing the results of the device from Bettencourt's hotel room to leave on your desk. I happened to have with me my newest detection device. It was sitting in my shirt pocket. It started to go off. I found that under Fenwick's desk."

"I feel special."

Turner asked, "If you found it, why did we have to keep silent and come here?"

"Because I need to do a full sweep of the whole building. I got this one about half an hour ago. I rushed down here, checked it out, and was on my way back up just now. I've got more to do."

"How long has it been there?"

"Not sure."

"Hours, days, weeks, months?" Fenwick asked.

Turner said, "Maybe they'll have a record of all of your farts, belches, and grumbles."

Fong said, "Something to record for the ages."

Fenwick said, "I see an HBO special in my future. A mini-series at least. And more dramatic than half their stuff."

Fong said, "A dream come true."

Turner asked, "What about the one in the hotel room?"

"Like this one, an audio device that recorded for a short while then sent a signal to a remote location, some computer somewhere on the planet, which presumably was also saving it somewhere."

"That's what I like," Fenwick said, "specific."

"I'll work on the origins of both devices and try to get their remote hubs. I don't hold out much hope. Here." From the top of his desk, he picked up two objects that looked like pagers out of the '80s. "Hook these to a belt loop. Wear them at all times. They're old but effective. They'll block anybody's signal who is trying to record you in any way."

"Can they tell us who is doing it?"

"No, they just jam signals of any kind, but don't record. You want to wear recorders or cameras? I can wire you up so that you'd get a 360° view and perfect audio. I can do lapel, belt buckle, shoe laces, whatever."

"Why would you need 360°?" Fenwick asked.

"It would cover everything. It's really cool."

Turner and Fenwick shook their heads. Turner said, "Maybe some other time."

Fenwick said, "Not yet."

"Up to you guys. I also downloaded all the video from the public areas here at the station. You can look at them to see if you notice anything suspicious. I've gone through them and don't see anyone out of place." Area Ten headquarters had cameras in all public areas, but none anywhere else.

He handed that flash drive to Turner, then plugged a separate one into a USB port on his computer. "This is the data from the hotel room."

Fenwick said, "Was that one there all the time, or was this just put there in that hotel room in time for the conference?"

Fong said, "Couldn't have been there long since it only has this little bit of two separate guys arriving on it."

Turner said, "If it was deliberate, someone would have to know the guests lists and the room assignments."

"We'll have to find out who knew that," Fenwick said. "Maybe they all knew where everyone was. An egalitarian protest group."

Fong said, "I'll see if there's security camera devices in the hotel.

Later, you or I or both can check them against the security devices here to see if someone was in both places. Won't prove they put it there, but if someone here is out of place in the hotel, you might be a step ahead."

"If they even had cameras, or devices that saved the recordings."

Fong added, "I'll get more work done on all the stuff you gave me, after I sweep the whole station and all the cars in the parking lot."

Fenwick asked, "Our homes, our phones?"

Fong said, "I'll take care of it."

Turner said, "Should we leave this under Fenwick's desk. They won't know we know it's there?"

Fong held it up. "I already turned it off. They know it's been compromised. Sorry."

"You tell Molton?" Fenwick asked.

"He's not in. Another meeting at downtown headquarters. Barb Dams said she texted him to call her immediately after the meeting."

Fenwick said, "Let's try the hotel room tape."

Fong tapped at his keyboard for a few seconds and the flash drive began to disgorge data. Fong pointed, "Nothing. And there's lots of it until you get to here." He moved the cursor forward.

They heard a door opening. A few minutes later a toilet flushing. Faint footsteps. A zipper maybe on a backpack.

Fong asked, "How much nothing you want to listen to?"

"Not much," Fenwick said.

"Same for the other guy?" Turner asked.

"Yep."

Westerman said he arrived last.

Turner asked, "Anything on the dash cams we found under the desk in Shaitan's room?"

"Those are good enough to be encrypted. I can't tell by whom.

I'll keep at it."

Fenwick said, "What the hell would he be doing with them, and if they are official and if from some department, then which official and which department?"

They all shrugged.

"What were all the rest of the electronics in his suitcase?"

"I'm still working on that as well."

They helped Fong drag electronic equipment up from the basement. Turner and Fenwick stood out in the parking lot while he swept the detectives' squad room. The wind was now a breeze with occasional puffs of gusts. A few high clouds scudded with the currents of air high above.

Friday 9:47 A.M.

Molton's car, tires squealing as he took the turn into the lot, came to an abrupt halt five feet from them. He jumped out.

Turner had never seen him look so angry.

Molton said, "You're out here."

Fenwick said, "Fong's sweeping the squad room for listening devices."

"Who the hell?"

Turner said, "Fong's working on it."

Molton shook his head then sighed. "There is some news from the usually useless meetings at headquarters. Carruthers has been relieved of his police powers and assigned to administrative duties. All the dash-cams from the incident on Harrison have been collected. They have to download all that footage as well as anything that may be found from non-police people during the canvass."

Such investigations were currently done by the Independent Police Review Authority. It replaced the often criticized Office of Professional Standards. The new group rarely found misconduct by police, and yet millions got paid out by the City Council to victims of that same misconduct. The mayor had now proposed a Civilian Police Accountability watchdog agency.

Nowadays, any department employee may have violated police department policy by discharging their weapon. Just because you discharge your weapon, didn't mean you were going to be reassigned.

Although Turner remembered the idiots a few months back who were caught on tape firing at a fleeing car. Firing randomly into the streets was a big no-no. It seldom actually stopped a fleeing vehicle, presumably the point of the operation, but even more it was a danger to every random passerby or people sitting watching television in the chairs in their own homes.

Fenwick asked, "You gonna evacuate the whole place?"

"Only if I have to." Molton left and stormed into the station.

Barb Dams came out of the building and walked over to them and said, "You heard about the speech the Commander is giving at each roll call?"

They shook their heads.

"He was talking about the damage to Rodriguez's car and I quote, 'If you want to walk a beat in the dead of winter and the heat of summer from here to the end of your career, let me find out it was you.'"

"Will it help?" Fenwick asked.

Barb shrugged. "I don't know. A few seconds ago just before I came out here, he told me to order new surveillance cameras throughout this building inside and out."

Fenwick said, "I hope it catches some asshole."

Three cars pulled up and took the three spaces marked for handicapped parking. Five sport coat wearing men emerged from the separate cars. There was one woman in a back business suit. None evinced any need for using such a designated spot.

They strode into the station. All had briefcases capable of carrying laptops.

Dams said, "Review board. They're meeting with everyone here."

"Carruthers will be here again?" Fenwick asked.

"Him specifically, not sure," Dams said, "but I am going to make sure each of those cars gets tickets for parking in those spots."

"Will it do any good?" Fenwick asked.

"The question is will having done that make me feel better, and it will." Dams added, "I know you know this, but you need to call a union rep."

Turner said, "Already called before I left home."

Fenwick nodded, "Me too."

She smiled at them. "I thought you might. I guess I just mean I'm worried, or at least concerned."

"Neither Buck nor I did anything wrong."

"And since when did that ever stop the Chicago Police department from fucking things up?"

The use of the profanity was rare from Barb.

A portly older gentleman in faded jeans and khaki shirt shuffled up to them. He lowered his sunglasses and peered at them. He said, "I'm looking for Detectives Turner and Fenwick."

Fenwick said, "You found them."

"I'm your union rep, Frank Yutka."

Dams left.

Turner and Fenwick answered his questions. He nodded a lot. Early on, he took off his backpack and, using the trunk of the nearest car as a table, took notes.

When the detectives finished, he said, "During the meeting, keep your goddamn mouths shut unless I tell you to speak or ask you a specific question then keep your answers short and to the point. Do that, and you'll be fine."

As direct as a Fenwick grouse but more effective than most.

Turner and Fenwick nodded acquiescence.

Friday 10:01 A.M.

The three of them walked into the station.

The meeting with the Independent Police Review Authority was in the Commander's conference room instead of an interrogation room. The main difference was this had fake wood panel walls, two windows that let in outside light, a larger table, and slightly more comfy chairs.

The six board personnel were arrayed on one side of the table. All had their laptops open.

Before he even sat down, Yutka took his time replacing his sun glasses with a pair of trifocals that glinted in the sunlight from outside. Finished with this ritual, or annoying habit, or affectation that gave him time to think, he said, "Six of you. That strikes me as odd. Very odd. Is there a problem here?"

The man furthest on the right end said, "I'm Lyal DeGroot. These guys are heroes. We all wanted our picture taken with them."

Turner wondered if there was any sarcasm left anywhere on the planet since DeGroot had imbued his crack with vats and vats of it.

Yutka harrumphed. "So we can all just go home?"

"No," DeGroot snapped. "I'll be leading the interrogation today."

Yutka took the central chair on the opposite side of the table. Turner and Fenwick flanked him one on each side.

Yutka spent an inordinate amount of time opening his laptop, bringing up any number of files on it, adjusting the screen, taking off his glasses, polishing them, putting them back on, adjusting the screen again, taking a legal pad out of his backpack, fishing out three pens from the depths of said backpack, then arranging them in various triangles around his computer.

The six on the other side of the table gave expressions varying from bored to annoyed.

Finished, Yutka leaned back in his chair and said, “Six?”

“That’s how it’s going to be.”

Yutka returned to fussing.

Lyal DeGroot was an older man with a handlebar mustache. Turner thought it must be the first one of those he’d seen outside of a Western movie in years or ever. Turner realized if he was thinking about something that inconsequential at a time like this, he must be more nervous than he thought.

The woman next to DeGroot spoke. She said, “I’m Mildred Sploe. We need to go over your statement from last night.” She was a tall woman with dark black hair pulled back into a tight bun from which Turner doubted any hair ever dared escape.

Yutka said, “Six?”

Glares from the other side of the table. Yutka fished in his backpack and came out with recording devices. He said, “I see you don’t have these, so I’m sure you’ll be happy to know I came equipped for us to start after four of you leave. My computer will also record this event. I like to have two devices. I never trust one set of electronics.”

DeGroot growled and asked if they’d give them time for a conference.

In the hall, Fenwick opened his mouth to speak, but Yutka held up a hand and said, “Shut up.”

Fenwick did. Turner knew that his partner could grumble to the point of maddening insidiousness and drive him and probably half the planet nuts, but Fenwick did know when to bow to the experts.

A few minutes later, four of the men trooped out of the

conference room.

Yutka, Fenwick, and Turner returned to their seats.

DeGroot greeted them with, “Happy now?” He’d saved a reservoir of sarcasm.

Yutka said nothing.

Sploe said, “Like I said, we need to go over last night’s statements.”

Yutka pointed to her laptop and then her briefcase and then said, “I assume you have all the casework electronically and on hardcopy and had the good sense to read it before you got here.” Yutka’s voice sounded like a grizzled old marine drill-sergeant in the baritone range.

Sploe said, “We need to talk about it.”

Yutka said, “Perhaps what you mean to say is, we have your statement from last night, would you look at it please, and tell us if there’s anything you wish to add, delete, change.”

Sploe and DeGroot both gave him looks that, which might not kill, were certainly designed to maim. Yutka just sat there with his hands folded on the table in front of him. Turner would call Yutka’s expression a benevolent glare.

Sploe pulled a sheaf of papers out of her folder. Barb Dams had forwarded all the paperwork to Turner and Fenwick early this morning. Turner and Fenwick spent time reading. Turner had gone over all of it, which was as correct this morning as when he and Fenwick gave their statements yesterday afternoon and evening.

Turner was no fool. He read the document as if it were for the first time then nodded.

DeGroot asked, “Any additions or corrections?”

Both detectives looked at Yutka whose head nodded about a sixteen of an inch.

Both detectives said, “No.”

Sploe said, “Are you sure?”

Yutka said, “Any other questions?”

DeGroot said, "Remember it's the lies and cover ups that get most cops in trouble in what they say."

Yutka asked, "Are you accusing Detective Turner or Detective Fenwick of lying?"

"We have different versions of events."

Yutka nodded, "And different versions of body cams and dash cams?"

"Those can be a problem."

Yutka said, "Yes, they can."

DeGroot said, "We're concerned about the Taser that went missing and was later found at a separate crime scene."

Yutka said, "So are we."

DeGroot pointed at Turner. "We understand you talked with Detective Carruthers last night."

Yutka said, "It's all in there."

Sploe said, "You realize the criminal Detective Carruthers and the others were chasing has connections to a terrorist organization."

Yutka laughed. "You mean he belongs to the NRA?"

DeGroot's voice rose, "Your clients protected a terrorist."

Yutka said, "I'll need your proof that he was a terrorist. I'll need to find where in the law it says that it's okay to gun down unarmed civilians no matter what their background."

DeGroot said, "The kid was armed."

"According to whom?" Yutka asked.

"Several witnesses."

"Name them."

"That's confidential."

"Then they don't exist."

"Oh, they exist."

"You either produce them or their names or the documentation from them, or they don't exist. You know better than that. What are you trying to pull here?"

Turner wondered very much the same thing.

DeGroot said, "Your guys could have backed away from the confrontation."

"And let the kid die?" Yutka demanded. "Let that moron keep firing? Are you mad?"

"Just asking questions."

"When do we see copies of what the dash-cams show?" Yutka asked.

"We're working on it."

Neither Turner nor Fenwick said a word about what Fong might or might not be able to accomplish.

Sploe asked, "Is it true you hated Detective Carruthers?"

Yutka asked, "How do their personal feelings affect their report of the facts of last night's incident?"

Sploe said, "If they hated him, maybe they want him to look bad."

Yutka replied, "We've all heard numerous rumors about numerous detectives. I assumed you've checked Carruthers's file, and the files of both of these detectives. You've seen the numerous complaints about Carruthers. The very few against these two."

Yutka and the two Internal Affairs people spent fifteen more futile minutes going round and round. When they were done, Turner, Fenwick, and Yutka stood together out in the hall.

Yutka said, "You both kept your mouths shut. Good." He glanced at Fenwick, "Although I was told I'd need to put a muzzle on you."

Fenwick growled. "I'm not stupid."

Turner asked, "What's next?"

Yutka shook his head. "The Taser shit has me worried."

"Why?"

"Their side claims the kid did have a gun. You say he didn't. Fine, but your case gets weaker with the missing, but since found, Taser. They can claim the same person took the gun as the Taser to make them look bad. You do know it being missing makes you look bad."

Fenwick said, "We had other things to think about."

Yutka frowned. "Makes no difference. They're looking for any edge they can get."

"Yeah," Fenwick said. "It almost sounded like they were taking Carruthers's side."

Turner added, "That bothered me, too."

Yutka said, "I'll check into it. For now they just might be being thorough. I haven't worked with these two before. I'll find out what I can. Maybe they think it's like some old Perry Mason show or story where at the last second they find a one/eighth inch discrepancy in the placement of a piece of evidence, and poof the case goes to hell."

Fenwick said, "It's not like that."

"It can be if they can make it stick."

"They'd have to get enough guys to lie."

"And you think there aren't enough cops on the force who would lie for each other?"

Fenwick said, "But in this case against us, we're one of their own."

Yutka said, "You know the court cases. Settlements won by the good guys, but that still didn't keep cops who broke the Code of Silence from being frozen out."

Fenwick told him about the beat cop from the night before.

Yutka said, "And there's been no report about it. So far. A little odd. Maybe they're saving it to use against you."

"Just like with the gun, they've got no tape."

"There is that." Yutka shrugged, "If they come around, call me, but you know that. Be careful. The Independent Police Review Authority, like the Police Board investigations, are seldom friendly, cheery affairs, but I got the impression that both of them didn't like you already."

Turner asked, "Could any of this have anything to do with that fact that I'm gay?"

"Doubtful, but anything's possible. They could also be friends of Carruthers. He must have some." Yutka shrugged. "Or as is more likely somebody is trying to cover their asses. Switch the blame of what happened to you. Keep themselves from being sued and maybe fired for all the years-long Carruthers fuckups, and I presume cover-ups. Remember, until last night, he had never actually physically assaulted someone."

Fenwick touched his wounded arm. "And he did it to a cop."

Yutka shook his head. "No matter how big an asshole someone is, if he has someone protecting him, that's who you should be afraid of. You're lucky. Your Commander's in your corner."

Turner said, "What was with the terrorist bullshit, and the he was armed bullshit."

Yutka shook his head. "That was actually the most worrisome. They've got people willing to lie." He shook his head then reiterated. "Whoever is behind Carruthers, that's who you have to be afraid of."

Fenwick asked, "Are we going to face criminal charges?"

"Good question. Have you done something criminal?"

"No."

"Then let's hope they don't twist it into that." He reminded them again to keep him informed and left.

Friday 11:17 A.M.

Yutka had just turned a corner when Fong, pushing a cart crammed with electronics, rushed up to them. "Your desks are clear. The Commander's office, too. I got tons more to go over." He hurried on.

Barb Dams approached their desks. "You guys okay?" she asked.

She knew better than to ask them how the just-finished interview went.

They both shrugged.

Turner asked, "Where's the Commander?"

"He's got a publicity person from downtown in with him along with a grandstanding alderman, and a few other people. They want to see you."

Fenwick raised an eyebrow. "Grandstanding alderman? Isn't that kind of redundant?"

"Grandstanding about saving the kid."

Fenwick said, "Just what we need, more distraction. We've got a case to solve."

Dams raised an eyebrow. "Did you just start yesterday or have you been working here long?"

Fenwick subsided. There were always ramifications and permutations to everything they did.

They paused outside the Commander's door. Fenwick raised an

eyebrow, "Publicity?"

"You're the famous one."

Dams shook her head. "Don't you get it? The community thinks you took a bullet for one of their own, and actually you did." She tapped Turner on the arm. "And you Tased one of the evil ones. They're falling all over themselves. Hero is as hero does."

In Molton's office were three men Turner recognized. Adam Edberg from the mayor's office from the bridge incident just before they got to the crime scene last night. He was joined by Clayton Griffin, who they all knew as the Assistant Chief of Detectives. He was a short, thin man with blond hair.

The third man was Gerald Palakowski, the District Commander where the Tasing of Carruthers had occurred, the subsequent murder scene, and bridge crossing moment.

The fourth man whom Turner had never met was Alderman Frank Bortz who wore a suit that he seemed a few pounds away from bursting the seams. It was in his Ward that Carruthers had been Tased.

The fifth person was Sela Jones, the head of the CPD press office. She was a blond-haired woman in her forties.

Everybody stood up to greet them. The alderman pumped their hands as if he was holding on to a lifeline to save him from deep water. He talked at a great rate. "So good to see you. How are you? You guys are such heroes. The department doesn't have enough people like you. We want you on the front page of the papers. You should have been already."

Molton managed to interrupt this discourse long enough to get them seated.

Bortz went on. Turner looked at Fenwick whose teeth were clamped and his lips pursed. Fenwick did not suffer fools gladly. Maybe the guy was just trying to be nice? In Chicago? With headlines to grab?

Bortz did finally wind down.

Griffin spoke up, "We do have a great chance to get some good publicity for the department."

Griffin, Bortz, Jones, and Edberg went on at length about ceremonies, a parade, community outreach. Turner noted Palakowski said not a word. Mostly, he looked like he was trying to smile while holding back an enormous fart.

Edberg and Jones took voluminous notes. When they finished, they turned to the two detectives. Edberg asked, "What do you guys think?"

Fenwick said, "No."

Turner said, "If there's some appropriate time in the future, we can get back to you."

Molton said, "This all sounds premature."

Palakowski said, "We need to see what all the investigations show. We need to not act too quickly."

Had the beat cop complained to him about Fenwick's actions the night before? He didn't say so, and this would be a time to speak up if he had.

Molton said, "The detectives have work to do."

The meeting broke up.

Griffin followed the two detectives onto the stairs that led up to their desks. He tapped each of their elbows and said, "I wanted to talk to you for a moment." They all stopped on the third step from the top. Palakowski stood directly behind Griffin who said, "You guys aren't really team players." Any affability from the Commander's office was gone.

Palakowski added, "Shown by your response to working with the department to get something good out of this."

"You've gotten complaints from Commander Molton?" Fenwick's voice was inching into snarl territory. "Our yearly reviews are excellent, so it's not him. He could just tell us. Our colleagues? Who? Roosevelt? Wilson? Rodriguez?" Fenwick thumped the wall he was standing next to. "Carruthers," he guessed. "You're a friend of Carruthers. Or you both are? Or you've been part of covering up for him for years, and you're worried about your own jobs and pensions."

Both men looked furious. There were times Turner wished his buddy would shut up. This was one of them. Griffin had something to say, and he thought it might be best to hear it all before making judgments and leaping to sarcasm or beyond to anger and bombast.

Griffin shook his head. "No, I'm just saying there are friends of Carruthers around, and you guys should be careful. You really should think about doing all this publicity stuff."

Fenwick scoffed, "What could they do to us if we don't?"

Griffin said, "It wouldn't be public, and it wouldn't be pretty. You know that. Be careful."

Palakowski said, "If I were you, I'd be very careful of anything I did or said."

Without waiting for a response from the detectives, they turned away and stalked off.

Turner gazed after them. "What was their game?"

"Friendly warning?" Fenwick proffered.

"Or additions to mountains of bullshit."

Molton came out of his office while they were still mulling. He asked, "You guys okay?" He too knew better than to ask about what had happened with the review board. Things could get tainted very quickly.

Fenwick asked, "What was all that publicity shit really all about?"

Molton shook his head. "This is out of control. I'm not sure who is talking to whom about what. I've got meetings back downtown all afternoon. Call me if you need me." He left.

Fenwick said, "Who the hell are all these people?"

"Who people?"

"Just the assholes who were here this morning. Am I supposed to remember all their names?"

"I don't remember their names, and I'm not complaining about it or them, so I'm a step ahead of you."

"Show off." After several more loud grumbles, Fenwick said, "Where the hell are we with the goddamn case? We've got fucking real work to do."

Turner said, "Interviews. Data collection."

Fenwick said, "I think we should become tortured cops like on television."

Turner snorted. "I'm not interested in your sexual peccadilloes."

"No, no. That gritty, doubt-ridden, anxiety-infested shit."

Turner asked, "Why bother?"

That stopped Fenwick for only a moment. After a couple seconds silence, he said, "We'd please the critics more."

"Now you care about what critics say? Now? Little late for that."

"I'm sensitive."

Turner did not burst out laughing.

Barb Dams hurried up to them. "Mrs. Bettencourt is here with a friend. I put them at your desks."

Turner did not relish meeting with those who had loved the departed. Before they moved, he asked, "How'd she know to come here?"

"They went to his hotel room. The cop on duty sent them here with Sanchez and Deveneaux."

Friday 11:35 A.M.

Two women sat in chairs facing the side of their desks. As they approached, the two women stood up.

The woman closest to Fenwick's desk said, "I'm Helena Avila." She was a waif of a woman. Turner saw that she was maybe in her early forties with blond hair in a ponytail that draped down her back to below her waist.

The other said, "I'm Susan Bettencourt." She was a tall, woman. She wore a plain back dress with a small string of pearls that would have done June Cleaver proud.

Both detectives said, "We're sorry for your loss."

Both women said, "Thank you." They all shook hands, then sat.

Turner saw that Barb Dams had gotten the visitors coffee. The women held hands as they sat. Both looked like they hadn't had much sleep.

Mrs. Bettencourt asked, "What's going on with the investigation?"

Turner said, "We're still talking to people. We're trying to find out what they were doing up on that roof. First off, why was he staying at a hotel instead of driving in?"

Mrs. Bettencourt said, "He didn't want to deal with driving in and out, avoiding rush hour. He liked to be right on the scene. He liked to talk. People opened up to him. He hated to stop the flow of rhetoric, good or bad. He didn't want to be driving home late at night all exhausted."

"He was one of the organizers of this meeting?" Turner asked.

Mrs. Bettencourt said, "Oh, yes, a driving force. He wanted to create a new order of politics in this country. This was going to be a foundational set of meetings and talks."

Turner asked, "Why did they invite all these violent groups?"

Mrs. Bettencourt said, "He wanted to work with them. He wanted to show them the way that peace could work. He's the one who organized that silent protest against Preston Shaitan."

"They knew each other before this conference?"

Mrs. Bettencourt nodded. "Oh, yes."

"How did they get along?" Turner asked.

Mrs. Bettencourt said, "Henry always thought of Shaitan and all the rest as a challenge. He had goals with each person he met. He always said, even if they couldn't agree on anything, a discussion always made him a better person."

"And was he?" Fenwick asked.

"Was he what?" Mrs. Bettencourt asked.

"A better person after each encounter?"

"He tried to be."

Fenwick asked, "What was the point of getting all these people together?"

She said, "Simply that, to get them all together. That was a triumph in itself. Accomplishing an actual result was often secondary to a we-were-all-together-and-didn't-kill-each-other scenario."

Turner said, "He was a peaceful man, but who gave him the hardest time in these groups, who were the biggest rivals or most recalcitrant about working together? Anyone that would want to harm him?"

"Anyone could be difficult at any time."

Turner asked, "How did that silent protest work?"

A ghost of a smile appeared at one corner of Mrs. Bettencourt's lips. "Henry and I worked on that together, but it was really Helena who implemented the whole scheme." She smiled at her friend. "Tell them about it."

Helena spoke for the first time. "Oh, the meetings we attended. The anger! Shaitan was such a complete and utter shit, and I say that as one who knows not to speak ill of the dead. The actual problem was twofold: to get people to show up and then to get them to be silent. So many wanted to scream, and shout, and fight back. But the idea of being peaceful caught on. We filled the admittedly smallish auditorium. He came out to speak, and there was this vast silence. A few scattered people clapped but then stopped after a few seconds. We caught them off guard. It was hell getting so many of the tickets. Even though they were free, we had to circumvent the few protections the organizers had in place. They didn't know what was happening."

Mrs. Bettencourt said, "I bet he didn't think he was going to get more than twenty people. Back then, he usually didn't."

Helena Avila nodded and resumed. "At first, he looked pleased and smiled as he walked to the podium, but then he got there and realized there was only a scattering of applause from the back. Our people had gotten there early. He went nuts. He raved. In what little he said, he took positions even more extreme than he had before. But the response was silence. Can you imagine? When the silence became overwhelming, Shaitan ran from the stage. Even his fans gave up. They were too scattered, too startled. They came for violence and rhetoric. They got nothing."

Turner said, "I admire that."

"It was all Henry's idea. He was a good man. I just helped."

"Would he have been going to meet Shaitan last night and if so why?"

Mrs. Bettencourt said, "Specifically, I have no idea. He didn't say anything to me about meeting him, but Henry thought he could talk to anybody."

Helena Avila said, "Shaitan was evil incarnate. I've found it's always better, if you can, to out-organize the opposition. That crowd was easy. See, they're all about their own egos, but you probably know that." She smiled again. A gentle smile. "We weren't going to make the same mistakes as those who are violent do."

"What were those?" Fenwick asked.

Ms. Avila said, "We weren't going to let it be known beforehand how many of us there were. If someone became violent toward us, we were going to surround them with peace and love. See, so many of those who attend rallies want violence, are looking for violence. Of course, it's gotten much worse in the past few years. When they discover that there are others who may outnumber them and who could do violence to them successfully, they tend to back down."

"You threaten violence?" Fenwick asked.

Mrs. Bettencourt said, "I think our very presence threatens them."

Ms. Avila shook her head. "It was exhausting. All that planning." She sighed. "We did so much work, but it helped for only that one evening. It didn't stop him in the slightest from going right on with his speaking tour. I'm not sure any of these protests do any good. In his case, he just went on to his next venue in the next city."

Mrs. Bettencourt patted her arm. "There was no violence. And remember we heard that when he got backstage, first he cried then he nearly broke down from rage."

"But we didn't stop him."

"You know what Henry always said, baby steps."

Turner asked, "Were there rivalries among the protesters?"

Avila said, "Shaitan was rivals with everyone. If you had an ego, the slightest bit of intelligence, you and he clashed."

"About what?"

"It didn't make any difference, I don't think," Avila said. "I think he just took contrary positions. If one day you said the sky was blue, he'd say it was pink. And the next day, if he felt like it, he switched sides."

"Who were Henry Bettencourt's other rivals? Or who among the people at the groups were rivals and might be willing to do violence?"

"You should talk to all of them. Every single one of them in that tent-city had an agenda. So few wanted to talk about non-violence. You've got to interview the protesters. The administration let that tent-city be on campus, and it expanded from there. The local police District wants to get rid of them. The school won so far, but you've got to talk to them. Both sides. They're all there. They're all upset by these killings, left and right."

"Did Mr. Bettencourt have specific enemies or friends?" Turner asked.

Mrs. Bettencourt said, "Henry thought of everyone as a friend. He could be trying that way."

"Anyone specific?" Turner asked.

Mrs. Bettencourt shrugged. "You could talk to Andy Siedel. He was Henry's right-hand man. He might be a good person to start with."

Avila spoke up. "And you should probably check with the infiltrators from the FBI, and presumably the Chicago police department. You should know those or be able to find out who they were."

Mrs. Bettencourt added, "And private investigators hired by big businesses who wanted to make sure the 1% had an in to what was going on."

Fenwick said, "Were they there to disrupt things?"

They both nodded. Mrs. Bettencourt said, "Of course."

"How did you know who they were?"

"You go to enough of these, you begin to learn who is really with you and who isn't."

"Do you know their names?" Fenwick asked.

"Not their real ones."

"We found guns in the safe in your husband's room."

"They weren't his. We don't own any guns. He made the mistake of caring and working hard for people. He wanted peace, not violence." She wiped away a tear with a tattered tissue. Turner moved the box on his desk closer to her. "I told him to be careful."

Fenwick asked, "What was the relationship between the three of you?"

Avila looked to Bettencourt whose cheeks turned slightly pink. She said, "We were in a polyamorous relationship."

Fenwick said, "I'm not sure what that means."

Mrs. Bettencourt said, "He and I were married, but we were free to date other women. The three of us have been in a relationship for two years now."

"You live together?"

"Most weekends."

"Did he date other men?"

"Not that he talked about. He was straight."

The detectives didn't mention Ian's confessed interlude with Bettencourt.

Friday 12:02 P.M.

As their heads disappeared down the stairs, Fenwick said, "Were all these people screwing each other?"

"Apparently."

"I must run in the wrong circles."

"The right circles all screw?"

"Apparently."

Turner said, "And at least some of the protesters were all mad at each other?"

"Except Saint Henry Bettencourt."

"But it sure sounds like some could have been mad at him. We got left and right going nuts on each other. Or at least a lot of possibilities."

"So can we say the protesters are upset because people are being murdered left and right?"

Before Turner could strangle him for the horrible pun, Fenwick said, "Maybe that's why people are shooting at me, to stop me from being funny."

Turner muttered, "Justifiable homicide if I ever heard it."

"I heard that," Fenwick said.

"You were supposed to." Turner sighed then said, "One thing about you being wounded and both of us being pissed off about all this, is that when you are in that mood, you tend to make fewer stupid puns."

"They aren't stupid."

"Some totally stupid. Some less stupid. But all stupid."

"You liked one."

"Once."

"You've laughed."

"I can't help myself, and laughing isn't liking." Turner sighed. "We gotta go talk to these tent people, protesters. See if we can find the FBI informant and the 1% person. See if there was a Chicago police presence."

Fenwick said, "If we didn't have a presence, we were criminally negligent."

"As long as they weren't agent provocateurs."

"But would any of this cause these two specific guys to be killed?"

"I guess that's what we need to find out."

Barb Dams appeared at the top of the stairs. She had a ream-thick stack of papers in her hands. She flopped them onto Fenwick's desk. "These are all the reports on all the groups of and individual protesters from any kind of law enforcement agency I could think of and that I could get info from. Fong helped as well." She held out a flash drive. "All that's on this as well. Fong and I flagged the ones who had any history of violence." She picked up about half a ream of paper from the top of the stack. "That's these. I flagged them on the flash drive as well, and emailed the whole thing to you."

They both thanked her.

Dams shrugged. "There's a Code of Silence, and it cuts both ways. There's also real police work that gets to the bottom of this shit." She thumped the stack of papers, turned, and marched away.

Turner said, "I'm glad she's on our side."

Fenwick said, "If she and Fong are traitors, we're lost."

Friday 12:15 P.M.

Roosevelt and Wilson hurried into the squad room and rushed over to Turner and Fenwick.

Wilson said, "We heard you found the Taser."

Fenwick said, "More like it found us."

Roosevelt said, "And you're not dead." Wilson whacked Fenwick on his not-wounded arm.

Wilson asked, "You know what this means?"

Fenwick said, "A shit stream of trouble for all of us?"

Wilson said, "And it's not funny."

Fenwick said, "I'm working on it." He got glared at. He shrugged. "They can't all be gems."

Turner said, "It means somebody's out to get us. The most obvious thing is that somehow it's connected to Carruthers."

"He was in custody," Wilson said. "He couldn't have planted the Taser on that roof."

Turner said, "Yeah, but he has defenders."

Roosevelt said, "But I don't get this. The killer put the Taser up there? Has to be. Why?"

Turner and Fenwick shook their heads.

Turner guessed. "To create uncertainty? But the deeper meaning of course, is that the killer was at the scene of the Carruthers fiasco.

Or the killer had a friend or at least someone he or she knew at the earlier scene, who just happened to pick up the Taser and choose to give it to him or her."

Fenwick said, "Begins to strain credulity."

Turner said, "Or it wasn't the killer, and someone is fucking with us just for the hell of it. Unless this whole thing is being well-planned and strategically organized from one central point."

Roosevelt said, "I just find it so hard to think of that whole Carruthers incident as little more than a joke."

Fenwick held up his wounded arm.

"Okay, wrong again," Roosevelt admitted.

Wilson said, "Any one of a number of people could have died."

Turner said, "When he took the Taser, if it was the killer, was he planning to kill these two guys at that time? That's an awful lot of forward planning."

Fenwick shook his head. "Fortuitous happenstance."

Turner said, "It's not making sense."

Dams hustled up the stairs and over to Turner and Fenwick. "You didn't hear this from me, but word from the secretary's network, is that the U.S. Attorney Walter Whitaker is going to 'investigate' the Carruthers incident."

"How many is that now?" Fenwick asked.

Turner said, "According to what I can gather from Yutka and Molton, and the usual procedures and the new practices, at the moment, we've got a Cook County criminal court investigation about an attempted murder charge against Carruthers for the kid and/or Fenwick." Turner continued to name and tick off the investigations on his fingers. "The Bureau of Internal Affairs, the Independent Police Review Authority, and the Chicago Police Board. A Cook County Grand Jury is investigating if cops lied about any of this, and now the U.S. Attorney, Whitaker."

Dams added, "Don't forget the Justice Department's Civil Rights Division."

Fenwick groaned. "They're all going to want to talk to us." He pointed to Roosevelt and Wilson. "They're going to go after you guys. You did the initial on-scene investigation."

Roosevelt said, "I don't give a shit. We wrote reality. We wrote what we saw. We wrote what people said, what you guys said. We submitted dash cams and crowd cams. Bullshit. We did right."

Dams said, "They're all fighting about who is going to investigate first. And who can screw up each other's investigation. I'm sure you're right about a civil rights investigation."

"Against Carruthers or us?" Turner asked.

Fenwick sighed.

Turner shook his head. He said, "It's perfect."

They all gaped at him.

Turner continued, "If you wanted to delay, obfuscate, get away with murder or attempted murder, you do a Keystone Kops thing. You announce you're all running around like mad. Hell, even open a few things that aren't investigations. If some time in the future a random victim gets a few million from the City Council, who cares? The Code of Silence has won. That's how it usually works. That's how it always has worked."

Dams nodded at Turner. "It's what they'll try. It's been their pattern. I will keep you posted when I hear anything." She left.

Friday 12:32 P.M.

On their way out, they stopped in Molton's office. They gave him a brief summary of the interview with the wife and their plan for the afternoon.

Molton said, "I've got more meetings downtown. What a crock."

Turner said, "Could you get us the name of the Chicago police infiltrators into the tent city?"

Molton said, "No problem."

Next, they stopped at Chicago Central Hospital to see DeShawn Jackson, the kid they saved. The wind had begun to gust. It felt good as it attempted to dry the dampness on every inch of their skin. Puffy white clouds had begun to appear.

The information they got from Roosevelt and Wilson's report said the boy's mom was a nurse and his dad was a postal worker on the south side of the city.

As they neared the room, a tall woman emerged. She spotted the detectives, hesitated a second, then rushed past the guard at the door, and hurried to them. "I'm Doris Jackson. You saved our son." The mother crushed Fenwick in an embrace. She had a figure of some heft, at least as much as Fenwick, perhaps a bit more. As much as anyone ever could, Turner supposed, she enveloped him in an embrace. Fenwick smiled and crushed her back. Then said, "My arm."

"Oh, I'm so sorry. You were hurt."

"Just a couple scratches, but the arm does ache when pressed."

She patted his good arm. Then enveloped Turner in a less full embrace. "And you were there. You stopped that awful police officer. Was he insane?"

"Just doing my job," Turner said.

Once in the room, they were introduced to Lionel Jackson, the father, a man with grizzled white hair who stood up and said, "Thank you." He extended his hand which Turner and Fenwick shook.

"How is he?" Turner asked.

They looked at the sleeping kid.

"Mostly just scared," Mrs. Jackson said. "They're a little afraid of a concussion after the two of you fell and bashed into that car. How is your head?"

Fenwick pointed to the small bandage on his scalp. "I've got a hard head. For me, the headlight lost. I'm sorry I couldn't prevent him from hitting the fender."

"You couldn't know. You saved him from a hail of bullets. Nothing is more important."

Mr. Jackson leaned closer and whispered, "They've been hovering around trying to scare us."

"Who?" Fenwick asked.

Mr. Jackson said, "Lawyers, people from the police department. Our lawyer is meeting with them right now."

Mrs. Jackson sat next to her son on the bed and held his hand. She said, "They've already been to court trying to get my boy's juvenile records. There was a lawyer in here, good thing our attorney was here. He said he was going to subpoena my son's juvenile record plus he wanted to know if my son had a medical condition or was on medication or was a drug user. Or a drug dealer. And about his connection to terrorist organizations."

"Your attorney was here?"

"Yes." The mom heaved a sigh worthy of Fenwick. "It was a good thing. He told that lawyer to go to hell."

"Who was the lawyer?" Turner asked.

A tall, African-American man entered. He wore a charcoal gray suit with a white shirt and dark tie.

Introductions were made. The new guy was Harold Furman. He said, "I'm the lawyer for the family. I'm not sure you should be here."

Mr. Jackson said, "They saved my boy's life."

Turner said, "It's probably best to listen to your attorney."

Turner and Fenwick retreated to the corridor. The lawyer followed. The three took several steps away from the door to the kid's room, in the direction away from the police officer on duty. Furman said, "Sorry to be officious."

"We understand," Turner said.

Furman said, "We're going to sue."

Fenwick nodded. "Many people have, and have won large sums."

Furman shook his head. "We get rumors about this Carruthers guy, about false arrests, searches without warrants, not reading suspects their rights, a host of other complaints. But even worse, there may be no charges against him at all. In fact, some are claiming he didn't hit the kid, just you."

The detectives nodded. They knew better than to open their mouths.

Turner asked, "Would you be willing to tell us who from the department has been here to talk to you?"

"A raft of lawyers. One from the city. Another one I think represented Carruthers, Cannon something. Then there were people from the police, a gentleman named Adam Edberg from the mayor's office, Lyal DeGroot from that police review board, and then the local alderman, Frank Bortz."

"They all came together?"

"No. They've been in and out. I happened to be here when the first one appeared, which was lucky. It's like I'm on guard against madness."

"Should they be talking to you?" Turner asked.

"I sure don't think so, but they keep asking questions. All seemed designed in some way to smear DeShawn. They'd ask, 'how long has he been a drug addict'. Not did he do drugs, but with a presumption that he did. Or 'how many of his friends are known terrorists'? Just nutty stuff. I told them all to go to hell. Even the alderman seemed to be strained by the whole affair."

"Something is odd," Fenwick said.

"They came here to threaten and frighten," Furman said. "A lot of these questions are normally done in court proceedings that take months." He shook his head. "Thanks for saving DeShawn's life."

They left.

Friday 12:45 P.M.

At the last second, just as the elevator doors were closing, a fist was shoved between the doors, which instantly reopened. A short, scrawny man scuttled in. He wore a white, short sleeve shirt, red bowtie, and black pants. They were the only three in the elevator. When the doors shut, he said, "I'm Ronald Cannon, Randy Carruthers's lawyer."

Turner said, "We shouldn't be talking to you. You shouldn't be talking to us."

"Oh, I think you'll want to hear what I have to say. Besides all that don't-talk-to-anybody-on-either-side? That's all bullshit. That's all to save their jobs, and has nothing to do with legal or illegal."

Turner assumed the guy was lying. He was also willing to play out a string to see if the guy could turn it into rope and hang himself or his client. It was a dangerous game to play.

Turner caught Fenwick looking at him out of the corner of his eye. They both gave the slightest of nods to each other.

Cannon pointed at Turner. "We're going to release it that you're a gay cop."

"So what?" Fenwick asked.

"Ah, but we're not going to call a press conference. We're going to whisper it to a few bigoted, but sympathetic reporters. See, we want it to look like a secret. We don't care if it is or not."

"There are protections in this city and this state," Fenwick said.

"We don't care. We don't want your job. Not right away, or that's not a specific goal. The idea is to discredit you. And you're right, being gay doesn't discredit people in the eyes of the law, not in Illinois, but we don't care about the law. We care about public perception and how we can turn it against you. There will be enough homophobes to ease off at least some of the pressure."

"How do you live with yourself at night?" Fenwick asked.

"I'm giving my client the best possible defense."

"Do you think that's what this is about, a defense?"

"If it works, I don't care."

Fenwick said, "I don't like you."

"Not an issue for me." They reached the ground floor. The doors opened, and they walked out. The lawyer followed them to their car. Upon arrival there, the lawyer asked, "Have you heard from the city's law department?"

"What do we have to do with them?" Fenwick asked.

"They're the ones who represent you. They're fighting with each other about what to do about this case." When Fenwick began to speak, he held up his hand. "And the Independent Police Review Board is split about what to do about you two." The lawyer leaned toward them. "You do know the video isn't clear. We've got an affidavit from a cop who says the kid had a gun or was going for a gun. Cops are threatening to sue both you guys. Word is damage was done to Carruthers, and you refused to treat him."

Fenwick snorted, "He refused transport to the hospital or an offer to have a doctor examine him. Refused on scene."

The lawyer said, "We'll find out what's true. We'll also be suing Detective Rodriguez."

Turner asked, "Why are you telling us all this?" He'd been content to let his partner take the lead in responding.

"Because I want you to realize who is really on your side."

"Who is that?" Turner asked.

"No one. I know you think you have friends in high places, but they'll drop you so fast. No one wants to deal with the Fenwick garbage. No one."

"You are," Fenwick pointed out. "What garbage?"

"You'll see."

Turner said, "I can see them arguing about what to do about Carruthers, maybe a little, but us? We're not in trouble."

"Or so you think."

Fenwick said, "What I would find surprising is that those groups would be confiding in you, the lawyer for someone who has a case coming before each of them."

Turner said, "Unless you had an informant in each of those groups, more loyal to you and/or to Carruthers. What does Carruthers have? Pictures of all of you naked in Daley Plaza attacking a group of nuns?"

Canon jammed his index finger at them. "You're in way over your heads. You have no idea who you're dealing with. If you both had brains in your head, you'd quit. It's going to get ugly, and it's going to get ugly very fast."

"This is news?" Turner asked.

Cannon shook his head then pointed a finger first at Fenwick then Turner. "I can't believe you haven't realized this."

"What?" Fenwick asked.

"About your Commander. If you don't think Molton isn't part of Carruthers's clout, you're naïve. You don't get away with that much when he's directly under your command. You just don't. Not unless there's direct collusion, and if he's been protecting him all these years, then you're further out on a limb than you think. Molton will abandon you. Right now, you think he's all that stands between you and perdition. Ha!"

Turner wondered if he practiced making his laughter grating.

Cannon did another round of finger pointing then said, "I'm surprised you haven't been suspicious of Molton."

Turner and Fenwick exchanged confused looks.

"Who has enough clout to save somebody's ass? The first person to look to is the immediate supervisor. Or who the immediate supervisor is afraid of. Or is beholden to. You guys are stupid. At the very least, he's been told to tow the line."

Fenwick said, "My guess is your design here is to sow doubt and dissension. Why would anybody be confiding in you?"

"I'm representing Carruthers."

Fenwick said, "The question still stands. In fact, they shouldn't be confiding in you because here you are blabbing. Unless you're part of the vast conspiracy to protect a fool. Why would you do that?"

"Everybody deserves a lawyer. I hope you've got a good one." More nasty chortling. "We're filing a number of lawsuits. His firing would be unconstitutional."

Fenwick asked, "He has a right to be stupid? Which amendment is that?"

Turner tried to glare and stop himself from smiling at the same time. It came across as a grimace. He said, "You know your client asked to talk to me."

"No, he didn't."

"Are you delusional?" Turner asked.

"Did you tape it?"

Turner asked, "Which answer will annoy you more?"

"He isn't that stupid."

Fenwick guffawed for a few seconds then burst into laughter. He stopped only when he stepped the wrong way and banged his wounded arm against the car.

Turner asked, "Why did you come here? Why did you even want to meet? The best I can gather is you wanted to frighten us, scare us off."

Fenwick added, "Have you lost your mind?"

Cannon pointed at Fenwick. "You can't scare me."

Fenwick said, "I think I'm going to put you on a suspect list."

The lawyer said, "I tried to do a good deed. I tried to warn you. You weren't willing to listen."

Fenwick said, "You're out to help your client, and fucking with our minds is one of your ways of doing that. Go away."

He left.

Fenwick said, "They're all lurking at every scene we go to?"

"Can be if they want, I guess."

"Now we mistrust Molton?" Fenwick asked.

"No."

Friday 1:15 P.M.

Fenwick took a gargantuan bite out of his extra colossal Italian sub from Romana's. They'd gotten to-go sandwiches and were eating at their desks. Fenwick chewed, swallowed, guzzled a third of a liter of diet soda, and said, "The dog did nothing in the night time."

Turner raised an eyebrow. He knew the Sherlock Holmes reference from the story "Silver Blaze."

Fenwick said, "Blawn, the beat cop from last night didn't file a report. That's not normal. I like normal."

"Yes," Turner said looking at his extra-hefty friend, "I know that one look at you and people think 'normal'. And why wouldn't they?" He shook his head then said, "I wish we could find one connection between all these events. I can't name one."

Fenwick said, "We keep looking. We got the financials on Bettencourt and Shaitan yet?"

Turner tapped a folder on the side of his desk. "Fong sent up what he got from the credit cards and bank statements." He shoved over Bettencourt's file to Fenwick's desk and opened Shaitan's. They glanced while they ate.

After a few minutes and a quarter of a sandwich, Turner said, "I guess yurts in India don't cost much to maintain. He's got very few charges in India. A few that prove he actually does go there. Other than that, I don't see much here, but his income is a little startling."

"How much does he make?"

"He gets large deposits of money, a couple as big as a hundred thousand dollars. Let me check these dates against the Internet." He called one of them up on his lap top. "This payment came right after he gave a talk at a college."

"Those college groups can afford a hundred thousand bucks? I don't believe that."

"Nor do I. Let's see." Turner hunted through the Internet checking Shaitan's schedule against the deposits to his account. "Yep," he reporter, "big bucks for these talks."

"So who was paying if it wasn't the college groups?"

"The actual checks are from the website he worked for, but are timed with the talks. My guess is whoever owns, or someone who likes what the website does was paying."

"If he was getting paid that much, why would he care who or how many showed up or whether or not there were protests?"

"Lot of money." Turner shrugged. "Doesn't give us evidence or motive for murder."

"Unless someone was jealous."

"If they even knew he was making this much."

Fenwick wolfed down a pickle spear then wiped his hands with several napkins. He said, "Our friend Bettencourt could be more ordinary, but I don't see how. Simple credit card charges, gas, groceries." He flipped several pages. "Income regular, making about five thousand a month. No large payments of any kind." He took another bite. "What's next this afternoon?"

"Protesters." Turner called up the email with all the information on the protesters. "We should look at these." It was the same information Dams had gotten them hardcopies of.

Fenwick put down the remainder of his sandwich and pulled up the data on the protesters on his iPad.

The detectives ate in silence as they scrolled and read through sets of information on the leaders who they hoped to meet that afternoon at the tent city. Before they began, they agreed that

Fenwick would start at the beginning of the alphabet, Turner from the end. They trusted each other to note significant oddities. They'd go over each other's work if they had to.

Turner's cell phone buzzed with a message from Barb Dams. He glanced at it and said, "Peter Eisenberg was in charge of the CPD presence in the tent city."

"Do they have their own little pup tent? Have a barbeque grill? Give out brochures for touring the city?"

"Beats the hell out of me. We'll have to hunt for them."

They ate and read some more.

Fenwick finished his sandwich and drained the last of his soda. He wiped his fingers, pressed the front of his iPad, and said, "Some of these people strike me as nuts."

"No doubt they've been waiting for your opinion and your approval. Probably sitting breathlessly on the edge of their chairs."

Fenwick glared at him.

"Or not."

"Come on," Fenwick said. "Look at these groups with real live people who deny these mass killings, saying they're all staged by the government as an excuse to take away their guns."

Turner said, "It's all fear. Live your lives in fear. It doesn't matter what the issue is. It doesn't matter how crazy it is. The more your fear spreads, the more donations you get. Fear sells. You know that."

Fenwick snorted. "I don't think they have enough self-awareness to realize what crazy is."

"Probably not. There's lots of good groups, too," Turner said. "Trying to get money out of politics, or do eco-friendly things."

Fenwick said, "I'd like to have a pet wolf."

This was new. "What?"

"Can't you picture it? And what could be more eco-friendly? We're on patrol. We come upon a scene where, I don't know, some numbnuts dumbfuck is firing a gun towards an unarmed suspect and we're right behind him. Can't you picture telling a wolf to sic em?"

"I think harboring wild creatures is at the least illegal, and probably cruel to them. And with Carruthers's luck up to yesterday, he'd probably accidentally hit the wolf."

"Look at this bunch." Fenwick waved his phone at Turner. It showed a manifesto from a group calling itself The Benevolent Association for Supporting Your Local Sheriff. "If you're a member of this group, why would you bother to show up? These people with their Second Amendment solutions. Pah."

Fenwick was off on one of his favorite rants. Turner knew better than to try to interrupt or change the subject.

Fenwick said, "If you believe there are so-called Second Amendment solutions to everything, why even bother going to a meeting? Or rather, I'd think you'd only ever go to a meeting to begin shooting people. Either you get your way or you start killing people? The whole wild-west solution to our existence. Plus, you wouldn't need cops, just coroners. Save taxpayer's money. No government, just death squads."

"You done?"

"Just raveling a thread."

"I do not want to debate these people. I do not want you debating these people, or we'll be here until… Well, too long."

"I could bore them to tears."

"Tell them some of your jokes."

Fenwick got a gleam in his eyes. "I just go from group to group telling the wrist joke."

Turner shook his head. "We'd either get mass suicide or cop-i-cide."

Fenwick raised an eyebrow. "Cop-i-cide?"

"I'd shoot you myself."

"You hate the joke that much?"

"You can't imagine."

Friday 2:07 P.M.

Turner said, "We should stop at the ME's office. It's on our way to see the protesters."

At Cook County Morgue, they wound their way through the tiled halls. They found Kent Duffy scrubbing instruments. No bodies were on any of the stainless steel slabs.

"You got anything on our guys?" Fenwick asked.

Duffy said, "They're still dead."

"Old joke," Fenwick said.

Duffy said, "I've got a few oddities but nothing that stuck out to me that would help lead to figuring out who killed them."

"What have you got?" Fenwick asked.

"Within twenty-four hours before they died, they'd both been penetrated and had anal intercourse. I found residue in their anal cavities. Semen that was not each other's and that does not match anyone in our data systems so far. But the semen was from the same person. Far as I know, Bettencourt was married to a woman."

Turner said, "We already know who did that. The guy who found the bodies. Anything else?"

"Shaitan had his pubes shaved like a male Eastern European porn star."

"What does that mean?" Fenwick asked.

Turner let Duffy explain. Duffy said, "His pelvic area was

completely hairless, and while he may have been without crotch hair, the area from his nipples to his knees was almost a solid mass of tattoos made up of Nazi symbols, Hitler's birth date, spider webs, that kind of stuff. He ever in prison?"

"Not that we've found in his record."

"Bettencourt had no tattoos. Stomach food contents for both a couple hours old. Sushi for Bettencourt, steak for Shaitan. No name or motive for who would want to shoot either one of them. Your shooter would have had to have been a very good shot, but with scopes so well-developed these days, he might have been close enough to not need to be an expert marksman, although with four shots that precise and that rapid, he or she had to be pretty damn good. On the other hand, your boy Carruthers, our colossal dumb fuck, got off fifteen shots. He managed to wing your partner, miss the kid, kill a street light and two car headlights, and put three shots in a car door just over Fenwick's head as he lay on top of the kid, two others that might have just missed you both, and random shots into a warehouse nearby. We're still missing some of the bullets, embedded into the ground or hell, knowing Carruthers, embedded in the atmosphere from which they may never come down." He paused looked at each of them. "You're lucky you're not dead." He cleared his throat. "Your Tasing him?"

"Yeah," Turner said.

"It almost certainly saved the kid from a direct shot. After that, his continuous firing endangered everyone in that entire block."

"Moving from deliberate to random. Which is better on the streets of Chicago? Are you saying I shouldn't have Tased him?"

"I'm saying it was a tough decision with unintended consequences, which, lucky for the good guys, did not redound to come back and bite you in the ass."

Turner thought, more random chance intruding into their lives. He shivered. Duffy knew no more. The detectives left.

On the way to the car, Fenwick said, "I like that Duffy guy, the new ME."

"Well, new to us. You like him because he's a Fenwick joke virgin? There aren't many of those left around. You are kind of prolific, and not much stops you. Ever."

"I like to spread myself around."

"As Madge said in a slightly different context not that many hours ago, there's so much of you to spread around."

"And the world is better for it."

Friday 2:14 P.M.

In the car, Turner's cell phone rang. He was driving, so he handed it to Fenwick who glanced at the readout. He said, "The station." He put it on speaker-phone. It was Barb Dams. "Paul, you've got an urgent call from Mrs. Carruthers. She wants to meet."

They were sitting at a red light so had a moment to gape at each other.

"Why?" Turner asked.

Barb said, "She wouldn't say. You want me to text you her number?"

"You tell the Commander?"

"The call came in for you."

Turner said, "Yeah, send the number, please, but also put me on with the Commander." He pulled into a bus stop.

Molton came on the line. Turner explained. Molton mused out loud, "Can it hurt? Can it help? If she brings a lawyer or a witness, leave."

Turner agreed. He hung up. Seconds later the text with the number appeared. He punched it in and put it on speaker.

They'd met Mrs. Nancy Carruthers at several Area Ten functions: retirement parties, funerals, and a few less grim occasions, many of these last her husband organized. Poorly.

"What can I do for you Mrs. Carruthers?"

"Nancy, please."

"Nancy."

"I'd like to meet and talk."

"About what?"

"This whole situation is out of control. I'd like to help. I think we should get together in person. I don't think over the phone is appropriate."

Turner agreed.

She added, "Please don't bring the mean fat one with you."

Turner said, "Not a problem." They agreed to meet in half an hour on the near southwest side.

Turner hung up and said, "You got told."

"I shall weep."

"She knew or guessed you were listening."

"So what?"

"You want to wait in the car?"

"Nah. There's tons of stuff to do at the station. I can make sure we've got all the latest reports, check in with Fong and the Commander."

Turner dropped Fenwick off at the station. Among other things, his partner would spend time with all of Fong's tapes looking for anomalies.

Turner had agreed to meet Mrs. Carruthers at Nick's Coffee Shop. It was on the bottom floor of an old factory just south of 22nd Street along the Chicago River. To get to the entrance, you walked down a narrow path built of oak planks recovered from the Great Chicago fire. The wind was blowing hard in the canyon of the river. Darker clouds had begun to appear.

The coffee shop itself was a long, narrow room, small tables along one wall going straight back fifty feet. Two people standing next to each other with arms extended could span the width of the place. Inside the front door were the beverage-making machines.

Lots of good coffee and the best hot chocolate in the city.

Nick Buscher and his assistant manager, Dave Lundquist, were the only two in the place. It was dark and cool. The walls were burgundy brick illuminated at intervals with low lights. On the wall under each table were outlets. Nick was willing to let his customers plug in and charge their electronics as conveniently as possible. The pattern on the rug was too faded to make out. It might have been maroon roses at one time.

Turner took his coffee to the last table in the back.

A few minutes later, Nancy Carruthers appeared. She was a middle-aged woman on the unfortunate side of dowdy. She wore a gray house dress with patches of sweat under each armpit visible from as far back as Turner sat. She wore red shower clogs.

She stopped for a beverage at the counter then peered into the dark ambience of the coffee shop.

Turner held up a hand.

She hurried forward, shower clogs flopping noisily.

He stood as she neared the table.

She held out hand and said, "Thank you for coming."

They sat and sipped their drinks.

She said, "How are you?"

Turner said, "Yesterday I looked down the barrel of a gun and lived."

"There's many a time Randy's said that you're the only friend he's got at work."

Turner wondered how his lack of open hostility had translated into friendship. Then again, if Carruthers was as oblivious as they all thought, why should he be surprised?

Turner said, "He's gotten in trouble so often, I'm not sure there's anything anyone could do to help."

"He always tries to do his best to do better. He always does what his boss tells him to do. He's religious about it." She gave him a wan smile. "I'm not naïve. I know he has problems. It's just his best isn't always as good as it should be. I know you've tried to help."

Turner couldn't actually remember a specific instance where he tried to help Carruthers. He remembered times he didn't pile on as others made comments about the inept detective's odd behaviors. Was he responsible, at least in some small way for Carruthers's spiral into the slough of stupidity? Maybe if he had reached out in some amorphous way. Then he figured, the guy had to take some responsibility.

She was continuing, "Like yesterday, Randy doesn't mean to do these things. He gets excited."

Turner wondered if she wanted to meet to convince him to excuse her husband. He said, "How can I help you, Nancy?"

She took a sip of coffee and leaned toward him. "They're going to destroy you just like you're trying to destroy my husband."

"Who is trying to destroy him?"

"Commander Molton for one. He's always disliked him."

Turner knew that Molton, as he did with all the personnel under him, went out of his way to be fair, including to Carruthers in his many difficult situations. Molton believed most adults could learn.

Turner said, "If he's disliked him all these years, how has Randy escaped being suspended? He must have someone who backs him up at higher levels. Maybe more than one someone."

"I don't know how all that department intrigue works."

Her eyes shifted as she said it. She's lying, Turner thought. She knows damn well what's going on. Why the hell am I here?

He asked again, "What can I do for you?"

She leaned close again. "He's down," she whispered. "I've never seen him this depressed. He won't talk except to his gun."

"Has he threatened suicide?"

"He usually talks to me. I don't know what's going on in the investigation. I've always known before. He tells me."

Turner took a guess. "You've had people you could talk to before. They aren't taking your calls."

She lowered her head and whispered, "No."

Turner had begun to wonder how much of all of this was a tremendous lie. He did catch a glimmer that Carruthers himself had contacts, and now maybe that she had contacts. Were they the same connections? Did she know more than her husband? Was she a bigger help to him than he was to himself? He tried to concentrate on her words. He said, "He's always been kind of up and down at work. Some days up, some days down."

"It's worse. His partner, Rodriguez, won't take Randy's calls. And nobody's called Randy. I'd know. He always knows when his friends are working for him. You've done things to help him before."

"I've never called him. Never called someone on his behalf."

Again she leaned towards him. "I've been threatened."

He caught her eye.

"Over the phone. I didn't recognize the voice. I've gotten hang-up calls with the Caller ID saying 'unavailable.' I'm scared."

"You should report it."

"I will. I have. I don't think they're going to do anything."

"Did Randy get any threats?"

"Not that I know of. Not that's he's told me. He just won't talk." She gulped some coffee then said, "You've made mistakes on the job. Everyone does."

Turner said, "Randy seems to have a long list of complaints going back a long time."

"There were thirty thousand complaints in the past five years. His are only a fraction of all those."

"Anybody's would be only a fraction. I'm not sure that's a good defense."

"The job warps your mind and heart. It does that to anyone who cares and who tries to do his best."

The problem, Turner thought, was that Carruthers's best just wasn't very good.

She continued, "You know how every decision you make is instant, involves life and death."

"Some decisions can. Most don't. Usually, it's pretty cut and dried. You get evidence, and you arrest somebody."

Her voice became more insistent. "Yesterday, Randy made a good decision."

Was she as delusional as her husband?

Turner said, "If it's a choice between Tasing your husband and innocent people dying or me getting shot, I choose Tasing."

Turner didn't think debating Carruthers's actions made a lot of sense. He said, "I don't think we should be debating what happened."

"Randy was trying to save your life, and you attacked him."

Turner wasn't going to get further into this nonsensical debate, but his innate politeness caused him to put it this way, "I think it's best not to discuss the specifics of a case in the middle of an ongoing investigation."

"You're right. You're right. Of course. I know better, but there's nothing you can tell me about what's going on?"

"I don't know what's going on."

"That's how they want you. They want you to have terror in your soul."

At this point Turner guessed Fenwick would begin a debate about the existence of a soul. Turner was in no mood for theological or philosophical debates and was glad his partner wasn't present.

They left a few moments later.

Friday 3:15 P.M.

As he walked out of the coffee shop, the hot afternoon clouds had begun to obscure large parts of the sky. He saw no thunderheads or shelf clouds. It felt like the skies were being lowered and the atmosphere was being compressed long past the point of oppressive. The radar on his phone showed no storms in the immediate vicinity.

At the station, he joined Fenwick. His partner looked up and asked, "What did she want?"

"Mostly, I think she wanted to scare me, or for me, us, to be frightened. If what she's saying is true, Randy has lost what few friends he had, and/or is more depressed and alone than ever. That he's a good guy and always does what he's told." He shook his head. "Claims he's talking to his gun."

Fenwick looked him full in the face. Cop's suicide was an issue they'd dealt with among their colleagues.

"I stopped in Molton's office before I came up here. Barb was there as well. I told them about the mention of suicide in connection with Carruthers, the way we're supposed to report hearing anything remotely like it about co-workers. I don't want him choosing to kill himself, and it coming back in any way to my conscience. Molton and Barb will know what to do. Molton's the right person to set things in motion. You know, handle all the paperwork and procedures on that."

Fenwick asked, "Was Mrs. Carruthers serious?"

"I can believe he's seriously depressed, and that he and his wife would have the kind of relationship that won't allow him to talk to her." Turner shook his head. "I don't know how much of the truth she was telling me. The other thing I thought she was trying to do was get information about what's going on with the incident investigation."

"How would you know about that, and why would she think you would know it, and why, if you knew it, did she think you'd be willing to tell her?"

"My guess is she, he, or both of them are desperate. She claimed she'd received threatening phone calls."

"What kind of threats?"

"For Randy to do what's right."

"What the hell does that mean?"

"Beats me. There is a chance that all of his fuck ups and all the cover-ups to all those fuck ups are going to come out. All those lies, along with, possibly his years of other violations of procedures, maybe violence to suspects. With maybe anyone who's been protecting him running for cover. Who knows?" Turner shook his head. "Hell of a way to choose to exist in this world."

Fenwick said, "When we were at the hospital, his lawyer wasn't running away from him."

"He's getting paid to stick with him." Turner added, "One last thing, I think she may have her own sources in the department. I have no idea what that means in terms of his future on the job, or…"

Fenwick said, "Beats the hell out of me."

Turner pointed to the laptop and stacks of papers on Fenwick's desk. "What have you got?"

"I got a lot of little stuff. Most of which doesn't add up to a solution, but what the hell."

As he reached for a stack of papers, Fenwick yelped, "Ouch."

"Still hurt?"

"Starting to stiffen up and to itch. Madge says that means it's starting to heal."

"I tell my kids the same thing with all their scrapes and bruises. They've always bought it."

Fenwick grimaced. "I took a few more aspirins." He spent more time moving the next papers before holding up a few. "I sent a bunch of stuff to your cell phone just before you arrived. Let me start with the simple stuff." He read, "Taser, no prints."

"Figures."

"Nothing definitive from the crime scene or the shooting scene. Some small bits of debris but no way to tell if any of it connects to the murder."

Fenwick pulled out several new sets of papers on his desk. "We got a follow-up on guns in the safe. None had been fired in quite a while."

"Well, we didn't think they were the murder weapon. For that, we need a rifle."

"No prints on the guns."

"Not even from them being put in the safe?"

"No prints is no prints."

"Huh."

"Nothing more from their motel rooms, Bettencourt or Shaitan. No suspicious prints. A few from housekeeping. No secret messages. No other recording devices."

"Financials?"

Fenwick pulled out another few sheets of paper. "Confirmation of Shaitan's electronic charges in India, so possibly or even presumably the yurt thing is true."

"It says yurt supplies?"

"I said possibly and presumably. You want to go yurt hunting in India?"

"Not today."

He held up another sheet of paper. "Shaitan had $43,953 in the safe."

"Where'd he get it? You don't walk into any average bank at get that much cash."

"India?"

"US currency in India?"

"Why not?"

Turner said, "I've got a better question, what for?"

"Crime scene folks only counted and inventoried. We also have cell phone records. I had time to go though some but not nearly all. Nothing suspicious so far. We'll have to get to all of them later."

Fenwick moved his monitor so Turner could see it. "I set up a grid of the shooting. Both buildings. I traced the most logical movements of their routes to the building and to the top of the building, both for the victims and the shooter in their respective buildings. Beat cops are finishing calls back on the canvass in both places. Nothing in interviews of all the people in the building."

"That map is kind of good."

"I got a new app on my phone."

"I'm still getting used to you making peace with technology."

"It's more a fragile coalition." Fenwick tapped for several seconds. "I've also got all the major players placed in terms of geography and time."

"If they were telling the truth, if someone can verify them, and, of course, maybe one of the major players didn't kill them."

"I can do minor players."

"You're just showing off. And there are too many of them. I think they should rise to suspecthood before we add them."

"Is suspecthood a word?"

"It is now. You're not the only poet in this bunch."

"Is two a bunch?"

"If we want it to be."

"That's all I've got."

"We should check in with Fong. Any information on who shot at our car?"

"Nothing."

Friday 3:44 P.M.

Downstairs, Fong was in front of his main monitor. He looked over and smiled at Turner and Fenwick. "I've been waiting for you guys. I wanted both of you to be the first to see this. It's so cool."

He clicked several keys on his keyboard. All the lights dimmed and then every wall and even the floor and ceiling showed what had until a second ago been on just his monitor. Fong said, "The whole room is a monitor now, walls, ceiling, floor. I've been working on it forever. Finally got the linoleum replaced yesterday. The floor is of polycarbonate plastic in case something heavy needs to be on it."

He looked at Fenwick then pointed to the far wall. "The driver circuit board is concealed behind that old fire extinguisher emergency holder box. It draws on a separate power source than the whole rest of the building. I had to hack into the electric grid to set it up." Turner thought he recognized the new ambient hum as the soundtrack from *The Hobbit* movies.

Turner said, "Congratulations."

Fenwick murmured, "Wow."

Fong said, "I just wish it guaranteed we'd catch more criminals."

Fenwick said, "You found anything so far?"

Fong cut the monitor back so the image was only on the large one above his desk. "Let's start here. Took some leg work, but I've been to every place between the two crime scenes. I've got tons of video footage. Here's what we've got from police dash cams, the public, any random cameras from businesses around. It's going to take you a while."

Fenwick said, "Doesn't everything?"

Turner bit down any comment about how fast Fenwick could devour a pint of chocolate-chocolate chip ice cream. A high powered vacuum cleaner would be slower.

"You got time to go through it now?" Fong asked.

"Now is as good as ever," Fenwick said.

"You're not going to get continuous action from camera to camera. This is from the time of the Carruthers incident to the time of the shooting, between the two venues. So far I haven't found anything that looks suspicious."

Turner and Fenwick sat together to look at footage. Fong assisted them. After half an hour, Fenwick said, "We got nothing."

"Sorry," Fong said.

"Not your fault," Turner said.

"For the actual Carruthers incident, I've checked CPD dash cams and all the footage from the people at the scene." He motioned them closer. "The official investigation seems to be missing a few. I, however, got all of them from everywhere and made copies. You know Carruthers claims the kid had a gun?"

"That's what he told me, too," Turner said.

Fong shook his head. "Ain't no gun. Nowhere. No how." He showed them the DeShawn Jackson footage he had. "No gun."

Turner said, "They had the perimeter set up pretty quick, and I trust Roosevelt and Wilson to find that kind of thing."

They checked the footage. The Taser didn't reappear after the first few seconds of use on Carruthers. There was only footage of what they had reported. Nothing with someone walking off with the Taser. They finished and sat back.

Fong said, "I traced the call threatening Rodriguez." He paused. The detectives waited. "It came from this building."

"Who?"

"I can only get to here. Beyond that, I haven't been able to trace it. I'm still working on it."

"Bullshit," Fenwick snapped. "Double and triple bullshit."

Turner asked, "Anything on that recording device from Bettencourt's room, and those wires and shit?"

"All I've got so far is that it's not a standard issue for the CPD. If it's ours, it's either very new or very old. I'm voting for new."

"FBI? CIA?" Fenwick asked.

"Or none of the above. I'll tell you when I've figured it out. As for the wires and shit." He shrugged. "Right now, they're just wires and shit."

The detectives nodded.

Fong said, "There's another thing."

They looked at him.

"You guys seen these sites?"

"What sites?"

"You know those pissed-off-cop sites?"

They nodded. Angry cops could post anonymously, snarling and snapping back at those who dared to criticize them.

Fong said, "There are cops pissed at you for tasering Carruthers."

Turner said, "There's all kinds of those sites. They go in and out."

"These mention you specifically. The Commander has me monitoring them. If I find anything, I'll let you know."

They left.

As they walked to the car, Fenwick said, "This is not the day I'm going to start worrying about what the Internet says about me."

"Still, I'm glad Fong is monitoring it. We don't have the time."

Friday 5:31 P.M.

It was late afternoon, long before sunset, but the sky had continued to darken. The wind was now gusting gale force from the south. Turner checked the local radar on his phone. A ragged line of storms from the Wisconsin border to down past Peoria was just beginning to cross Interstate 39 in a number of places. Summer storms covered some of the far north and west suburbs.

A few stray wisps of illumined cloud seeped out of the cloud banks. The branches and leaves swayed in the breeze that did little to ease the humidity.

In deference to the heat, they wore short sleeve shirts and had their ties undone. As far as Turner could see, Fenwick wore a size tent shirt.

The protesters' encampment spread over several acres and included the commons of the college, a part of a neighborhood park, and then ran around and down an old alley with trees that met overhead. A large parking structure, where they left their car, served as boundary at the south end of the complex of tents. They walked from there.

The first thing Turner noted was there seemed to be numerous clots of unsupervised little kids running up and down all over everywhere. One of the larger groups was in a circle seeming to try and twirl with the wind. Another cluster jumped up and down to music Turner didn't recognize. He couldn't see an adult who was actively supervising any of them.

Vendors dotted the area selling everything from scones and vegetables to untraceable phones.

As they approached, they saw a row of news vans from all the local stations posted along one side of the nearest street. Reporters and camera people bustled about in and out of van doors.

As they walked closer to the nearest tents, a few fat drops of rain studded the sidewalk. The black clouds hurried through the early evening dimness.

The grass was trampled to mud.

Fenwick sniffed. "It kind of stinks."

Turner pointed. "Port-a-potties line the sidewalk over there."

Fenwick added, "And unwashed people."

Ian stood at the entrance as they neared it.

The short fat man he was talking to was speaking in a voice just short of a shout. "You don't know anything about our real goals and ambitions. You don't know what's wrong with the world. You haven't gotten beyond your own ego."

Ian said, "You are so right," and turned his back on the guy. He spotted Turner and Fenwick and strode over. In one of the rare changes in his attire, instead of long pants, Ian was in khaki cargo shorts. The shorts revealed his extremely hairy legs which Turner knew matched the fur on his stomach, chest, shoulders, and back. Ian still wore his slouch fedora, clamped low on his head against the wind.

The short fat guy scuttled after Ian and got between him and the detectives. The short man wasn't through. He said, "You will be sorry if you write anything about us. We have powerful friends. We won the election. You'll be sorry." He wagged a finger in Ian's face. "So, so sorry."

"Thank you," Ian said.

In the face of such benignity, the man ran down, looked at Turner and Fenwick, and with a last sneer at Ian, harrumphed away.

"People threatening you?" Fenwick asked.

"No more than usual. Then again, for as many here who think you are heroes, there are those who wish you two had been shot."

"Who?" Fenwick asked.

Ian checked his notes. "How much good is this going to do to give you those names?"

"Probably none," Fenwick said.

Turner kept his residual annoyance with Ian at bay. He asked, "Anything helpful to an investigation?"

"I can't tell. If you try to talk to them, mostly they rant about their cause or causes."

Turner said, "We're looking for Andy Siedel, supposedly second in command to Bettencourt."

Ian said, "I haven't heard of him. I'm not sure these people have a structured hierarchy." He pointed to a circle of people a third of the way down the alley of trees. "If there's a leadership council, that's it. I got pitched from their gathering. It wasn't pretty. That last guy was the final remnant of snarl I got from them. Oh, and be careful of everything you say or do. Assume these people have phones out recording things."

Fenwick said, "We always do."

Turner nodded in agreement. He thought anyone who didn't presume so and act accordingly was some kind of special stupid. Although he wondered what 24-7 cop cameras would really show. How helpful would it be for the world to see them doing tedious paperwork, or watching Fenwick eat gargantuan quantities of food?

Ian said, "You'll be seen as police outsiders."

Fenwick said, "Try to tell me something I don't know."

As they strode down the alley, Turner noticed underneath all the nearby odor was the scent of fresh rain.

As they neared the circle of people, they heard shouts and saw people waving fists.

Fenwick sighed. "I wonder what great philosophical argument has brought them to this point."

They stood just outside the circle and listened. Various members of the group were screaming and hurling accusations about sanitation.

After a few moments, they stepped forward and introduced themselves as detectives and showed ID. They were quickly circled by about fifteen protesters.

A tall, young guy spoke loudest, "Can't you do something about the washrooms?"

Fenwick said, "We're looking for…"

But the young man interrupted him, "They keep moving the port-a-potties back making us go farther and farther to use the washroom, and those aren't really washrooms."

A young woman standing next to him said, "And they're jammed. The lines are immense. And they reek. There's a washroom in the parking garage. The guy says he won't let us use it because they didn't repeal that part of the Affordable Care Act."

Fenwick said, "Huh?"

"He told us that the Affordable Care Act mandates all washrooms must be handicap accessible and any ones that are not can't be used by anybody."

Fenwick said, "You do realize that's a bullshit excuse? There is no such provision repealed or unrepealed."

"Fine. You do something to help us."

Fenwick called Barb Dams at the station and asked her to find out who to contact. She put him on hold for a minute then got right back on the line. She said, "I'll call. I'll get someone in charge to you fast."

While they waited, they asked for Andy Siedel. Pointing, murmurs, and shrugs occurred.

Dams was as good as her word. A few minutes later, a hefty man in blue bib overalls strode purposefully from the parking structure. He walked up to the circle of protesters and said, "I won't have you people using those washrooms."

Turner and Fenwick identified themselves as detectives and asked him to step inside a nearby tent.

Once inside, Fenwick said, "You're under arrest."

"Wha! For what?"

"Gross stupidity. Causing a public nuisance. Blatantly lying when you have no knowledge of the law."

"Wha! You can't."

Fenwick pulled out his handcuffs. Turner pulled out his cuffs and moved to the other side of the man.

Fenwick got up close to the man and whispered in his ear, "Unless you'd like to find a way to let these people use the washrooms in the parking garage."

"They'll make them dirty."

Fenwick rattled the handcuffs and said, "We'll assign a male and female beat cop to be right outside the doors. They can monitor any difficulties."

The bib overall guy said, "Fine."

They stepped outside the tent. Fenwick looked at the crowd and nudged Mr. Biboveralls. Fenwick whispered, "Tell them."

The guy said, "You can use the parking garage washroom."

The protesters cheered. Cameras flashed. Video was taped.

Fenwick mumbled, "This is nuts."

He got hold of Sanchez and Deveneaux to organize shifts of beat cops for the washrooms.

Moments later, a short thin man who hadn't been present came forward and said, "I'm Andy Siedel." He wore a T-shirt that said, "Human Rights for Jesus."

They introduced themselves and asked to talk to him.

He nodded and led them twenty feet away to a tent with its canvas flapping in the wind. They stepped a few feet inside. Without waiting for the questions from Turner and Fenwick, Siedel began, "You're the first cops who actually identified themselves. Sometimes I think there are more cops here than protesters. I know we've seen FBI guys and Chicago police in plainclothes." He waved his arm toward the parking structure. "Homeland security has a van in there. They might as well have labels on the side panels."

Turner said, "We're investigating the murders of Shaitan and Bettencourt. We were told you were Bettencourt's second in command."

"You could call it that. It was more we agreed on a lot of issues and worked together often."

Turner asked, "How did Shaitan and Bettencourt get along?"

Siedel scratched his head. "This place is as rife with gossip as a Peyton Place. You get all kinds of rumors. Before yesterday, it was they hated each other. Now it's like they're martyrs to the cause."

Fenwick said, "We thought Bettencourt was the leader of the peace and light faction."

"He was. Shaitan was leader of the idiots and egomaniacs. If you can call what he did 'leading.'"

"Did they clash openly?"

"Bettencourt didn't do a lot of open clashing. He worked like mad behind the scenes to get people to come to agreements."

"Did Shaitan prevent some of those agreements?"

He sighed. "Depends on who you believed and how much power they thought they had, how much power other people thought they had, and how much power they really did have. Shaitan was reasonably delusional. He was in the camp that believed the dictum, 'if I write for a website, therefore I am,' which is sort of true in our world here."

"You know where they were yesterday?"

"Giving small talks to groups of people in their tents, outside their tents, in rooms at the university, and around the city in people's homes. Hell, if you held still long enough, they'd find you and talk to you. It wasn't just those two. People just kept trying to talk. That's what we all do. Most of us are good people trying to make the world a little bit of a better place. Other than that we sweat. Try to find water, and stay just outside the tents. The interiors get pretty ripe in this heat. Might not be bad if we had a real storm. Now that we can use those washrooms in the parking structure, we can at least take sponge baths. Thanks for that, by the way." He shrugged. "Much of the time, most of us ran off to anything that looked remotely like a demonstration. People would hear about something on their phones and go running. Then people got wise that there were a lot of fake postings."

"Fake postings?" Turner asked.

"Yeah, like a confrontation with police at some random spot, and people would rush to cars, or buses, or trains, or taxis. And they'd get there, and there'd be nothing."

"Sabotage," Turner said.

"Yeah. Or triumph by exhaustion, wear us all out. Or just keeping people confused. Then again, I don't think some of these people care which cause, or what side they are on in that cause."

"Must be some true believers," Turner said.

Siedel nodded. "Sure. Lots of those." He shrugged. "What most of them were doing specifically, I have no idea."

Fenwick asked, "Why even bother to have this conference?"

Siedel gave him a blank look.

Fenwick said, "So many protests these day seem to emanate from one person, or one small group posting, then poof, everybody shows up. Spontaneous."

Siedel nodded, "That can work, but see, there's long term things that need to be done. Sure, you get a few hundred thousand people on a Saturday, but it's the organizers and planners that make things happen in the long run."

Turner asked, "Did you know Shaitan was making a hundred thousand dollars per talk?"

Siedel shrugged and scratched his beard. "Doesn't make him sound like one of the people."

"Who's behind him and all that money?"

"As far as I know, he has a Russian billionaire who is madly in love with him, guy named Pashton Kashnikoliv who is also supposedly a transgender transitioning person."

"Is he here?"

"Not likely. I understand he owns several private islands in various oceans around the globe."

Turner asked, "Were they lovers?"

"Not according to the rumors I heard. Or at least that Shaitan put up enough of a front so the money kept coming. Not enough to move in with him at random places on the globe."

Fenwick asked, "That much money doesn't make him a traitor to the cause?"

"His cause was himself. Our causes are our own. I'd met him. I didn't like him. Not enough to kill him." He shook his head. "Bettencourt was a good man in the best sense of that phrase. He had no enemies that I know of. He was always willing to help. I saw him in and out of the tent city the past few days. Shaitan barely gave me the time of day. He didn't think my organization was worth the time." He leaned closer to them. He smelled a little cleaner than most of the others, and at least he'd smeared some kind of deodorant or cologne over himself to offset the ripeness. Siedel said, "You should be investigating the infiltrators."

"You think you're that important?" Fenwick asked.

"We don't know what they think is important. We act on as many contingencies as we can. What do you think all of our groups have in common, left or right? Infiltration by the government. Or by big business interests." He scratched his beard again. "Hell, the various sides might have been trying to infiltrate each other, trying to videotape each other. We had one group trying to bribe people into causing riots during demonstrations and meetings. I'm reasonably certain Shaitan was behind that. We had another group trying to record them making those bribes, or trying to solicit them to solicit the bribes."

Fenwick and Turner exchanged a glance. Turner suspected they'd had the same thought, Shaitan was using the cash in his room for this.

Turner asked, "You're sure Shaitan was part of the group trying to get people to riot and cause trouble?"

"That's what I heard. He was spending a lot." Siedel gave a short chuckle. "Some of the people were taking his money and using it to have a big party, lots of booze and weed. Shaitan wasn't too bright. People would start to linc up when they saw him coming. Some went back several times. People were videotaping money changing hands both buying and selling, all supposedly very secret. It was kind of nuts. Hell, paying people to cause trouble? Agent provocateurs aren't new. Probably been around as long as there have been governments to protest. So, forever."

"Who else would be good to talk to about Shaitan and Bettencourt?"

"Adam Wolfe. This whole thing was his idea in the beginning. His tent is back toward the parking structure."

They stepped out of his tent. Siedel pointed. "Along the way, you might stop at that orange tent."

"Why's that?" Turner asked.

"It's the onsite police presence."

Turner said, "You'd think they'd be more circumspect."

Siedel shrugged. "Don't ask me to explain the police to you."

Turner and Fenwick strode back through the rising gale. The sky had darkened considerably. It was still over an hour to sunset. Turner checked his phone. The ragged line of storms continued to approach, at some points reaching the Tri-State Tollway. A few more drops plopped and thudded onto the ground around them. He looked up from his phone and said, "These people should start heading for shelter."

Fenwick nodded.

They stopped in front of the orange tent. Angry voices came

from inside. Fenwick knocked on the tent pole. The flap was thrust aside. The man who emerged snapped, "What the fuck are you doing here?"

They held out their IDs.

The guy snarled, "You want to blow our cover?"

"They all know who you are."

"No, they don't."

Fenwick laughed, "It's the only clean tent in the whole place. And it's new, and for some idiot reason, it's bright orange. Not only that, the first person we talked to pointed you out to us."

"Did not."

Fenwick let incredulity drip from his voice. "You do know you are conspicuous?"

"Are not."

Fenwick bellowed with laughter. A thin guy emerged and motioned them inside. He pointed to a bearded, even thinner guy with taut, wiry muscles sitting on a campstool in the back of the tent. With Turner and Fenwick it was crowded with nearly seven people in the tent. "He told us to keep it clean."

"You Peter Eisenberg?" Turner asked. The taut, wiry muscle guy nodded and said, "They call me Pete." He wore tight jeans that revealed an immense bulge at his crotch. He wore a T-shirt cut to reveal perfect six-pack abs.

Fenwick said, "And you look too good." He sniffed. "And you don't stink. All these people are scruffy, and except for a few of the hotter women, they haven't seen the inside of a gym since high school. You stick out."

"Sorry if I don't meet your stereotype." Pete's voice was basso-profundo.

A young guy stood up and swept a hand toward Turner and Fenwick. "These are the guys that turned on one of us."

Fenwick said, "I'm the one who got shot."

The guy pointed at Turner and said, "He Tased Carruthers."

Turner said, "He was shooting at us. You must know what a shit he was."

A portly man stood up and said, "These guys were just doing their job."

The youngest one stood up. He wagged a finger in the portly guys face. "You can't defend these guys."

The portly guy planted himself in front of the young guy. "You don't tell me what to do ever. You've been around a year, two, at most."

"I know what's right."

"You know shit."

"They roughed up Gary."

Fenwick spread his legs wide and went straight into high grumble. "You mean shit for brains from last night? The beat cop who gave us shit?" He pointed at them in turn then said, "You don't put up with anything from anybody. Why should we?"

All were silent. They listened to the wind. A few rain drops pelted the top and sides of the tent.

Turner switched topics. "Has any of the people you've run into here said anything that would help us in our investigation of Shaitan's and Bettencourt's murders?"

They all remained silent until Pete said, "On the surface, some of these people are trying to get along and sit in circles and sing songs and make nice. Others are trying to ravage the world with violence. They tend to be quiet about it, but frankly, I think they're all just an AK-47 short of an attack on each other or the rest of the world."

An older cop said, "And jealous. And mad at each other. And they never shut up."

Turner asked, "How did you find anything out? How did they trust you?"

Pete said, "They don't trust us, but like Al said, some of them just don't shut up. Not ever, I don't think. Some of them just keep talking to hear themselves. If we're lucky enough to get one of those, we listen." He sighed. "But specifically on your buddy Shaitan, people did hate him. I'm not sure any person said a nice thing about him. Ever. At all. Even after news spread that he was dead. At least I saw a few tears for Bettencourt."

They others nodded their heads.

"Lots of people liked him," Eisenberg said, "but lots of jealousy."

"Enough to kill him?"

"Who knows with these people? Some of them would be willing to take potshots at cops and have said so."

They knew nothing helpful. Turner thought their presence was an exercise in futility dreamed up by useless bureaucrats to try and control a situation.

As they walked away, Fenwick muttered, "That Pete guy must stuff his crotch."

"I watched him scratch. I think it may have been the real thing."

"You watched?"

"Genetic habit."

"Oh."

A man with a clerical collar ran up to them. "You have to talk to my people. I heard you were here. They may have information about your case, insights into your victims. I have a little tent chapel a few feet away over there." He pointed to their left. They began to walk toward it.

"Who are you?" Fenwick asked.

"Father Benedict. Yes, I know, like the Pope, but I came first."

They stopped and stood in the wind.

Turner asked, "What's your role here?"

"Mostly, I try to keep them from killing each other. I know you're the ones who saved DeShawn and arranged for better bathroom facilities. You're heroes."

Fenwick grumbled like distant thunder.

The priest wore vintage-style huarache sandals, a black shirt with a clerical collar, and black jeans cut off at the knees. Bits of cloth dangled from the shearing.

Father Benedict said, "I know you were the cops that exposed the church to that scandal a few weeks ago. Those people needed to be brought down, but you should talk to someone about that. You can't imagine the church would let go of that, not without exacting some kind of penance or even retribution?"

"From us?" Fenwick asked.

"You gave scandal to the faithful, as the right-wing Catholic cliché goes. That isn't easily forgiven."

They arrived at his tent. "It's a mixed group. Please be patient."

For ten minutes, they listened to a cacophony of complaints and pettiness, ranging from those who seemed genuinely aggrieved to the certifiably loony. They asked each person if they knew the victims or if they know who might want them dead.

Someone with a camera began taking pictures. Father Benedict ushered him away, and then took charge. He began bringing the inmates of the tent up to them one at time and introducing them.

Fenwick and Turner wrote down all their names and jotted down a few brief words, but none of them had anything useful to add about the murders.

One character accused them of hate speech and murder. He decreed, "You are responsible. You have preached hate and death. You are murderers. What do you have to say for yourselves?" A woman standing next to him tried to get him to shut up.

Another person said, "I'm against body cameras. Are you wearing body cameras?"

"Uh, no," Fenwick said.

"How do we know you're telling the truth?"

Fenwick asked, "Have I ever lied to you before?"

The guy said, "Huh?"

One protester said, "I know this guy Carruthers. He tried to frame me for a crime."

"When was this?" Fenwick asked.

"Many years ago. Carruthers had an informant, and the two of them wanted me off the streets. I was an honest drug dealer. They didn't like that. I tried to tell anybody and everybody it was a set-up. I went to a lawyer. Back then, it was even worse than now. I fled the city."

The detectives did not ask if he had current warrants out. If he committed crimes in Chicago, the statute of limitations was probably up long ago. Unless he committed murder.

Another man leaned close to both of them. Turner fought not to draw away from the smell of unwashed body. This one said, "I heard that Shaitan was gang raped by members of the Chicago police department. Maybe by some of those working here undercover."

But he had no names, specifics, or evidence.

The last one, a short stout man with gray whiskers and a bald head said, "We already talked to cops who said they were on the case."

"What were their names?"

"Same as yours."

"They showed you IDs?"

"Same as yours. Is this some kind of cop fuck up?"

Turner asked, "What did they look like?"

"Older than you guys. They wore fedoras. Maybe they were trying to hide their faces. The sat in our tent and stayed in the shadows."

"What did they ask about?"

"I guess the same as you."

When done, they thanked the priest and left.

Outside the tent, people scurried about. Some clutched heaps of belongings heading for better shelter than their sleeping bags. Others were pounding tent stakes farther into the ground attempting to secure these shelters against the rising wind. Some were running toward the not-too-distant campus buildings or back toward the parking structure.

Crackling thunder boomed. Lightning flashed.

They stopped at every tent they came to and asked for Alan Wolfe. At the sixth one, a man and woman huddled together with two small children. When they asked, the man pointed, "Try three tents over."

Turner said, "Maybe you should move to a more sheltered spot."

The woman said, "This tent is built to withstand an Arctic winter."

Gusts of wind tore at the tents. Lightning sparkled and flared. Thunder rumbled at a three count from the flashing. Turner knew the old tale, if you counted seconds between a flash and the thunder, that's how close the heart of the storm was.

Rain poured down.

Turner unzipped the third tent and looked inside. A gray-haired man sat on a camp stool with a lantern next to him on a table. He gripped a cane in one hand as if he would use it as a weapon.

"You Alan Wolfe?" Turner asked.

"Who the fuck are you?"

Emergency sirens began to wail.

Friday 6:52 P.M.

Turner pulled out his phone and punched the weather app from a local station. It showed a radar image of red bearing down on the city with cones of possible tornadic weather and severe storms. The nearest tornado sighting was at the southwest city limits about ten miles away. He shoved his phone in his pocket and said, "We should help these folks get to safety."

The man began to object. Then his tent and contents were taken by a gust of wind and blown three feet. Perhaps the only reason the tent didn't fly to the winds was that Fenwick had a foot inside. The detective began to trip, stumbled into Turner, whom he fell on top of. Fenwick's bulk and Turner's added weight anchored the tent for the moment as the gust passed. The man inside tried to scramble past them, but he was tangled in torn remnants of the side of his tent and by ropes tied to stakes now floating in the wind and rain.

Fenwick bellowed into the wind. He'd landed on his wounded shoulder. Turner scrambled out from under him then turned and yanked Fenwick up by his good arm. Turner wasn't about to wait for the next gust. He untangled the other man from the tent ropes and flaps.

They stood for a few seconds in the pouring maelstrom. Everyone was running for the nearest shelter, the parking structure still half a block away. The detectives joined the surging throng. Tents, camp stools, a grill; random bits of debris flying around were the biggest threat.

Fenwick moved as fast as his bulk would allow. The old man's cane was useless. He tried to totter on his own for several steps. A gust knocked him to his knees. He strained at his cane to no avail. Turner gave him a hand up. As soon as he let go, Wolfe began to tumble.

Wolfe whispered, "Help."

Turner picked him up and carried him. The three were among the last ones to safety.

In the parking garage, most people were crouched beneath any kind of wall or huddled around any kind of cement structure they could find. Turner made sure Fenwick and the old man were safe, then looked back over the wall.

The first thing he saw was the cops' huge orange tent flying off. He saw none of its denizens.

A few stragglers rushed in. Through the rain, now falling in sheets, he saw some kids huddling under a tree. He didn't stop to plan or decide, but found himself running toward them. Fenwick was at his side.

Through the rain, thunder, lightning, Turner heard Fenwick grumble, "Where are their goddamn parents?"

It was forty feet of a wild rush. Fenwick picked up the two smallest, maybe two years old. Turner picked up the third and last who looked about four.

They rushed back toward the parking garage. Two seconds after they dashed inside, lightning crashed down, split the tree the kids had been sheltering under. A flash of sparks followed, but were doused in seconds by the pouring rain. The kids would have been electrocuted or burnt to a crisp or both.

The detectives looked back and couldn't see if there was anyone else caught in the storm.

The wind howled.

Fenwick held the two whimpering kids. He looked up at Turner. "Anybody else out there?"

"Can't see anyone."

They were out of the worst of the wind and rain.

Turner patted the four-year-old who said, "I was supposed to watch them."

Turner said, "You got them to as much safety as you could. You're okay now."

Turner saw the old man shivering.

Turner realized he and Fenwick were soaking wet.

He lifted his head a few inches. To his left a few feet away, he saw a skinny man, his jeans and T-shirt soaked, who had a boy and a girl, both about four years old, huddled underneath him. The man patted both their backs. The kids whimpered.

To his right about seven feet away, a woman in a granny dress wailed over and over, "We're all going to die."

Fenwick caught his eye. "If the storm doesn't get her, I will."

Turner hunched down with the others and waited for the maelstrom to pass.

The worst of it lasted maybe three minutes. In ten minutes, the wind had eased. Although it was still raining, the sky lightened, and Turner realized the sun had not yet set on this long June day. He glanced at his phone. One radar loop showed the actual worst of the storm had passed two miles south of them. The line of the most severe storms had passed their area but was intensifying over northwest Indiana.

He and Fenwick began checking on the people nearest. Others were gathering themselves, checking on friends, punching at cell phones.

Beyond their shelter, the intensity of the rain continued to slacken. They saw shambles of strewn everything.

In a few more minutes, the rain let up, as often happened after the worst had happened, with surprising quickness.

Other than minor cuts and scratches, these people had survived. In the last light of the day, people began to straggle out to their nearly gone encampment. A girl about twelve ran up to the little kids

Turner and Fenwick had saved and gave them towels. She led them away.

Alan Wolfe gazed at them. Using his cane, he swayed, and shook his head. "You saved those children." He paused a moment. "And me." His eyes were moist and not from the rain. Someone gave him a blanket. He pulled it close around him.

Turner asked, "You want to go back to your tent and check your stuff?"

Wolfe shook his head. "This isn't my first camp-out. Anybody stupid enough to bring valuables to a protest is too stupid to care about. They might as well be Republicans."

Turner heard the sound of an emergency vehicle rise and fall. He and Fenwick called home. Their families were fine. Ben said, "We watched the radar on the television down in the basement. There was an actual brief tornado touchdown in Morgan Park. By the time the line of storms got to us, it was dissipating."

Jeff and Brian were outside helping Mrs. Talucci with branches that were strewn on her lawn from the aged oak tree in the front yard.

Turner's soaked clothes clung to his skin. Fenwick looked like a beached whale that had somehow gotten tangled in someone's side-yard laundry line.

Turner called the station. After ascertaining all was okay at both ends of the phone, Barb Dams told them Molton's orders were for them to stick to their case.

Friday 7:31 P.M.

They turned to Wolfe. The two detectives tottered with him to a bar on a nearby corner. The electricity was still on in this part of the city. They found a booth in the back. They ordered sandwiches and sodas. They sat in their squishy, wet clothes. Fenwick showed his cop ID and managed to get a couple of clean towels from the bartender. The three of them used the towels to remove the worst of the wet. Turner couldn't wait to change, but he wanted to get this interview in as quickly as he could.

Turner said, "We wanted to get some background on Preston Shaitan and Henry Bettencourt."

"They hated each other. They were traitors in league with each other. The more extreme Shaitan sounded, the more reasonable Bettencourt sounded. They raised money off of each other. Sometimes, I wonder why we even bother to protest. It's not like we're going to do much good."

Fenwick shook his head. "Some protests do make a difference. And why am I arguing their efficacy with you? You're the protester."

Turner returned them to questioning for the case. "How'd you get along with Shaitan?"

"Biggest asshole in the universe, but I never actually met him."

"Bettencourt?" Turner asked.

"He was an egomaniacal moron who didn't know how to organize his way out of a paper bag."

Turner knew Fenwick loved people they questioned who had nasty things to say about the victims. You rarely got good or useful information from those who loved the dead.

"We've been told by a number of people that he was a great guy, and that everybody loved him."

"Everybody but one, and anyone with sense."

"Why didn't you get along?"

"I was an idea guy. Bettencourt was practical, willing to sacrifice ideology to practicality."

Fenwick said, "We thought this whole protest was your idea."

"It was."

"But he got involved."

"I'm an idea man. I'm the starter."

"Ah," Fenwick said, "The guy in the background who urges others to go risk themselves."

Instead of the sharp rejoinder Turner expected, Wolfe smiled and said, "Safer that way."

"So who got invited, and how did they get invited?"

"My idea was to invite everyone, left, center, right. What's most surprising is the right wing showed up. The real enemy of all of us is the 1%. They're the ones who killed Bettencourt and Shaitan."

"Anyone specific on that?" Fenwick asked.

"No. And you'll never find anyone specific from the 1% to arrest and prosecute. You're not that naïve. I hope."

"Why kill them?"

"They're as semi-famous as anyone. Although Bettencourt would have been a specific kind of danger. He may actually have been able to get the groups to work together. The 1% doesn't like that." He took a sip of coffee. "See, they'd prefer us all to be working drones and slaves who the police can kill with impunity if they are inconvenienced."

For one of the rare moments Turner was aware of, Fenwick

didn't interrupt to debate.

The older man continued, "The 1% don't mind ravers and screamers. In the long run, they're ineffective and can be safely ignored. It's the hard workers and the organizers who are the danger."

"Danger to what or to whom?" Fenwick asked.

Turner wanted to nudge his partner's wounded arm to maybe shut him up.

"Danger to them. They really have nothing to fear, but keeping others afraid keeps them in business. Keeps me in business too, for that matter. It can be pretty symbiotic and incestuous."

Fenwick asked, "You meet with the 1% to plan all this?"

"Well, no, but it's kind of obvious what's going on to anyone who is paying attention."

"Did Bettencourt meet with them?"

Wolfe leaned over the table toward them. "The fixer for the 1% is in town. He's Danny Currington."

Turner noted down the name. "You know where he's staying?"

"With the 1%."

"How does anyone get in touch with him?"

"Find a mover and shaker in town. They'll know."

"You've never met with him?"

"Once in Key West when I was on vacation. Purely an accident."

"Who else?"

"It would be hard to pick specific leaders. Starts out as mostly disorganized, angry anarchists. Young protesters are mad at older protesters. They accuse them of being out of touch. Many of these groups were one or two people and even then they didn't last. Bored nut cases. They had fights over who was to be the designated speaker to the media."

Turner tried again, "How about a few names? Maybe a few of the angriest, or most out of touch, or most anarchistic?" He mentioned a couple who were the ones Father Benedict had brought to them.

Useless.

Fenwick asked, "How about this Guns for Gangs group?"

"Westerton's crowd? That started out as a joke."

Fenwick said, "I don't hear anyone laughing."

"Not now. But we were then."

They gave up on him. They helped him back to his tent. He picked out a few soaked belongings.

"Where will you go?" Turner asked.

"I have a suite in a quiet hotel just off Michigan Avenue. Nobody here knows about it. No way am I really going to sleep on the ground. I'm too old for that shit."

"You're all charlatans?" Fenwick asked.

"No more than the 1% who convince all those sheep to vote against their own interests. They get theirs. Why shouldn't I get mine."

"Did you kill them?"

"Why bother? We're all charlatans in some way."

Fenwick gaped at him and said, "You've swallowed your own Kool-Aid."

"Some of us have turned it into a lifestyle."

"Then why bother with any of this?" Fenwick asked.

"People want to. They're comfortable with this. It's fun to walk down the canyons of a big city and listen to your chants echo off the buildings."

Fenwick said, "Not everyone is that cynical."

Turner tried one last time. "Anyone specific either of these guys had fights with?"

Wolfe had no names.

They left. As they walked away in the still close air, Turner said, "I think the oddest thing we've got is someone else claiming to be us walking around asking questions."

"Who the hell thought that up?" Fenwick asked.

"More to find out," Turner said.

Sanchez and Deveneux came hustling up to them. Sanchez said, "We've been looking for you. The Commander wants to see you."

"Why didn't he just call us?"

"It's some secret thing. I don't know what. He trusted us not to blab."

A small child began trotting toward them as fast as its tiny legs would carry him. His mother chased after. The little kid kept looking at the ground near them and shouting, "Bear, bear."

Sanchez leaned down and picked up a child's teddy bear. He stood back up and then lurched forward.

Friday 8:27 P.M.

Then they heard the gunshot. They all saw Sanchez fall and start to bleed. He moaned. The woman picked up the kid and ran.

They all ducked down. They got themselves and Sanchez behind the nearest tree. He was hit just below his vest on his torso.

With one hand, Turner kept pressure on the wound. He said, "We're not going to get an ambulance with all this chaos. We'll take him ourselves. I'll keep pressure on the wound."

Fenwick agreed. Deveneaux rushed for the squad car, drove it over the grass to them.

While they waited, Turner noted that about a foot above the wound he was staunching, part of Sanchez's protective vest had been ripped and torn. So there had been at least two shots. Sanchez moaned. Turner kept repeating, "You're okay. We're getting you to a hospital. You're okay."

When they got Sanchez stretched out onto the back seat, he was unconscious but breathing. His blood only oozed slightly from the wound.

Deveneaux flipped on the siren and drove like mad to the hospital. Turner stayed in the backseat. Fenwick hustled for their car and drove over. They got Sanchez onto a gurney, into the hospital, and into an emergency bay with medical people in attendance.

Storm victims added to the wild crush at the hospital. In the chaotic waiting room all the seats were taken. People lined the corridors and clumped in the halls. Turner and Fenwick found a spot in an obscure corner and leaned against a wall.

Turner stared at the second hand of a clock high up on the wall. His clothes were wet. His hands covered in Sanchez's blood. He shut his eyes a moment, opened them, and said, "I can't wrap my head around it. We've had a number of deliberate attacks on us, or deliberate attempts to fuck up our case. Who the fuck benefits from doing both?"

Fenwick heaved his bulk away from the wall and paced twice up and down the hall. He stopped then said, "My clothes are too wet for me to pace in them. I think my underwear is permanently stuck in my crack."

"More information than I'd care to have at this moment or any moment."

Fenwick asked, "Why shoot at Sanchez?"

"Or were they shooting at us?"

"They're trying to kill us?"

"I'm trying to keep an open mind, but 'yes' strikes me as a logical answer to that."

"Who?" Fenwick asked.

"One of your better rhetorical questions."

Fenwick said, "I want to hurt someone or something."

"Not yet. First, we figure out what the fuck is going on and then we act."

"You're that calm?"

"I don't have someone to direct my anger against. If I direct it randomly outward, innocent people could be hurt."

Fenwick looked at his friend. He said, "I'm glad you're my partner."

"Mutual."

They stood in silence until some minutes later, Fenwick said, "They're all old."

"Huh?" Turner was semi-used to his partner's comments out of mid-air apropos of nothing.

"I expected young people. Isn't it the young who protest angrily?"

Turner asked, "How does that relate to murder and this case?"

"Motive. People get pissed."

Turner said, "I'd rather have forensic evidence."

"That is so like you. Proof. Tangible, something you can present in court. Sigh. You never change."

"It's a curse."

Friday 10:29 P.M.

Beat cops and detectives clustered around the emergency room doors. Turner and Fenwick joined them.

One guy asked, "Were they shooting at you guys or Sanchez or both?"

Turner said, "No one knows." He wasn't going to discuss any aspect of what was happening to a bunch of cops some of whom he did not know. He asked, "How is he?"

Deveneux said, "They're working on him."

A very skinny, heavily-bearded man rushed up to the desk. He wore tight cut-off jeans that clung to his butt and upper thighs. His T-shirt was paint splattered. He wore black socks and running shoes at the end of very hairy legs.

He announced, "I'm Dave Sanchez's husband, Alvi Baqri."

The nurse said, "One moment, sir."

Turner and Fenwick knew him. They hurried over.

Baqri asked, "What happened?"

Turner said, "We were there. We saw it happen. His vest saved him. He took two shots, direct hits. The vest got tore up but saved him from a torso shot. But one got him just below the vest, on the top of his butt."

It wasn't a secret where Sanchez was. A cordon of cops surrounded the bay where he was being tended to. Fenwick led the way. The group parted. Deveneux was just coming out of the room. He hugged Alvi. Deveneux led him into the room and then reemerged himself. He strode over to Turner and Fenwick. He said, "I wanted to give them some privacy."

"How is he?"

"Drugged up, but alert. Waiting for test results. He thinks the shots were meant for you guys and that his movement at the last second got in the killer's way."

"Possible," Fenwick said.

Turner thought this was likely, and that they were lucky.

Commander Molton rushed up to them. "How's Sanchez?"

"He should be done with the doctor soon. Nothing life threatening. He's being prepped to have surgery to take the bullet out. His husband is in there with him."

A beat cop stood guard.

Molton said, "I wanted to talk to you guys." He'd been carrying a bundle of clothes. "We got these from your lockers at the station. We used the master key to get in. I figured you'd want dry clothes."

They thanked him, changed in the washroom. Turner scrubbed at his hands, wrists, and arms. He tried running cold water on the spots of blood on the shirt he'd been wearing. Much of the blood sluiced away. They came back, and sat down next to Molton who had also brought sandwiches and soft drinks.

Molton turned to a passing hospital person and asked if there was a private room. They were led to one with no windows, blond furniture, and pale gray walls. The chairs had strips of leather on them. Not as uncomfortable as some hospital chairs.

"First, are you guys okay?"

Turner said, "I'm not sure."

Fenwick said, "Something is fucked up."

Turner said, "I agree."

Molton said, "We've got to figure out for sure if someone is trying to kill you two, and if so who. I know, none of us believes in random coincidence, but we can't absolutely rule it out. And then there's the goddamn murder case. And the tenuous, but I don't think we can ignore, too-much-of-a-coincidence, Carruthers incident. Either of you think the shot that hit Sanchez was meant for him, not you?"

They shook their heads.

Molton drummed his fingers on the table top, moved his chair back and forth.

Fenwick gobbled his sandwich. Turner nibbled his.

Turner asked Molton, "What's wrong?"

"I've been in meetings all day. About you guys, process, procedures, investigations, publicity. Meetings with just about everybody from the superintendent on down."

Fenwick said, "What the fuck?"

Molton said, "Precisely."

Turner put a restraining hand on Fenwick's arm. Turner asked, "What's going on?"

"What isn't? An example, you know how you guys did that huge computer monitor spread sheet for the case about the cardinal and his crew?"

Nods.

"You've heard of the Lavery incident, the cop back in 1982 who testified for the defense, and it all came out about Chicago cop secret files, and how we weren't supposed to do that anymore."

More nods.

"Well, your cardinal case is being used against you for keeping secrets."

Turner said, "We sent copies of all of that to everybody except the press. From the superintendent on down. We got commendations."

"It's being investigated."

Fenwick gaped. Not a curse escaped his lips. Turner guessed he was more flummoxed than he'd ever seen his partner.

"You know that rape case you guys solved a few years back?"

"Which one?"

"Where you found the DNA evidence to exonerate the guy. Supposedly there's a tape of a Cook County prosecutor feeding false information allegedly from you guys to the prosecutor to convict the guy instead of finding him innocent."

Fenwick banged his fist on the table. "Bullshit. We found the DNA to exonerate him."

"You've seen the tape?" Turner asked.

Molton nodded. "Mostly it shows a blur, but they want to use it against you."

"Who is against us?"

"It starts with Clayton Griffin, the assistant Chief of Detectives."

"We talked to him this morning," Fenwick said. "He warned us to be careful, but not specifically about himself."

Molton said, "The whole Carruthers case is being built up as one where you guys, his colleagues, are blowing the whistle on police corruption, so it's all your fault."

Fenwick said, "Carruthers is a colossal asshole who almost killed who knows how many people, and it's our fault?"

"You Tased him and saved a victim. It's being twisted against you."

Turner said, "It's a set-up. What has Carruthers got?"

"It's bigger than Carruthers," Molton said. "It's all those who've covered up for him over the years. All those he's been involved with. They're saying you've had complaints against you, both of you."

Fenwick said, "Complaints are part of the job."

Turner said, "I've had three, and Fenwick's had one. Those are incredibly low numbers for as long as we've been on the job."

"I know that. You know that. And Fenwick's is from one incident the first day he was a beat cop. His bulk bashed into a poor guy's street cart. The guy complained. A lot."

Fenwick scratched his head. "I apologized. The guy gives me free food to this day."

Molton said, "Makes no difference."

Fenwick asked, "How many complaints does Carruthers have?"

"I would never talk about other personnel. The disappeared ones or the real ones?" He didn't wait for them to answer but said, "According to Barb Dams's count, ninety-six."

Fenwick whistled.

Molton continued, "And Rodriguez has none. She said she gave you those records."

Turner said, "But they're after us."

"Yup."

"Is Rodriguez in trouble?" Fenwick asked.

"Not with me. And neither are you with me. But the three of you are on the hot-shit list, but not in a good way, but they have to be real careful about going after you two. You guys are heroes to the community."

"It'll be a slow death," Turner guessed. "A leak to the press here. Fake news there. You know how fake news is the rage these days."

"There are some on our side," Molton said, "but this is bigger than sides."

"They want us gone?" Turner asked.

"They want us dead," Fenwick said.

Molton didn't contradict him.

A nurse poked her head into the room and pointed at Turner and Fenwick. She said, "You guys are on the news."

They all stepped into the hallway to look at the nearest monitor. It was a local TV station with continuous coverage of the storm. They saw pictures of Turner and Fenwick carrying the kids to safety. There was a separate clip of Turner carrying Wolfe. The reporter giving a voice over said, "We've discovered these are the same two police detectives who saved DeShawn Jackson."

Fenwick said, "Fuck."

The nurse said to Fenwick, "You know you're bleeding."

Fenwick looked at his arm. "Double fuck."

The nurse took him into an emergency room bay where she removed his previous arm bandage, examined him for a few moments, and said, "A few of your stitches came loose. I can fix that right up." She even examined the wound on his head and said it was scabbing over nicely, and he didn't even need to wear a bandage on it if he didn't want to. Fenwick chose not to.

As she fussed, she said, "You guys are such heroes."

Fenwick had the sense to keep his mouth shut.

She gave him more pain pills.

After she left, Turner said, "They can tell it's us on the video. You've got all that bulk and that white bandage shows up clearly. I guess I'm playing Robin to your hefty Batman."

Fenwick said, "This heroic bullshit is driving me nuts."

Turner nodded.

Fenwick said, "We need to stop doing it."

"You know you grouse, but if it happened again you'd do the exact same things."

"Fine. I just don't want to hear about it, or be on someone's goddamn television."

"Even if you weren't a cop, and you were presented with an emergency, you'd still act."

"It's not my fault. I was born that way."

Molton said, "That's what they all say."

Turner tuned out the next five minutes of Fenwick complaining then returned to the information on Shaitan and Bettencourt's murders. They told Molton what they'd found at the encampment.

Molton shook his head about the duplicate cops. "That's nutty and dangerous."

"How so?" Fenwick asked.

"Sending someone to impersonate you? A decision to do that has to come from high up. That's even clearer evidence to me that the murder and the Carruthers incident are connected."

Turner and Fenwick nodded.

Molton continued. "What's worse for them, is the more people they get involved in whatever conspiracy is going on, the more likely it is to break against them. A conspiracy becomes unwieldy. Too many people know what's going on. Somebody blabs or breaks."

Fenwick said, "Soon, I hope."

Turner asked, "We're working both cases, aren't we? The Carruthers fiasco on the street and the killing of the protestors on the roof."

Molton said, "Yes. I can't believe they aren't connected. There's some shit going on and the three of us know it. We've all said a million times we don't believe in coincidences. We have no choice but to come down on the side that they're connected. Safer for us all around if we think of it that way. And if it turns out they aren't connected, it won't be the first time we chased our tails getting a case solved."

They emerged from the bay Fenwick had been treated in. Molton said, "If you want off the case at any point, please let me know. Otherwise, you are my guys and this is your case. Period." He promised to work on the duplicate cops issue from his end. He left.

Friday 11:28 P.M.

Turner and Fenwick stood in the hall. Judy Wilson stormed off the elevator, spotted them, and rushed forward. She barged through the knots of cops. Barb Dams emerged from the elevator a few seconds later. She stood there as if on guard.

Wilson got to them, looked around, and pulled them into the original room where they'd begun talking to Molton. She asked, "How's Sanchez?"

"Doctor said he's going to be okay," Turner said. "What's wrong?"

"Joe and I got a visit from Lyal DeGroot, the head of the Internal Review investigation. It was about an hour ago. He was working oddly late, I thought."

Fenwick said, "I thought we weren't supposed to talk to each other about contacts with them."

Wilson leaned close, Her voice was low and fierce. "Bullshit. It's all bullshit. They or he, only care about getting both of you. That even seems secondary to getting Carruthers off the hook."

"What did he say?" Turner asked.

"He asked questions about you guys. About how often you lied. If you guys covered for each other. He wanted to know if you'd used Tasers on children."

"We haven't," Fenwick began.

"Listen to me! They wanted to know if you'd ever fired your weapons."

"But that would be in reports," Fenwick said.

Wilson said, "I'm as exasperated as you. You've got to know this shit. It's like they're taking every complaint against Carruthers and trying to claim you were part of it or you did it."

Fenwick was not to be denied. "Bullshit! Bullshit! Bullshit!"

"Keep your voice down," Wilson said. "DeGroot claimed he came to question us about the Carruthers incident. He challenged every statement you gave us. He almost accused us of lying. You think I'm pissed. You should see Roosevelt." She shook her head. "It's all about you guys and anything you've done while you've been on the force. Frankly, I think if you took time on the job to breathe, they're going to try to get you for that."

Fenwick said, "I knew that breathing shit was overrated."

Barb Dams entered the room with a beat cop straggling behind her. She tapped him on the arm, "Officer Arnold was out here. He claims he was posted to this duty."

"What duty is that?" Fenwick demanded.

"I don't answer to you," Arnold said.

Commander Palakowski of the local district stuck his head in. "I need Officer Arnold out here now."

Palakowski and the beat cop left.

Dams said, "He was eavesdropping." She pointed at Wilson. "I noticed him follow you when you walked down the hall."

They reported Wilson's news to her.

Dams said, "We better read Molton into this." She and Wilson left. Dams was already on her phone as they waited for the elevator.

In the hall, Fenwick and Turner's union rep, Yutka, hurried up to them.

"What the hell is going on?" Fenwick asked.

Yutka said, "Everybody knows about the shooting. Everybody knows you're here. I have news that you need to hear."

They hustled back into the empty room.

"First of all, the investigation of the incident itself. I think that's the key or one of the main keys to why Carruthers has gotten away with so much for so long."

"How's that?"

"DeGroot has led the Carruthers investigations, if not all of them, close to all of them. Mostly what he does is nothing. He doesn't interview officers or witnesses. Or if he does, it's years later, or incompletely and in a slapdash way."

"But why?" Fenwick asked. "Who told him to do this?"

"I was not able to find that out. As far as I can tell, the word on what to do about Carruthers goes up the chain of command within the department itself." Yutka shook his head. "I have to admit, from the investigation reports I've seen, Carruthers has never said anything stupid."

Fenwick demanded, "How is that possible? He leads the world in stupidity."

"Before he answers, he always turns to his lawyer."

"Just smart enough," Turner said.

Fenwick said, "Wait a second. We showed up at the scene. Carruthers was bellowing. Are they going to what? Arrest us for failure to obey a police officer? Resisting arrest?"

"If they could, they would have already. I don't know what they're crazy enough to try. Your Commander is fighting madly for you in every forum. You're lucky."

"If he wasn't behind us?"

"You'd be toast."

Both detectives raised their eyebrows.

Turner said, "We're only being saved because we have a boss who is on our side?"

"There's your reputations, which they will do their best to destroy. There's your records, which they will lie about. There's who and what you are, as regular guys doing their jobs who stumbled into heroism, twice now in two days, all of which they will try to sully. But you knew that, right?"

Turner asked, "How do you sully saving kids from a lightning storm?"

"Give them a chance."

Turner was exasperated. "There's video."

"I'm giving you the worst case scenarios."

Fenwick said, "I'm not sure who to be angriest at."

Yutka asked, "Did you really arrange for the protesters to be able to use the washroom in the parking garage?"

"Yeah."

Yutka pointed at Fenwick. "Some guy in bib overalls tried to say you threatened him, but he had no witnesses, plus it seems there was a crowd of protesters around when he was complaining. The crowd was on your side claiming you were saints."

"Saint Fenwick. I like the sound of that."

Turner said, "Spare me."

"What do you suggest we do?" Fenwick asked.

"Nothing."

"All of that?" Fenwick asked.

"It's got to come crashing down on them."

"It hasn't so far," Turner said.

"There's more. There's talk of destroying the tent city. That the protesters are taking pot shots at Chicago cops."

"Somebody took pot shots at two of the protesters. They're dead. Sanchez will recover."

"They don't care. They want to respond to violence with violence. So far the mayor's office has kept a lid on it."

Turner said, "Just more violence."

Fenwick said, "And we've got a place in this? Sanchez made a sudden move. Not that he heard a shot and moved, but he was leaning over to pick up the teddy bear for that kid. The movement probably saved himself as well as Paul."

Turner nodded. "Sure feels like that to me."

Yutka said, "If they don't clear out the tent city, that will tell you something as well."

"What?"

Yutka said, "That someone high up in the CPD wants that group there, or hell, even wanted the protesters here. People are still furious over that Department of Justice report. There are all kinds of ways to fight back on that. You guys have a couple of the cleanest records on the force, that itself is easily a threat to some people."

"We're no threat," Fenwick said.

"It's the perception of your persona."

Fenwick said, "Huh?"

Yutka said, "You look like good guys."

Fenwick asked, "Who are we making look bad?"

"All the assholes who've been lying all these years. Someone or maybe lots of someones want to drag you down with them."

They agreed to keep in touch. Yutka left.

They checked on Sanchez. He was on his way to surgery to remove the bullet.

Fenwick and Turner leaned against the wall in the corridor. Fenwick said, "I'm bushed."

"Me too."

Friday 11:59 P.M.

Turner and Fenwick returned to the station. They sat with Molton in his office staring at the streetlights over the parking lot.

They drank hot coffee and gazed.

Finally, Fenwick asked, "So what are we investigating?"

Molton said, "Some members of the department are using these protesters as scapegoats, to expand the pool of suspects, to send you in wildly different directions. Maybe, somehow, getting you by killing them."

Turner asked, "How could it be protesters?"

Fenwick asked, "Do they have the wherewithal to move evidence from crime scene to crime scene?"

Turner said, "It would require near perfect placement or a lot of luck."

Molton added, "Or expertise which cops would have."

Fenwick said, "If I was a smart protester killer, I'd do it the opposite way. Use the chaos in the police department to get away with murder."

"But the planting of so much evidence?" Molton asked.

Turner said, "There's skill involved. Protesters, some of them, know how to shoot high-powered rifles. So would, or could, a member of the CPD."

Fenwick asked, "We've got infiltrators in the protesters. Are they acting as agent provocateurs?"

Molton said, "No evidence of that, yet."

Turner asked, "What about the rumor we got that Chicago police gang-raped Shaitan?"

Molton said, "He didn't report anything. Maybe he happened to be at a consensual orgy where absolutely no one knew who he was. Or it's fake news."

Fenwick said, "Or they all knew and wanted to fuck him until it hurt."

Turner asked, "What's going to happen to the protester's tent city?"

Molton shrugged. "I have no idea."

At their desks, exhausted as they were, they did an hour of paperwork. There was an odd comfort in the relentlessness of bureaucracy. They worked mostly in silence. The day had them both down. The humidity seemed to increase with each second they spent at their desks. Turner thought that the amount of relief the fans provided felt as useless as all the work they had done so far on the case.

Saturday 1:05 A.M.

Paul sat with his butt on his front porch, his feet reached to the second step down. He reflected, listened to his house, his neighborhood, his life. He saw no extraneous patrol cars or police officers. He didn't see much debris. In the far distance, he saw periodic lightning flashes from storms that were now far out over the Lake. He heard no thunder. He saw lights in houses the way they'd always been since he could remember as a child. A few lights dim behind curtains, wind in the trees, the distant sounds of the city, an occasional emergency vehicle, a truck rumbling by on Taylor Street. He leaned forward, put his chin in his hand. It had been a hell of a day, and tomorrow didn't look much brighter.

Ben came out and sat next to Paul and put his arm around him. Ben wore baggy basketball shorts, a crisp, clean T-shirt, and his favorite running shoes.

Ben caressed his husband's arm for a moment, rubbed his back for a few seconds, then said, "Are you okay?"

"I don't know."

"You just missed being shot."

Paul shut his eyes and leaned back into his husband's arm. "Yeah." He was silent for a moment. "I want to hit out. Worse than Jeff in one of his fits of temper." They'd been working on the boy's display of bits of violence since they began to appear about a year ago, perhaps coinciding with the onset of puberty, or simply his way of testing his parents. Paul said, "I don't believe in violence. I don't.

I'm just so angry. If I could figure out something to go after, I could apply logic to solving the case."

Ben sat close.

"You okay?" Paul asked.

"Just worried about you." That sat in silence for a few moments. Ben cleared his throat, "Mrs. Talucci asked if you would stop by as soon as you got home."

As tired as Paul was, he recognized a low key request from Mrs. Talucci as if it were news of a five alarm fire. She made few requests.

"She tell you what it is?" Paul asked.

Ben shook his head. "She suggested I come with."

They walked over to Mrs. Talucci's. The front door was open behind a latched screen door. Graciola, one of the grand-nieces let them in.

Mrs. Talucci was in her kitchen. The ceiling fan was on low. She sat with a woman Paul didn't know. A silver tea service was spread between them.

Mrs. Talucci stood and took Paul's hand. "Are you okay? I heard they just missed you."

"They missed Fenwick and me. A friend of ours, a beat cop we know, Mike Sanchez, was hit. He's going to be okay."

The woman who was a stranger said, "I believe I know his family. Good people."

Mrs. Talucci said, "This is Florence Wolchevitz. She was involved in the Beat Representative program with the CPD back in the day, and the CAPS program. She's been a neighborhood activist on the far southeast side for years, still is. We've known each other since before she began working with the police. We take some of the over-90 travel trips together. I talked to her. She's willing to help you. I trust her implicitly."

Paul said, "Thank you."

Mrs. Wolchevitz had a bouffant of white hair. Both she and Mrs. Talucci wore white summer shawls over faded flower print dresses.

While Mrs. Talucci served tea, Paul asked, "You all came through the storm okay?"

Mrs. Talucci nodded. Mrs. Wolchevitz said, "Everything seemed remarkably clean after the rain, but the worst hasn't passed according to the weather forecasts. At least another day of this."

When everyone had a cup of tea, and they all had access to scones, Mrs. Talucci began, "Why don't you give us a summary of what happened today? We saw you on the local news saving some kids. You and Fenwick deserve medals."

Paul summarized for them. He finished, "The questions are two-fold, one about activists in the city, and the other about the police department itself."

Wolchevitz put her teacup down, pulled her shawl a bit closer around her, and said, "Now, as for the activists. Andy Siedel, I've worked with a few times. He seemed reasonable. Adam Wolfe is an old charlatan. He'd be in the middle, or he always was back in the day, of every conspiracy, plot or plan."

"Motivated enough for murder?" Paul asked.

"He's a complicated man. I could never figure him out. I don't really know most of the new crowd, and I know nothing about Shaitan and Bettencourt."

Mrs. Talucci said, "I think she can help most with connections within the department."

Paul nodded.

Mrs. Wolchevitz began, "First of all, you have to understand that power structures within the upper echelons of the department are fighting all the time."

"About what?"

"Power. Influence. Jobs. Prestige. Reputation. Jobs they'd like after their own retirement. Or moving up in other cities if the way is blocked here. You probably already have some sense that this occurs."

Turner nodded and said, "But I'm nothing to that."

"Ah, my dear, I wish that were so. My guess from decades of observation, is that they are angry to the point of irrationality. You're seen as thwarting them. And they don't like to be thwarted by anyone, any time." She broke a corner off of a scone and nibbled at it. "What you've got to realize is that anyone whom you have seen, you must presume is part of a conspiracy to get you."

Turner nodded.

Ben asked, "But what is this about?"

Mrs. Wolchevitz sighed, sipped tea, and resumed. "What you and your partner have done is violate some of the most inviolate rules of the hierarchy. The most basic is, 'I can make you.' This is not new. The spirit of the Chicago police department, 'do as you're told,' doesn't happen by accident. From the silly orders to protesters, to ordinary encounters with civilians, too often too many of them have been irrationally harsh. This started long before the '68 convention. The police in Chicago have treated the public as those who must shut up and obey."

Ben said, "You worked with them all these years."

"And some are good men and women, and sometimes I made things a little better for both sides. As you know, it's not just this city. It's all over. And the convention in '68 just revealed for the world a real attitude of society, not just police."

Ben said, "But there seems to be so much anger and rage these days."

Mrs. Wolchevitz said, "I'd hate to make comparisons through the history of the city or down through the ages for that matter. If you were in the Park in 1968, you hated the police and Mayor Daley in equal measure."

"You were there?" Ben asked.

She nodded. "Very much in the background. I didn't get arrested or beaten." She sighed. "Nowadays, with fake news fighting with real news, it's hard to tell who is really more or less angry. And does it make a lot of difference? So the crazies don't just march around some forest in the Rocky Mountains, now they're at our doorstep.

The attitude that created them has been with us for a very long time." She shrugged. "Those whom you've met or know high up in the department, so many are among the newly aggrieved, hiding their need to cling to privilege and power behind a racist buffoon."

Ben asked, "Can we do anything?"

Mrs. Talucci said, "We do what we always have. Whatever we must. Whatever we can."

Paul said, "Anything specific about who we've met." He gave her a list of names.

Mrs. Wolchevitz said, "DeGroot is not head of the investigation by accident. He's been the head of the Carruthers investigations for years."

"Our lawyer said that as well."

Mrs. Wolchevitz said, "And the State's Attorney who just happens to wind up with so many of his cases, gentleman named Brandon Smeek. That's another name to check into."

Ben asked, "Who the hell is Carruthers and why do so many people risk so much for him?"

Mrs. Wolchevitz said, "I can help you with that. The Carruthers family goes back a long, long time in this department. They first came to major notice at the time of the 1968 Convention. The grandfather and great uncle of your current asshole, both got reputations for beating up protesters but not being caught doing so. The mayor heard of it. They got rewarded. They continued to be loyal through the years. They got more rewards. Since then, it's intertwined. Lucrative contracts for concessions at the airports to close relatives of theirs. For example, DeGroot's father, who is a distant cousin of the current Carruthers iteration, got some of the biggest concessions at both airports for incredible bargains." She sipped some tea. "I do believe the connections go deep into several Cook County departments as well. Those connections, I've heard, are on his wife's side."

Paul said, "Supremely connected. I got that impression about Carruthers and his wife, separate and together."

"Yes." She thought a moment. "You could follow the command structure above DeGroot, but my guess is, the higher up you go, the more danger you'll be in."

"Do we trust Commander Molton?"

"A good man and an honest cop. I would think so." Mrs. Wolchevitz picked up her coffee cup, took a sip, put it down. "There is a rumor that things at home for Carruthers are deteriorating rapidly. His protectors may be abandoning him. He may be suicidal."

"His wife mentioned that."

"It could be true." Mrs. Wolchevitz sighed. "Double and triple your vigilance. There is that much real danger. As for your basic questions. Remember it took a year and a new superintendent for a recommendation to fire seven officers for lying about the LaQuan McDonald case. They will play with time." She smiled at them. "I know you know all of this."

Paul said, "Everything you've said has been a help."

Mrs. Wolchevitz said, "Your more important problem isn't those who might or might not have lied for Carruthers about what happened at that scene. They've got to find a gun with the kid's fingerprints on it."

"They won't," Paul said. "There wasn't one."

"They can manufacture a great deal," Mrs. Wolchevitz said. "I hope you're right. No, I think what you've now run up against, or will be running up against are who in the brass has been covering up for this Carruthers all these years. People have heard rumors about him probably in the whole department. You also might check into the influence of the church in this. I think at least a few higher-ups are smarting from your last case, and remember Carruthers was their spy in your camp. There is likely to be some loyalty there. I might be able to help you a tiny bit there."

Mrs. Talucci said, "I'm not sure I can get you much information about that anymore. I spent a lot of years of built up good will on your last case." She smiled. "My power is not infinite."

Mrs. Wolchevitz smiled as well. She knew no more. Ben and

Paul thanked them both. As they walked out of the kitchen, Paul turned at the door and asked Mrs. Wolchevitz, "Why do you still go to meetings?"

"Because in spite of it all, I still believe people are good at heart."

Ben said, "Anne Frank in her diary."

Mrs. Wolchevitz smiled. "Yes."

Saturday 1:00 A.M.

When he got into his own house, Paul thanked the blessed air-conditioning. He and Ben checked Jeff's room. Brian was asleep on his brother's bed. His tall, athletic body sprawled wide, a copy of the third Harry Potter book open on the sheet next to his left elbow. Jeff was asleep in his wheelchair. If Brian had no date and Jeff had no late meetings, they spent many evenings reading to each other in Jeff's room. Of late, they often fell asleep like this.

Upstairs, Paul clutched Ben. After holding each other for several minutes, they undressed, and got into bed. Propped on elbows, they faced each other.

Ben asked, "You okay?"

"I'm not sure."

"You saved those kids and the old man. It was on the news."

"Just doing my job."

Ben hugged him and asked, "Do you know what you're going to do next?"

"No. I'm just exhausted. I need to shut my mind down and get some rest."

In minutes, they were both asleep.

Saturday 6:17 A.M.

Paul's phone buzzed. Before getting into bed, as he always did, he'd turned it to its lowest level of sound. He glanced out the window. The first shreds of dawn's light poked through heavy clouds. He looked at the phone. Mrs. Talucci's number.

Paul got up as quietly as he could. He didn't want to wake Ben. His husband snorted but slept on.

He pulled on jeans, shoes, and a T-shirt. He clipped his gun and Fong's jamming device to his belt then hurried down the stairs and eased open the front door. He looked across at Mrs. Talucci's front porch. He saw her rocking in her chair. She had her shotgun across her lap.

Paul hurried over. He heard morning birds chirping as if a great storm was nearby.

In the shadows of the porch, Paul saw another figure. He got to the top step of the porch before he could make out the figure in the shadow. It was Peter Eisenberg, the plainclothes cop from the protester encampment. He still wore the tight jeans, T-shirt, and athletic shoes he'd had on the day before. The jeans looked to have dried on him.

Mrs. Talucci said, "This man chose to disturb our neighborhood this morning." Usually, Mrs. Talucci sounded like someone's grandmother who was in a kitchen humming while making chocolate chip cookies. She had other voices. Today's was what Paul referred to as her royal voice, that is, he could imagine Queen Victoria saying in just that soft, icy tone, "We are not amused."

Eisenberg scuffed his shoe on the porch. "If we could talk please, and not so openly as this."

Mrs. Talucci nodded. Paul opened the screen door. Eisenberg preceded him in. They sat at the kitchen table. Mrs. Talucci joined them for a minute. She put out pitchers of breakfast juices and glasses, and cups for coffee, made sure they took what they wanted, then left.

"How the hell did she know I was here?" Eisenberg asked.

Paul said, "Better not to know, I suspect. It's her neighborhood."

"Jesus, she scared the hell out of me. There was no one there and then there were these big, hulky guys, and I was on that porch."

"You didn't think it was odd to show up at this hour of the morning in any neighborhood?"

"Bad decision. Dumb. I'm sorry."

"How'd you survive the storm yesterday?"

"Our tent is gone. Most of us ran. Two of the ones who stayed are in the hospital, but are supposed to be okay."

Paul sipped the always excellent coffee. "What can I do for you?"

"I was a shit to you yesterday. I'm sorry. I should have been braver. I want to apologize."

"I appreciate the apology."

"I couldn't say this in front of the guys."

"Say what?"

"I think you and your partner did right, saving that kid, Tasing Carruthers. I don't know him. I do know his reputation. I don't get why everybody is rushing to hold up the wall of silence for him but not for you guys."

"Why did you come see me now?"

"I'm still not that brave. I wanted to see you outside of work." He adjusted his pants, pulled at his T-shirt. "Last night, we helped people. That took hours. Then we went drinking. I haven't been home. I also came to warn you."

"About what?"

Eisenberg sipped coffee. "See, I'm gay. There's still a lot of prejudice in the regular rank and file. I mean nothing openly homophobic, but kind of casual-like. And we talked about you. One of the guys is connected to DeGroot and the Carruthers investigation."

"Nothing about the death of the two protesters?"

"They think protesters are too disorganized to plan and carry out a bake sale much less a murder. The scuttlebutt I've got is that cops way up are behind planning everything that's happened, no matter how weird and convoluted. That Carruthers, he's too stupid to plan all this."

"All that's happened has been part of a plot to get me and Fenwick?"

Eisenberg said, "That's what I've got. Some central point in the CPD. No way could it be the protesters."

Turner said, "Some of them have been organizing for years. Many of them marched with the women after the inauguration and helped put that together. Some of them have been marching since the sixties."

"But this is trying to get such disparate groups to come together. That women's march was almost spontaneous and powerful. I think the intention here was right, but the road to hell here was exceptionally bumpy. I think everybody wanted to sabotage it."

Turner asked, "Including members of your detail?"

"Acting on the orders of our higher ups."

"Who?"

"Commander Palakowski for one. It's not DeGroot's assignment, but he hung around a lot. And that guy from the mayor's office, Edberg, seemed to be at every debriefing. And Bortz, that idiot alderman."

"How about the FBI, Homeland, or a rep from the 1%?"

"The FBI guys were all secretive and superior. I suppose you could call on the FBI, but I don't think they'd give you much. Or, at least, they never gave us anything. The one we dealt with from the FBI was Chris Randall. We never saw Homeland, just the van we all assumed was theirs. The 1% guy was Danny Currington. He was secretive, superior, and a snot. He has a suite at the top of one of the towers at the Chicago Extravaganza Hotel on State Street."

"Was anybody around pretending to be Fenwick and me asking questions about the murder case?"

"Not that I heard of." He caught Turner's eye. "That would be special bold. They trying to screw up you guys' investigation?"

"Presumably."

"I doubt if it was the protesters. They knew who we were early on. Before they knew who we were, some would talk to us and even after they knew, a few would still talk to us. Some wouldn't shut up. A few were generally pleasant, trying to make peace with the world, trying to make the world a little kinder. I shouldn't make fun. The gun-nut hate factions would go on at great length just like any other group. Endlessly, repetitiously. It seemed at times they were in a competition to come talk to us. As if they were afraid of some rival getting a leg up."

"Nothing specific on Shaitan or Bettencourt?"

"The few that mentioned either one said they didn't like Shaitan, and they liked Bettencourt, but it was only a couple people, and it was mostly passing references, but like I said, word I heard is that this is all being orchestrated from high up in the department." He paused a moment and then his face turned red. "I should have told you this next bit already." He hesitated again.

Turner waited.

"Some of the guys in our group were working with Shaitan. They gave him recording devices."

"Why?"

"As far as I could tell, it was convoluted bullshit. Supposedly if we were nice to him, he'd give us inside information. I think there pretty much wasn't inside information, not of the seriously criminal kind, more of the usual mix of kind and good hearted people trafficking with delusional morons."

Turner thought, Shaitan was in it with delusional Chicago cops. He certainly wasn't surprised. He asked, "Anything else?"

"That's all I know." He hung his head. "Well, except, you're a gay cop and that seems to work for you. I'd like it to work for me."

"It will."

He glanced up and looked down. His hand inched towards Paul's knee. "You wouldn't be interested in…"

Paul drew his knee back an inch or so and said, "I'm flattered that you asked, but I'm happily married."

"Okay."

They walked out to the porch and shook hands on the top step.

Paul said, "Thanks for coming."

"Be careful."

Paul sat with Mrs. Talucci. Morning sun was trying to poke through the clouds. She moved her shoulder and winced. "Probably the worst storms coming today."

He said, "Thanks for your help."

"Just being a good neighbor. He was right. Please, be careful."

"I always do my best to be."

Saturday 7:03 A.M.

When he got back home, it was just after seven. Ben was still asleep. Paul didn't hear the boys stirring. In the laundry room, he found a pair of freshly washed and dried gym shorts from when he was in high school. He changed out of his jeans. He liked the well-worn cottony feel. He made himself a cup of coffee and sat on the back porch. With the shorts on, what little breeze there was outside stirred the hair on his arms and legs.

The humidity seemed almost close to bearable. The garden needed weeding. He'd have to get to that. Ben tilled and planted. Paul tended and harvested. The tall fence, the garage, and the large trees in full leaf screened the porch from any prying neighbors.

Paul watched the summer light spread around the yard. He was tired from stress, the long hours of work, and lack of sleep. He sat and mulled until he heard Jeff's wheelchair. It stopped in the kitchen at the espresso maker for a minute or two. Then the back door swung open, and Jeff wheeled out.

"Morning," Paul said.

"Morning." The boy busied himself balancing his small cup of coffee as he transferred himself to the swing next to Paul. His dad was careful not to help without asking first. The boy was sensitive about doing things on his own. It took longer, but Paul figured if the boy needed a few extra moments, as a dad, he could spare the time. Paul took off his shirt and wiped sweat off. He draped it on his chair to be tossed in the laundry hamper later.

Jeff settled then said, "You got in after I fell asleep."

"It was late."

"You're up early again. What's wrong?"

"Things at work are complicated."

"I read all the reports on the Internet including from the local newspapers. Are you part of the Code of Silence in the department? Is that what's happening in this case? Does the Code of Silence work for you or against you since it's a fight between detectives?"

"What do you know about it?"

"Just what was in the papers."

"And what did it say?"

Jeff began to recite chapter and verse from what he read. The boy's memory was phenomenal. As for his understanding of what he read, he still often needed help. He continued for several minutes, paused, sipped from his espresso cup, then finished with, "Are you going to be okay? Are you okay?"

"On the job, I'm going to do my work as best I can. I'll talk to who I have to talk to. It's more complicated now because there's been a history, then again, come to think of it, there's always a history that makes things complicated."

"You're not going to get fired?"

"No." Paul knew that as long as Molton was his Commander, he was reasonably safe.

Jeff said, "The bullies always win. The rich always lie. Are they going to try to kill you?" At the end, the boy could not suppress a plaintive tremble in his voice.

Paul put his hand on his son's arm, looked him in the eyes. He said, "I'm going to do the best I can to keep you, Brian, Ben, and myself safe. After that, I catch bad guys. Today will be the same as any other." Paul hoped this was true.

Jeff nodded, which Paul took to mean acceptance of what he'd said. The boy asked, "What does it mean when it says a police officer has been 'stripped of his police powers?'"

"That he or she sits at a desk doing boring work for hours on end."

"But still gets a paycheck."

"For now."

"Is Mr. Fenwick okay?"

"As much as he ever is."

"They've got all those review boards. Do you have to face them?"

"Anyone can face them at any time. I haven't done anything wrong, so there's nothing to fear." He hoped that was true. For now, it was enough truth for his son.

"But you saved that kid from Carruthers. You saved those kids from the storm."

"Just doing my job," Paul said.

Jeff said, "Why doesn't the Code of Silence work both ways?"

"What do you mean?" Paul asked.

"The Code of Silence hushes up mistreatment of minorities and tolerates misconduct. Those guys won a lawsuit against the Code of Silence. Costs the city two million bucks. But even so, whoever snitches is a 'rat motherfucker'. I can say that in this case right?"

"For now."

"Well, if Carruthers is one of their own and they rally around to protect him, and if you and Mr. Fenwick are ones of their own, why don't they rally around to protect you? Why doesn't it work both ways? I think they might contradict each other. You can't be on both sides at once."

Paul said, "Sometimes people feel they have to choose, or feel they need to."

"They think you broke the Code of Silence by saving that kid?" Jeff banged the arm of the swing. "That makes no sense. You saved somebody's life. Carruthers's reputation is more important than that kid's life?"

"It's what each person has invested in Carruthers's reputation that makes a difference."

Jeff banged the arm of the swing again. "That's bullshit."

Paul said, "Besides making your hand and wrist sore, what good does banging it do?"

"I'm mad. It makes me feel better."

"Is that the best way to deal with frustration?"

"You know I get mad."

"And I know this isn't the only time we've talked about this."

"I'm defending you."

"And I appreciate it. Do we bang things, throw things, hit out?"

Paul got a whispered, "No." Jeff paused for a moment than asked, "Don't you get mad? Don't you get angry?"

"Yep."

"So what do you do?"

"I work even harder to be logical, do research, and make sense and take deliberate, useful action. It's the difference between President Obama and his predecessor and his successor."

"But that's distant and far. I'm talking about us."

Paul sighed, "Sometimes when I'm angry, very angry, frustrated, the question for me is what can I do about the anger, how can I ease the frustration? I've never found hitting something made a problem any better."

"But wouldn't you feel better?"

"I feel better when I can solve the problem."

"I'm a kid."

"Took me a while to learn as well." Paul paused then said, "I will listen to you explain your anger for as long as you like. Please don't hit."

A teenage pause and a mumbled, "Okay."

The two sat in companionable silence.

Ben, wearing a pair of baggy basketball shorts, showed up and stood next to Jeff. The three chatted for a while. Jeff had to get to his Saturday morning chess league meeting. He did his wheelchair thing in reverse and then trundled off.

Ben sat next to Paul. "You okay?"

"As much as I can be with work a mess."

"Is Carruthers suicidal?"

"I never thought so before these events. His wife certainly gave that impression."

"The world is against him. From what you described, his wife isn't very fond of him. Why does she stay married to him?"

"Who knows? But suicidal? Beats the hell out of me. He's so relentlessly Carruthers, it's hard to think of him as anything else. I reported it to the Commander and let Barb Dams know. I did my part. They'll follow all the procedures."

"Are his protectors abandoning him? I would if I were them."

"I don't know because I'm not sure who his protectors are. Certainly they're going to try to save their own skins, their own jobs, their own careers. They wouldn't let Carruthers threaten that. I don't think."

"But you're a threat to all that is theirs. That's what I worry about. What if they want to get you out of the way?"

"We've got Molton, and now that Carruthers is gone, according to Barb Dams, all the detectives on the squad at Area Ten."

"There've been random killings and random shootings."

"That's what makes them so hard to solve."

"But they could become specific to you."

As they sat, their elbows and arms touched, they could feel the hair on each other's legs. Paul loved the warmth and masculinity. Neither wore a shirt, so their hairy-chests and six-pack abs stood out.

Paul said, "That's one of the reasons Fenwick and I are going in early again today. We want to solve the murder case so we can concentrate on the Carruthers bullshit. Although as far as Molton, Fenwick, and I can see, it's all one big case."

Saturday 8:38 A.M.

Turner and Fenwick met up a little after eight thirty in the headquarters parking lot. As they walked in, Dams caught them in the hall. "You might want to watch this."

The television in Molton's office was on. It showed Griffin, the assistant Chief of Detectives, giving a press briefing. He was saying, "Well, we don't know exactly what happened."

"After all this time?" shouted a reporter.

Griffin ignored him. "They are many unanswered questions that we need answers to."

Fenwick muttered at the screen, "Bullshit."

Griffin went on, "By talking to you now and at periodic intervals, we're showing all of you how transparent we are trying to be. We've got evidence techs and crews, even as we speak, going through surveillance video. It takes time."

They chose not to listen to any more and turned to go up to their desks. Dams motioned them over to her desk. She picked up two thick manila envelopes. She gave one to each of them. Turner glanced inside. He said, "This is Carruthers's file."

Dams said, "The real one. I also cut and pasted the thing onto emails that I sent you both."

"We never got this from you," Fenwick said.

"Announce it to the world for all I care."

"How'd you get it?" Fenwick asked.

Dams gave him a grim smile. "Sometimes people are stupid. When we digitized everything, we didn't destroy everything, at least not my backups. Nobody gets to my files, and if they try to, I have backups to the backups. Never fuck with an all-powerful secretary."

The detectives knew this to be true, even to the point of never fucking with a less than all-powerful secretary.

Turner said, "Thank you."

They walked upstairs to their desks. Five feet from his, Fenwick halted, then asked in his deepest rumble, "Why is there a broken lock in the center of my desk?"

Turner stopped. He whispered, "It can't be from the door that led onto the roof where the shots came from."

"It can," Fenwick whispered back.

"More proof the two cases are connected? Or it's our fellow cops out to get us?" He shook his head. "Or more likely both."

Fenwick said, "I was depressed before this."

Turner said, "I'm just totally pissed."

Molton wasn't in. They called Dams, Fong, and crime scene technicians.

Saturday 9:03 A.M.

They headed for the nearest Starbucks, three blocks away. They took great care to be sure they weren't followed.

This morning, the sun shone brightly. After the few short blocks, Fenwick's clothes showed nearly as much dampness as after they'd been in the rain last night. The air-conditioned coffee shop was fabulous. Severe storms were predicted for that evening. A tornado watch had been posted from noon today to noon tomorrow.

In the crowded establishment, a table came open in the back.

Fenwick stirred his sugar and cream-filled coffee then slammed the wooden stir sticks down hard enough on the table top to splinter them.

Turner said, "I agree."

They drank, watched the crowd, gazed out the windows, and mulled their situation.

Fenwick said, "I am not happy about this. Somewhere, somebody else is going to be unhappy when we get to the bottom of this. And when we do, it's going to hurt. Them. A lot."

Turner said, "Yep."

More coffee drinking and mulling.

Fenwick said, "They've got us dizzing around here, and we're buying into all this stupidity. I feel like I could drown in stupidity that's as thick as all this humidity."

Turner said, "We need to go one incident at a time. Sort them out."

They opened their laptops and began taking notes and jotting perspectives as each other spoke.

Turner told him about the visit that morning from Pete Eisenberg, the Chicago police undercover guy.

Fenwick said, "You keep getting visits in the middle of the night."

"This was early morning. You jealous?"

"I might be. Is this like the international gay conspiracy?" Fenwick asked.

"Only if I want it to be."

More tapping on keyboards making notes.

Fenwick said, "It almost feels like these guys didn't really care."

"Who?"

"The CPD brass, whoever set up this thing. From the gaudiness of the tent to what seemed to be a poor choice of personnel. It all seems sort of slapdash."

"Somebody wanted there to be violence? Somebody wanted the conference to fail? They didn't care how many innocent people died while they tried to kill us?"

Fenwick asked, "Who? Why?"

"Wasn't me. I don't know yet." Turner paused a moment then said, "As long as we're listing odd things how about this. We've got every stripe of radical who have all learned to take pictures of police and every other speck of dust on the streets of Chicago except nobody got the picture of the killer nor did the killer post pictures of his work. Why then is he/she the only one at the convention not so posting?"

He tapped his coffee cup then said, "Can we draw the conclusion that the killer wasn't part of the wild camera work, because he wasn't at the conference or part of the conference or connected to the conference."

Fenwick said, "The radicals and protesters have nothing to do with any of the killings and shots. The whole radical conference thing is a convenient red-herring? Why kill the activists? A cover-up? A diversion? Or what the hell, just randomly kill two people. Just for us."

"You're a cop, and you've read history. People have done far more cruel things for no apparent reasons. Sometimes, they're just nuts."

"And someone, those nuts or that nut, is in a powerful position in the city of Chicago or in the Chicago Police Department? And we've met a lot of nutty administrators."

"That nutty?"

"Maybe our experience just got broadened. Yeah. I think they're nuts enough."

Turner said, "Using the deaths to confuse the issue. There was one target, and having two die confuses the issue even more."

"Great. Which one was the cover up?" Fenwick asked.

"Yes."

"And the presence of Ian?"

"A bonus for the confusion sweepstakes? Pure dumb luck? Stop me when you think I've gotten to something that works."

Fenwick said, "I'm stumped."

Turner said, "Let's go back to another oddity. No one has reported the beat cop incident. Not officially. Sure, like those cops in the tent, they'd heard about it, but silence from all official channels. Possible logical conclusion, the cop involved knows something."

"We gotta talk to him."

Turner asked, "Why was there a guard on your cubicle in the hospital?"

"Huh?"

"If we're being watched, and we're suspicious of everyone, let's go back and examine what we might think of as the slightest oddity. First one I thought of was the cop at the cubicle when you were getting stitched up. Who assigned him there and why? We weren't in danger. We were cops. We weren't going to be arrested. We were the good guys. Who the hell was he?"

"Someone is desperate?" Fenwick suggested. "Or stupid?"

"Or both," Turner said. "Okay, and why was there a guard outside the kid's room?" He didn't wait for an answer. "Then there were all those cops hanging around Sanchez's room, but there was one official guard."

"They were always watching us. Always trying to listen in. What the fuck were we saying that was so fucking important?"

Turner said, "They cared about what we might say. If this was all about us, if every action on their part was to catch us, if this was all a set-up, then they could be fishing for anything random. They've been monitoring every incident of our day since this all started. Since the first moment of Carruthers's first shift back from vacation." He mused for a moment. "Who has the ability for such monitoring?" He answered his own question. "The CPD."

"Doesn't strike me as efficient."

"Has anything about what has been happening since we stopped Carruthers struck you as efficient?"

"Well. No." Fenwick sighed. Gave his coffee cup a slow twirl, took a huge gulp, and said, "Although somehow, if it involves Carruthers, and friends who can't be much above his level of intelligence, I assume it would be fucked up. They keep shooting at us. And they keep missing me. How? Or they're only shooting at one of us?"

"We actually only got shot at once. We weren't there when they attacked the car."

Fenwick said, "The storm nearly got us."

"You saying the storm was orchestrated by evil forces?"

"Not today. Give me time. Just because we're paranoid, doesn't mean we don't have enemies."

"The storm happened just to get us wet?" Turner asked.

"How paranoid do we want to be?"

"I don't know," Turner said. "Having an enemy that controls the weather? Wouldn't that make us kind of special?"

"Not special enough."

Turner tapped at the keys on his laptop. "Why did the kid DeShawn have a guard? Who ordered it?"

Fenwick said, "The bridge."

Turner raised his eyebrow at his friend.

Fenwick said, "If we're going to be paranoid about everything, we should add that, too. Why was that crowd there at that time? To give me a chance to be heroic?"

"The world plans things just for you?" Turner asked.

"If it doesn't, it should."

Turner asked, "Why was Carruthers shooting that kid at just that time?"

Fenwick said, "Carruthers isn't capable of that kind of evil plotting. Someone higher up, but we need evidence, not conspiracy theories. We've got enough people in town to twirl such theories into madness. My question is why bother?"

"Huh?"

Fenwick said, "It's not as if these conspiracy people have the wherewithal to organize themselves into power."

"Can you say presidential election?" Turner asked.

"Oh. We're looking for a killer who is an orange haired presidential candidate?"

"I doubt it. Real planners aren't that stupid," Turner said.

Fenwick asked, "Why are Henry Bettencourt and Preston Shaitan dead?"

"Random chance? They were both at the wrong place at the wrong time?" Turner paused and gazed thoughtfully into his coffee cup. "I think it's usually the innocent who die at all the mass killings from Sandy Hook to Orlando."

Fenwick nodded, sat back, let out a deep breath. "Yeah, but not always this virulent. Why just those two? Why not more? The murders are connected to the Carruthers mess? How can they not be?" Fenwick stated it, "This all has to do with us."

"Why kill those two on the roof? The killer couldn't know we'd investigate."

"Unless he could."

Turner asked, "Why'd we get the case?"

"Because we're the best?"

"We know that. What did Molton say that first time?"

"Pressure had come from downtown." Fenwick stopped mid-sip. He put his coffee cup down. "You know, before this moment, I sort of figured it was all of one piece, all this shit, but now, I'm convinced. The killer is connected to downtown, police headquarters. The mayor's office."

Turner said, "We don't know specifics, but it's just a solution that seems plausible. You know the old Sherlock Holmes saying, when you eliminate the impossible, whatever else is left, no matter how improbable, must be the truth."

"So they're out to get you and me and don't care who else dies?"

Turner said, "You want more weird? If it's Carruthers, it's likely to be connected to our last case with all that church corruption."

Fenwick took a long gulp of his coffee then whispered, "Mother fucker. This can't just be all anti-us. Can it?"

Turner shrugged. "It depends, I think, on which of them have heard the wrist joke and those who feared they might soon be told the wrist joke."

The line for the counter had thinned out for the moment, and Fenwick got up and ordered himself two breakfast sandwiches and more coffee for Turner and himself.

He sat back down and gobbled a sandwich, sipped coffee, stared out the window a few minutes. He finally said, "Who has the wherewithal to do all this? Plant evidence. Use high-powered rifles. Get to as many scenes as they've gotten to. To know where we are."

"Chicago police, or the protesters have gotten very sophisticated."

"We've seen that some of them are."

"A conspiracy so immense," Fenwick said.

Turner said, "Or a mix of protesters and cops and the church."

"In league to do what? Get us? It's worth that much to go through all this?"

Turner told him about Mrs. Wolchevitz from the night before and her theory of power and corruption among the top CPD brass. He finished, "Carruthers's support system was even more powerful than we imagined. Or maybe the support system isn't for Carruthers. Maybe he's just caught up in it. There's a Code of Silence that he's in on that we aren't. What makes him so special?"

"That's what we have to find out."

"Being pro-Carruthers is a bullshit motive. We got no forensics. We're nowhere."

Fenwick gazed evenly at his partner, and said, "There are big plausibility gaps to overcome."

"We've been asking the wrong people the wrong questions."

"You can ask the Superintendent of Police if he'd mind answering a few questions?"

"Maybe we won't start quite that high up."

"No matter how low we start, as soon as we stop questioning that person and leave, that person will report our activity to higher ups." He offered Turner a bite of his other sandwich. Turner said no thanks.

Fenwick gobbled, swallowed, gulped more coffee, and said, "I don't see a way out of this."

Turner said, "I'm not ready for despair."

Fenwick said, "Me neither. What the hell, let's try the shit we got from Dams on Carruthers."

Turner's phone buzzed. It was a text from Barb Dams that said, "Friendly visitors on their way." Turner told Fenwick and finished, "Doesn't say who."

Fenwick said, “I guess we’ll find out soon enough.”

While they waited, they connected to the Internet, downloaded, and began to read what Barb had sent them.

After several minutes Turner said, “Discipline has been recommended for Carruthers, but the recommended discipline was never imposed.”

Fenwick asked, “How do people get away with that?”

Turner shrugged and read. “And he was supposed to get specific new training. Didn’t happen. The guy is a walking, losing lawsuit.”

Saturday 9:35 A.M.

Ian and a man dressed as a monsignor in the Catholic Church, white collar, red piping on his cassock, walked in. Ian nodded to them. He and his companion got coffee. The Monsignor went to add cream and sugar to his. Ian came directly over to their table. Ian said, "Barb Dams told me you were here."

Fenwick asked, "Who is he?"

"Monsignor Schneider with the Catholic Church. He was at the station looking for you. Says he knows a buddy of yours, a Mrs. Wolchevitz. He'd taken a cab to the station, but he was leery of walking the few blocks here in the rising wind."

Turner had seen healthy people blown over after being caught in the cross-canyon winds of the tall buildings of Chicago. Monsignor Schneider looked to be close to ninety.

Turner swallowed his anger. He guessed that this was part of Ian trying to say he was sorry, by trying to help with the case. Right now, he'd take help from wherever he could get it.

The Monsignor tottered over to them.

Turner and Fenwick stood and introduced themselves. Everyone sat.

Schneider said, "I work in the Diocese Central Office. I'm semi-retired, but I hear everything, and have excellent sources. I got a call from Mrs. Wolchevitz early this morning." He pointed at Ian. "This gentleman was kind enough to help me struggle the few blocks over here. The wind is up." He gave a small cough. "I was told to talk to the two detectives." He raised an eyebrow.

Ian began to stand up.

Turner said, "It's okay. He's helped us with a few cases."

Schneider said, "Very well. I may have some information for you."

Turner said, "Thank you for coming."

The Monsignor nodded. "Mrs. Wolchevitz is a dear woman. I hope I can help."

Turner said, "We talked to Father Benedict last night. He was helpful in putting together a bunch of people to talk to."

The Monsignor gave a discreet cough, sipped his coffee, and said, "I know. I was his Master of Novices during his novitiate year in the seminary. He called me. We are old friends. He is a true believer in causes. I admire him. I'm not sure how effective he really is, but the man believes in real tenets of Christianity, and actually tries to treat all people he meets by them. So many of us get caught up in fund-raising and petty disputes. Benedict believes and tries. He's a good man. He said kind things about you as well. And I saw you on television saving that young man."

He sipped more coffee. The detectives waited.

"I have some inside information for you. A few members high up in the church are trying to influence your careers including this Carruthers mess and your current investigation, at least enough to make you fail and look bad." He paused, took another sip. "Or kill you."

"Why?"

"Because, in their view, you disgraced the church in that investigation of the murdered bishop."

Fenwick said, "We just worked the case, followed leads."

Schneider said, "As the old cliché goes, you gave scandal to the faithful."

Fenwick said, "I can dish out scandal with the best of them."

Turner said, "They're hiring people to shoot at us?"

Ian said, "Are you suggesting the Catholic Church is hiring terrorists to kill non-believers?" He finished with a mutter under his breath, "Wouldn't be the first time."

Fenwick asked, "Anything specific since the Inquisition or specific to this case?"

Turner ignored Ian and Fenwick and asked his question again.

The Monsignor shook his head. "No, they wouldn't hire people, not directly. That would be out of character, and if someone broke and told, it could be traced back to them. No, they'd work behind the scenes, as they most often do, first to help discredit you, if they could, but even more, to put pressure on those who did have the wherewithal to try to destroy you. They might also help with the planning, but not necessarily the execution of the plot. Remember, Carruthers is one of theirs."

Fenwick shook his head. "That we are perceived as such a threat amazes me. In the long history of the Catholic Church, we're nobodies."

Monsignor Schneider said, "You know the quote, Emerson I think it was, 'If the single man plant himself indomitably on his instincts, and here abide, the huge world will come round to him.' That's you two."

Fenwick said, "Bullshit. We have no such power."

The Monsignor said, "Not quite as philosophical as I would have hoped, but what I was told to expect."

Fenwick said, "About as good as you're going to get this morning."

Turner said, "You know us?"

"I also have ways of getting information." He took another sip of coffee. Turner noticed the old hand trembled slightly as he raised the cup to his lips.

The Monsignor smiled, "You should have seen the Cardinal's residence as we watched the coverage of the storm from last night. Your rescue of those children was prominently played. You could have cut the hatred in that room with a knife."

Fenwick said, "I've got a quote for you. How many divisions does the Pope have?"

Another smile from the Monsignor. "Well played, but quoting Stalin to me may be clever, but not effective."

"They'd prefer that we let the kids die?"

"Well, no. They'd prefer you'd have been at the bottom of the tree when the lightning struck."

"They are that vindictive?" Fenwick asked.

The Monsignor said, "Somebody mentioned Inquisition earlier." He took a sip of his coffee. "Look, I came here to warn you. Part of the pressure you're getting is because the church still has influence, a great deal of influence."

"Specifically, with whom?" Turner asked.

"Start with Commander Palakowski. He and the new Cardinal talk. There is also someone high up in the mayor's office. I presume Edberg who is a church stooge. And then there's Clayton Griffin, the assistant Chief of Detectives. He and the priests in the central office go way back. They are out to get you and the planning is extensive."

Turner asked, "Enough influence to cause them to commit murder?"

"My opinion is unfortunately, maybe. And I can give you no direct proof. Just what I've gleaned, heard, summarized, and on a few occasions, been confided in. I know it's not enough."

"More than we had before," Turner said.

Ian asked, "Is Carruthers part of the planning?"

Schneider smiled. "I met him once. In that brief time, I was as unimpressed with his intelligence as anyone else. No one would be stupid enough to let him near the planning. I believe he played a part in the first scenario on the street. Even then he screwed it up. He was never part of planning. Now he's part of nothing."

"Why are you coming to us?"

"Because," the Monsignor said, "I can see a man, in this case, two, standing indomitably on their instincts. I wanted to be among the ones who come round to them."

Turner said, "I appreciate the compliment, but…"

The Monsignor interrupted. "Also, and this I only heard second hand, do not trust your Commander or the Superintendent of Police."

Fenwick asked, "And why should we trust you?"

The Monsignor said, "Touché. I can but say, I wish you well."

Turner and Fenwick were not going to discuss their Commander and their relationship with him with this stranger.

Ian said, "The Carruthers incident and these murders are connected." He looked to the two detectives. Ian had not been privy to the information and insights they'd gotten yesterday. Turner didn't have the time or inclination to go into all that, especially with the monsignor still present.

Turner and Fenwick shrugged. They thanked Schneider for his information. Ian offered to help the older man on his way. They left.

Turner and Fenwick gazed at each other for a few moments. Turner broke the silence. "It's confirmed. It's one huge incident."

Fenwick said, "We've got to figure out the specific details, and precisely who did what."

"Yeah, lots of convoluted shit."

Saturday 10:35 A.M.

They went back to the station. They were still hours early for their regular shift. They noticed a black Lincoln Town car with a bodyguard/driver standing watch at its front bumper.

Fenwick asked, "Could that be the Superintendent's car?"

"Don't know. He doesn't come visit me."

Barb Dams appeared at the entrance and hurried down to them. She said, "The Superintendent is here. He and Molton want to meet with you."

Fenwick said, "I feel more than special."

She said, "You saved those kids."

Fenwick said, "Next heroic thing, I walk away and leave the poor, innocent victim tied to the railroad tracks."

Barb hurried ahead. They drifted into the station. Just inside the door, Fenwick said, "We better be careful what we say."

Turner said, "Unfortunately, I agree."

As they entered Molton's office, both he and the Superintendent rose to greet them. Izzy Labato had become Superintendent of Police only a few months before. In the continuing uproar about the Chicago police, no one dared to take a bet on how long he would last in the job. He was a portly man in his late fifties with grizzled white hair. He extended his hand to them and said, "You both deserve the highest commendation and praise for a great many things." He ticked them off. "You saved that teenager. You defused the situation at the bridge. You made sure those washrooms in the parking garage were open. Last night, you saved those children and that old man. I thank you. The department thanks you."

They hadn't even told Molton about the parking garage. They looked to Molton then back to the Superintendent who said, "I try to keep myself informed. And now they're shooting at some of my best people. That pisses me off. I came down today to thank you for what you've done, and find out what I can do to help you out." He pointed at Fenwick, "And to see if we can't get you in front of the cameras. The press is hounding the mayor's office and my office to try and get you to do publicity. It's something positive, and we need positive, cops who the community trusts."

Fenwick said, "I really think that would be a bad idea."

The Superintendent said, "So I've heard."

They took seats. The Superintendent sat next to Molton. They were behind the Commander's desk. Turner and Fenwick sat in front. Barb Dams brought in servings of coffee for all. Drinks settled, the Superintendent asked, "What's going on with the case?"

They gave them broad outline of what they'd been doing. When they finished, the superintendent said, "How can I help you gentlemen?"

Turner said, "We're trying to clear a few things up. We're nowhere near having any kind of evidence to make an arrest or name a suspect."

He kept quiet about Monsignor Schneider's revelations of this morning. He wasn't about to over-confide in anybody.

"You think Carruthers killed those two men on the rooftop?"

Molton intervened, "Why don't we let them explain their concerns?"

The Superintendent nodded.

Turner asked, "How did we get picked for that case? We need to find out the chain of evidence, phone calls. Who knew, who could have planned to kill them, and then have us be there."

The Superintendent asked, "You really think this is that convoluted?"

Turner said, "We have to investigate it as if all of our paranoia is real. We can't be ruled by our paranoia, but we have to act as if everything that's happened is suspicious."

The Superintendent looked at Molton who said, "I was told directly by Clayton Griffin to assign Turner and Fenwick to the shootings on the rooftop."

The Superintendent said, "Yes, Griffin said he'd had calls from the local alderman, the district commander, and a slew of activists. I didn't think to question whether or not what he was telling me was true."

Fenwick asked, "Who put guards on me the first night in the hospital, on the Jackson family outside their kid's hospital room, and tried to have someone listen in on us with Sanchez?"

"I didn't," Molton said.

"Not I," the Superintendent said.

"Or put a guard on my street?" Turner asked.

Both officials shook their heads.

"Who would?"

"Most likely is Commander Palakowski of the local District."

Fenwick said, "We need the names of who was on duty at the hospital when I was first there, and outside DeShawn's room."

Turner shook his head, "Or just get us the yearbook for three Districts closest to the hospital. I think it was the same guy. We can look at pictures and identify him."

"We'll need background when we identify him or them," Molton said. "You sure it was the same guy both times?"

Turner said, "I think so."

Fenwick said, "I didn't see the guy when I was being treated. I'd recognize the other one."

Molton said, "Dams can get whatever we need."

Turner said, "We need to proceed as if this were a normal case, or cases. We need to talk to each of these people and find out which of them are connected with getting us put on this case."

Fenwick said, "If they've got brains, they'd call their lawyers right after hearing from us."

Turner said, "They will call to tattle on us."

"They might call me first," Molton said. "As a warning."

"Or take us as an even greater threat."

Fenwick brought up another point. "If we talk to them, they'll think we're wired."

Molton said, "At this point, they'd be stupid to presume you weren't."

"Is this hopeless?" Fenwick asked. "We'll meet the same Code of Silence that's supposed to be protecting us."

The Superintendent said, "They won't like to be challenged, but it will scare them. No one is that confident of their power in any bureaucracy."

"And the church?" Fenwick asked.

Molton said, "There's a new cardinal. What the hell, talk to him."

The Superintendent spoke. "You really think the Catholic Church is going to go that quietly? They're known for secrecy."

Fenwick said, "No one expects the Spanish Inquisition."

In spite of himself, Turner smiled. He knew Fenwick was referring to one of his favorite bits of television comedy on Monty Python. When the Cardinals rush in and claim the church has various powers, finally deciding on saying their chief weapons are, surprise, fear, ruthless efficiency, an almost fanatical devotion to the Pope, and nice red uniforms.

The Superintendent raised an eyebrow.

"Sorry," Fenwick said, "not important."

The Superintendent gave a ghost of a smile himself. He said, "I know Monty Python. Unfortunately, Carruthers is very Catholic and very much active in his church, and there is real power and real danger there." He harrumphed and took a sip of coffee then said, "We already presume there's a conspiracy against you, or the presumption that there is one is strong. To let them know we know, I don't think that gives them power."

Molton said, "It might scare some. The weak links. They'll be scrambling to destroy their weak links, or be certain of their silence, or assure the weak links that all will be well."

"Can the conspiracy be that immense?" Fenwick asked.

Shrugs around the room.

Turner said, "We've got to find out who the expert shots are in the department."

Molton said, "I can get you raw data on possibilities. The top sharpshooters in each class at the academy for the last fifty years."

The Superintendent asked, "Why bother to make this all that convoluted?"

Turner said, "My guess is, it didn't start out that way. They wanted to prevent what we're doing now. They wanted us scared and frightened."

Fenwick asked, "Why not just kill us and be done with it?"

Molton asked, "An outright murder of cops? Tough to sell. And you've got that heroic shit in the last couple days."

Fenwick asked, "A sneaky murder of cops is better?"

Nobody bothered to answer.

Turner asked, "We found those CPD dash cams in Shaitan's hotel room. What if he or some group of protesters were in it with the cops?"

Molton said, "All to protect Carruthers?"

Turner said, "So far we have no forensics or proof for any of this."

Fenwick asked, "When they call to complain about us, are you going to back us up?"

Both administrators said yes.

Fenwick said, “If these people are as all-powerful as we are positing, then will we live to see another day?”

The Superintendent said, “They can’t be omnipotent.”

Fenwick said, “All they need to do is either be a better shot, or stop trying to dick around with us.”

Molton said, “All of a sudden, they’re graced with omnipotence? I think not.”

The Superintendent said, “Enough potence to snuff you out, I’m guessing, or close to it. You know a bureaucracy can crush you as well as anyone.”

Fenwick said, “They haven’t been able to save Carruthers.”

“Yet.” The Superintendent mused. “You do know that dirt is flying in your direction as well. You saved yourselves by saving those kids.”

“Wasn’t our fault,” Fenwick said.

“But close enough to be heroes. Because you both made split second decisions that saved lives, you may have saved your own, or at least made it more complicated for powerful people in this town to get even with you.”

Saturday 12:12 P.M.

After the meeting, Turner and Fenwick trooped up to their desks.

Fenwick plunked into his chair. He said, “Maybe the ones who are working against us want me to do a press conference because they presume I will fuck up and embarrass myself, kind of the buffoon rule of intimidation.”

“Are we really that important?”

“Someone seems to think so.”

“We’ve wasted time on all these activists.”

“Maybe we’ve got both ends of the same thread, and we’re going to meet in the middle.”

Turner’s phone rang.

It was Fong. He said, “I’m in my basement. Would you guys please come down?”

Down they went.

The whole floor, ceiling, wall thing was turned off.

Fenwick said, “No special effects this morning?”

“I’m working on the next show.”

He pointed to his monitor. “I’ve been hunting the web for cop videos.”

Fenwick said, “More bullshit.”

Fong said, “At times, one must go to the bullshit and wade

through it." He tapped on his keys and seconds later rows of icons showed up. "I started with those angry-cop sites, all fighting back against perceived attacks, slights, and prejudice against cops. Then I began to go further. I've been looking for Carruthers on the dark web and the deep web. You know how there's a few big cases with payouts for victims, but the vast majority of police complaints are found in favor of the police?"

The detective nodded.

Fong said, "They're both right. All the complaints ignored, most of those, the vast majority of complaints are from assholes who are guilty. You know they used to yell 'police brutality', now they still yell it, but they have video. Or video they think backs them up. The problem is, the nuts and all their idiocy get in the way of real stuff."

Fenwick said, "We knew that."

"I hunted." Fong rubbed his hands across his face.

Turner realized the poor guy looked exhausted. He asked, "Have you slept?"

Fong said, "I like you guys. The stuff I found, while not profound, might start to give you leverage on Carruthers."

"What have you got?" Turner asked.

"On the dark web, on crazy sites. Hidden. Extreme. I found some Chicago cop sites. Video taken by Chicago cops. Bragging Chicago cops. You know how teenagers take video of themselves bullying somebody. Same kind of thing. I found several sites at around six this morning. I spent hours downloading, saving, sharing."

He pointed at his monitor. They watched. Fong explained as he went. "I started with right wing sites. They've been even more bold lately. Then I found Carruthers."

He came to a particular point, paused the tape, tapped the monitor. Turner and Fenwick moved in close. "Kind of blurry," Fenwick said.

"Most of them are," Fong admitted.

Scene after scene unfolded of cops using excessive force against civilians, mostly, sometimes each other. According to the data under each one, the scenes of cop-on-cop violence were the most clicked on.

Fong said, "Here. Now."

A series of scenes followed for eighteen minutes.

After they were done, Fenwick said, "It's just Carruthers. Rodriguez isn't in any of them." He sounded relieved.

"Rodriguez isn't a psychopath," Turner said. He tapped the monitor. "These could plausibly be seen to be identified as Carruthers, but I'd hate to have to rely on them in court."

"Maybe we don't need them in court," Fenwick suggested. "Just releasing them might be enough to scare people off."

Fong said, "Hell, I may release all this stuff when I can make sure no one can find out it came from me."

"Can you do that?" Fenwick asked.

Fong said, "I'll have to go to a cyber café or library and use a computer there, and I should be able hide it, or better yet, bring it back to Carruthers's laptop."

Turner mused, "It might take a lot of work, but maybe we can figure out the times when Carruthers and Rodriguez weren't working together."

Fenwick shook his head. "He could have done this any time, but we can let Rodriguez know. He might have an idea."

Fong said, "Simplest thing to do would be to start with Rodriguez. He's not in any of them. Do a process of elimination. Some of these are date and time stamped. Find out where Rodriguez knew Carruthers to be." He handed them a flash drive and several sheets of paper. "I've got that for you. I called Rodriguez. Most of those videos happened before they were partners."

Fenwick said, "Carruthers was smart enough not to try to involve him."

Fong asked, "You're wondering why Carruthers has so few successful official complaints against him?"

Fenwick said, "I was curious about that."

Turner said, "Well, we found he had a lot, but they went away."

Fong tapped more keys, called up some more files. Civilian complaint forms appeared. "He has. Somebody made a ton of them go away."

"How'd you find them?"

"Once it's on a computer, or worse, on the Net, you risk that for all time, someone can find it. I found it. I talked to Barb Dams. She says she gave you copies of the originals from her files as well. My stuff is more complete with paperwork above Area level. Barb wouldn't have that."

Fong handed them each a flash drive. "Those are your copies. I've saved it to every device here. I've saved this to my home machines. I've saved it to the cloud. I've emailed it to myself, to each of you, and to other people I trust."

"With so many people with copies, it will come out."

Fong shrugged.

Fenwick asked, "Why were they stupid enough to put those videos on the Internet?"

"They didn't think someone as smart as me would be after them? Who knows? Ego? Stupidity? People love to see themselves."

Turner shook his head. "Most of these are blurry. We've got to prove it's Carruthers."

Fenwick groused, "What about our goddamn crime scene? Everybody but the killer and his victims was taking pictures and video like mad. Everybody was following everybody else with a camera. Except our killer."

Fong tapped his screen, "That wasn't part of this. That was part of your protester murders."

Turner said, "Unless our killer wasn't part of the conference."

"Huh?"

"They're all running around like mad. Except our killer and

tormentor. The damn deaths have nothing to do with that conference."

Turner sat next to Fong on a stool that wobbled. "That you found all this could be dangerous to you. You could be a target."

"If I die, it's all set to come out to every website and broadcast network on the Internet."

"Every?" Fenwick asked.

Fong smiled. "More than they'd be able to count or stop."

Turner said, "Let's hold on to all this for as long as we can. We've got to figure out what the hell is going on." Then he asked, "You have anything more from all those surveillance cameras?"

"Nothing new. I've got a few more cameras to go through. You know how long it takes when I don't have someone I'm specifically looking for."

Turner and Fenwick knew how useless the search was without such.

"However, you may find it slightly odd, or even majorly odd, that the cameras in the most direct line from the crime scene to the encampment to the murder scene, and all the cameras around the encampment were all non-functional."

"Deliberately broken?" Fenwick asked.

"Can't tell you that. My guess is your average protester is bright enough to know there are cameras around and paranoid enough to want to make sure they aren't functioning. Not sure I blame them."

Turner asked, "How about that bugging device in Bettencourt's room?"

Fong said, "It is not ours. As far as I could find out, it is a type that can be purchased online by anyone."

Fenwick said, "Crap."

Fong said, "Precisely. I can try and narrow it down to a specific web site, but I doubt it. Some illicit gun shows sell them as well. They wouldn't advertise, so they'd be hard to find. Underground and that shit."

Fenwick said, "We need to find some Chicago cops. We don't have one of their names. He was outside of Fenwick's first hospital bay, and then DeShawn's hospital room."

Fong turned to his computer. "You want to find a cop in the city? So that's ten thousand, give or take. Can we narrow it down?"

"Male," Fenwick said. "White. Young maybe 25-30."

"Let's start with the local district," Turner said.

"You said he was young. Maybe he was on a sports team for the district." There were numerous police sports leagues. Fong called up the local district's sports page. Turner leaned close shook as the faces scrolled up. Then he pointed and said, "Him." Fenwick said, "That was the guy outside my room?"

Turner added, "And outside DeShawn's room."

Fong isolated the shot, enlarged the head, got the name, Bruce Deaton, from the caption under the photo. A few minutes later they had the names and addresses for both Deaton, who had been outside the first two hospital rooms and Arnold, first name Joe, who'd been dragged away by Palakowski at the Sanchez hospital room scene.

They stood up.

The detectives thanked him profusely. They left.

At their desks, they worked on preliminary data on who in the CPD had the expertise or background to fire a rifle the required distance. After half an hour, Turner said, "I'd say an estimate based on what we've done so far is over half the members of the department could have fired the rifle."

Then they called up as many of the cases that Carruthers had worked on that required a State's Attorney. They came up with one name. Brandon Smeek.

Turner asked, "How many detectives have one State's Attorney continuously on all their cases?" He turned his monitor so Fenwick could see.

Fenwick gazed for a moment. "These are the ones that didn't involve Rodriguez, all involved some kind of complaint against

Carruthers."

They read some more. Turner said, "They all went away."

Fenwick said, "Son of a bitch."

Turner said, "We need to talk to a friendly State's Attorney."

Fenwick said, "We've worked with that Robert Cardin for a few years. He's been a good guy. We could try him."

Turner said, "I'll call him."

They drew up a list of who else they needed to talk to.

Fenwick said, "It's a Saturday. A lot of these civilians will be at home." He paused. "I believe people will use any advantage they think they can get especially as they're backed into a corner." He sighed. "Then again, they may feel more invulnerable being in their own homes on their own turf. Screw it. Makes no difference. Fuck all. Let's go talk to these people no matter where they are."

Saturday 1:05 P.M.

Fenwick said, "Food."

They stopped for lunch at Petunia's on Division near Milwaukee Avenue. Fenwick ordered the full dinner loaded-meatloaf. Turner had avocado toast and a hearts of palm salad.

While they waited for their food, Turner fumed. "How could Ian be so stupid? How could he think we wouldn't find out? I'm still angry that he didn't tell us at the beginning?"

Fenwick said, "He has shit to answer for."

"Got that right."

Turner did a grouse almost as long as a Fenwick grumble. He stopped when their food arrived.

Moments later, they noticed Palakowski, the local district Commander, march in. Petunia's was known as a cop hangout. He looked around, spotted them, and surged to their booth.

Palakowski waved a finger in Fenwick's face. "We've gotten complaints about you." His voice was raised.

Fenwick said, "Would you care to join us?"

Palakowski said, "If I don't get you fired, you'll be busted to writing traffic tickets in Hegewisch."

Fenwick said, "You're upset. I got that part. So do all the patrons in this place. Anything else?"

As their food arrived, Palakowski plunked himself next to

Fenwick. As the detective bulked large, the Commander's butt flopped half off the bench. Palakowski rammed both elbows onto the table. Fenwick shook drops of hot sauce onto his meatloaf.

Turner looked up. The waitress held a container of coffee. She raised an eyebrow at them. Turner gave a slight shake of his head. He noted the rest of the patrons. The place was crowded since it was Saturday lunch in Chicago. A few cops in uniform stared blatantly. The rest ignored them.

Palakowski lowered his voice to a whisper which Turner thought he might be trying to make menacing, but came across more of a whistle from a teakettle well past its prime.

"I know what you did to Blawn on that rooftop the night of the murder."

"And yet this is the first we've heard about it," Fenwick said. He looked at Turner. "I find that odd."

Turner said, "Normal protocol is for a complaint to be filed and an investigation to be held. And yet, you're here in what strikes me as an unofficial capacity."

Palakowski sneered at Turner. "I expect you to cover for him."

"Cover that some asshole beat cop turned traitor on a couple of detectives? I thought the Code of Silence worked in favor of cops. Or are there sides of silence?"

"Fuck you, asshole. You'll be in as much trouble as your fat partner."

Fenwick said, "Yet, it's our word against your guy."

Palakowski pointed at Turner. "He just admitted it."

"You wearing a wire?" Fenwick asked. "I doubt it. Wires have to be made official, and if it involves cops, has to go through the Internal Review Authority, and you haven't had time for that. You'd have had to talk it over with Molton, and we'd have heard about it. Did you or your beat cop file paperwork or an official complaint?"

Neither detective was about to tell him about Fong's jamming devices they wore.

Palakowski looked down.

Turner asked, "Are you part of covering for Carruthers and why?"

"Fuck you." Palakowski stood up.

"How'd you find us here?" Fenwick asked.

Turner said, "Why would you be having us followed? How are you connected to all the cover ups?"

Palakowski put his fists on their table, leaned close, and rasped, "You two have no idea the forces you're dealing with." He whirled around, stood up, and twisted into a passing member of the wait staff. The resulting tumult of broken crockery drew the attention of all of the patrons. Palakowski stomped off.

After Palakowski was gone, Fenwick tasted his food then added more hot sauce. He looked at Turner. "That was bullshit."

"Yep."

"He's in on the cover up."

"Yep."

"We don't have to talk to Blawn or Arnold. We know they came from Palakowski."

"Two less assholes."

"Either one of them trying to kill us?"

Turner drew a deep breath, took a bite, and sipped coffee. He said, "His minions, no, but Palakowski has now moved to among the top suspects. We've got to find out who his clout is. Doesn't anybody move up in this department on merit?"

"How long have you worked here?"

"Sorry. Too long to be asking a question like that."

"We're in deep," Fenwick said.

"Hope we get out of it."

"I intend to, and if I don't, a whole lot of people are going down with me."

Saturday 2:15 P.M.

When they got outside, the gloom of the day had increased. Bits of misty raindrops, blasted by the wind, blew against them.

In the car, Turner said, "Let's start with the beat cop on guard in the hall. There must be a straight path from that guy to whoever is running things."

Fenwick shook his head. "It won't be a straight path. There will be layers of protection on this. Layers of deniability. Guy we want is this Officer Bruce Deaton from my room and DeShawn's."

Turner put on their siren and started the Mars lights rotating.

With the light Saturday traffic and bells and whistles clanging, they roared faster than usual down the Dan Ryan to 111th Street and headed west.

It was a typical Chicago bungalow. The cop answered the door. He wore madras shorts and a too tight T-shirt.

Fenwick said, "We need to talk to you."

Deaton growled, "Get the fuck away from my door." He reached back to grab it. Fenwick guessed quicker than Turner that he planned to slam it in their faces.

Fenwick kicked the door as it swung toward them. It flew backward and bashed against the wall.

Fenwick marched in. Turner followed. They stood in a short hall.

Deaton said, "Fuck you guys. You're toast."

Fenwick said, “Not according to the Superintendent.”

Deaton looked confused.

Fenwick went on. “We just met with him at the station. He seemed pretty supportive.”

Turner asked, “Who told you to spy on us?”

“Molton.”

Fenwick sneered, “Bullshit.”

Turner said, “Why would you tell us such an easily disprovable lie? Why bother?”

No one else had appeared in the hallway behind the cop. The home had decent air conditioning.

Fenwick said, “You are going to answer questions. We can do a great big showy arrest. We might even throw in one of those stupid perp walks the press loves.”

“You can’t arrest me.”

“But we can make it look like it.”

“And your career will be shit.”

“You’re part of trying to make ours shit only drip by drip. If we’re going to make it shit, we’re going to have one great flood of shit, a great big splashy flood of shit.”

“That’s disgusting.”

“But amazingly enough, not as disgusting as you.”

Deaton took out his phone. Fenwick grabbed it. “No phone calls.”

“If I’m under arrest, I get a call.”

Fenwick laughed. “Does this look like a normal situation to you?”

Turner said, “If you’re so confident of your positions and your support, why don’t you answer our questions? If we’re so friendless, what have you got to lose? And if we have support, and your side might be the ones to lose, shouldn’t you get out in front of all this and try to save your butt and even at this late date, show that you’re on our side?"

Deaton shrugged, "Fuck it. We were all just talking."

"We who?" Turner asked.

"The guys in the locker room before the shift. Most of us don't know Carruthers, but he was one of us. You can't be Tasing your own."

Fenwick lost it. "He was shooting at us, you numb nuts dumb fuck! Are you suggesting we should have just stood there! Are you the most brain dead person on the south side?"

"It was just us guys talking."

Turner said, "There wasn't an organized conspiracy? There wasn't one guy taking the lead?"

Deaton shook his head.

They left.

In the car, Fenwick said, "It's all bullshit about that locker room crap. Somebody gave him direct orders. How stupid does he think we are?"

Turner said, "They've all lied their way out of so much."

Fenwick remained in high dudgeon. "Bullshit, bullshit, bullshit."

Turner said, "If he knows who is next higher up in the anti-us conspiracy, he's calling him right now. They're all going to be expecting us."

"Maybe they'll bake a cake. Or hell, we can go in with guns blazing. We keep going, or we give up and go home and wait for the end."

"You ready to give up?"

Fenwick shook his head.

Turner gripped the steering wheel. "Who's next?"

Saturday 3:15 P.M.

The light rain had stopped. Clouds still loomed above. The wind howled.

Back in the Loop they stopped at the extraordinarily plush Chicago Extravaganza Hotel on State Street. In the lobby, they took note of the high-end furnishings, the waterfall, and the glass-enclosed elevators that went up fifty floors.

This was the headquarters of Danny Currington, the protester infiltrator for the 1%. He had a suite on the top floor.

They showed their badges and were brought to the office of the head of security. He cooperated completely without the slightest hesitation. Turner found this refreshing. He gave them Danny Currington's room number and wished them well. In the elevator, as they hit the fiftieth floor, Turner glanced down and asked, "What do they do with guests who're afraid of heights?"

Fenwick said, "Take them out and shoot them?"

They knocked at the door.

Fenwick asked the man who answered, "You Danny Currington?"

"How did you get up here past security?"

They held out badges. Currington made a show of inspecting each one then opened the door wide.

They walked in. Adam Edberg from the Mayor's office sat on a couch next to a man they didn't know.

Edberg stood up. He said, "I'm out of here." Without another word, he walked out.

Currington nodded toward the other man, “This is Chris Randall from the FBI. What can we do for you gentlemen?”

“What was Edberg doing here?”

“Liaising from the mayor’s office.”

“The mayor’s office is in charge of infiltrating?”

Randall spoke up. “We’re all interested in keeping terrorists from taking over the city.”

Fenwick went to the window and gazed down at the streets below. He said, “I see six terrorists running up State Street right now. Shouldn’t you be on it? Or them? Or maybe they’re hurrying to go shopping before the storms hit?”

“You joke about terrorists?”

“I’m not a right-wing propagandist. I believe in dealing with facts. Are you saying, in fact, there is a terrorist plot to take over the government of the City of Chicago? Are you delusional? How would they do that? Why? What difference would it make if they sat in the mayor’s office? Or they took over the city council chamber?”

“The city would look ridiculous.”

Turner said, “You’re supposed to be ferreting out plots. My guess is you’re still looking for cells willing to set off bombs and kill somebody. You find any of those with those protesters out there?”

“Not so far.”

“Who’s in charge of all this?”

They both sat silent.

Fenwick said, “You don’t know who your boss is? You don’t know who you report to?”

Currington said, “My bosses are not part of the city employees.”

Fenwick said to Randall, “And you report to your superior at the FBI. Who is that?”

“I’m sure if you check with the local office, they’d be happy to talk to you. We are not answerable to you.”

Fenwick asked, "You learned anything about the killing of the two protesters?"

Randall said, "No, just another example of Chicago violence run amok, your inability to protect your own citizens."

"Why does the 1% have a rep here?" Fenwick asked.

"I don't remember saying who my employer is."

"Any of you guys or the organizations you represent have people going around the tent city pretending to be detectives investigating the murders?"

They got nothing from them.

Saturday 3:49 P.M.

In the car, Fenwick said, "Assholes."

"Who's next?"

"The friendly State's Attorney."

Up Lake Shore Drive, the wind buffeted the car.

Turner had set up a meeting with Robert Cardin, the State's Attorney they both knew. They'd worked with him before. He'd been helpful and friendly in a number of cases.

They met in a darkened pub on the far north side of the city, on Howard Street a few blocks west of Sheridan Road. They were only a few feet from Evanston.

Robert Cardin was short and thin. When the cops entered, he raised a finger. Turner caught the movement. Cardin led them to a back booth.

He said, "I shouldn't be meeting you. I shouldn't have agreed to this."

Fenwick asked, "Carruthers is worth all these careers?"

Cardin glanced around the room, wrung his hands, leaned forward, and whispered. "You want to draw attention to yourselves, I don't give a shit. I've got a wife, kids, and a mortgage."

"You've helped us before."

"Not with something this big."

"What is it about Carruthers?" Fenwick asked.

Cardin's voice was an exasperated whisper. "Jesus, you guys are dumb. You think this is about Carruthers? Hell, I heard he was going to use the 'delusional disorder' defense."

"He is that," Fenwick said.

"You've heard of it?"

The detectives nodded.

"Probably his only chance of winning," Cardin said.

Fenwick said, "The video shows he was in the wrong."

"They'll have experts trying to turn that into a third-rate horror film." He leaned close to the table. "The silence on this one is complete. Complete. No one knows anything. We've all been told to mind our own business, and as far as I know, that was before anyone asked any questions." Cardin gulped, ran his finger under his collar. "I've always thought I could trust you."

"Yes," Turner said.

"No matter whose name is on the paperwork for Carruthers cases, only one guy ever handled them, Brandon Smeek."

Fenwick asked, "Who's Smeek, and what's his game? Why would he stick his neck out for Carruthers?"

"I've already stuck my own neck out too far."

"How do you know about him?" Turner asked.

"One of them was my case. I was going through some filing, and I found the name change. I took it to my immediate supervisor and brought it to her attention." He shook his head. "Just for noticing, I did bullshit in Hegewisch for two years. I was told to forget it. That it was a mistake. I certainly did that. Until today."

He sipped his beer, ran his gaze around the room, then said, "You ask what this is about? You know what it's about. They've all been lying for years. All the lies are going to come out. Normally, the low level cops who get caught lying on forms are the only ones who are fired. This time, it has to involve the higher ups. They're all going to lose their jobs. Maybe their pensions."

"Who is going after the higher ups?"

"I'm not sure. Most likely is the office of the U.S. Attorney for the Northern District of Illinois."

"The people protecting Carruthers don't have friends there as well?" Fenwick asked.

"I don't know who has friends anywhere any more. I gotta go. This is too much. You won't say anything, please?" Cardin leaned over the table. "I wish you guys all the best of luck, but frankly, I think you'll be lucky to be alive in a few weeks. If you try to talk to Brandon Smeek, you won't last the week." He scuttled out.

Saturday 4:22 P.M.

In the car, Fenwick said, "He's frightened out of his mind."

Turner said, "How about this for a notion? The ones who aren't frightened are the ones who are behind it all."

State's Attorney Brandon Smeek was at home on Lake Shore Drive just south of Fullerton. The wind howled through the canyons between the buildings. Smeek lived on the fifth floor of a century old, five-story luxury condo building. The detectives entered. The walls were all dark wood with framed paintings exquisitely lit. No outside noises filtered in. The air-conditioning was perfect.

They identified themselves. Smeek didn't seem surprised to see them.

He led them to chairs, offered them drinks. The detectives declined. He poured himself a finger of Scotch from a cut-glass crystal decanter into a cut-glass crystal tumbler. From his seat, Turner could see across the street to Lincoln Park. The tops of trees twisted and swayed in the harsh wind.

Turner said, "We're here about Carruthers."

Smeek said, "And you're both heroes. How far do you think that's going to get you?"

Fenwick said, "About as far as you trying to change the subject."

"Yeah, you want to get Carruthers."

"Just following the case. Carruthers's complaint cases got assigned to one guy in the department, Ken Coscarelli. The ones that all just disappeared or got buried or went nowhere."

"You two have been running around making fools of yourselves. You've got a case. Two dead protestors. And you've got Carruthers having problems which is not up to you to investigate." He looked at the two of them. "Wait a second. What the hell is going on here? You think these are connected? You think that top cops planned the killing of two activists? You think State's Attorneys are afraid of a few protesters? And then somehow before all that happened Carruthers, what? Took potshots at you. You guys are nuts."

"We haven't completely figured out how the two incidents are connected," Turner said, "Right now, we're just following the facts."

"Whose facts? Don't you know we're living in a post-fact world?"

"I'm not," Fenwick said. "So right now, you need to talk to us."

"No, I don't. You have no idea what you're doing."

"Why don't you tell us?" Fenwick said.

Smeek's smile held more sneer than humor. Smeek sipped his drink. It was at moments like this that Turner wished he was a violent person. If he was, he'd bash the glass out of the man's hands and enjoy wiping the smirk off his face.

Smeek said, "Tell you? As you wish. Since your buddy Rodriguez was Carruthers's partner on most of these cases, they were in it together. If Carruthers goes down, your buddy goes down."

"Rodriguez doesn't have the complaints against him that Carruthers does."

"Carruthers doesn't have complaints." He looked at them with another smirk.

Turner said, "We have all the original complaints."

Smeek snapped, "Those shouldn't exist."

"Ah, but they do," Fenwick said. "You the one that made all those complaints disappear?"

"Don't be absurd."

Turner said, "You had help. DeGroot for one. You must have

been colluding. Why is Carruthers worth so much that you're willing to lie and risk your career?"

Fenwick added, "Why keep up with this Code of Silence for such a dumb fuck?"

Smeek's sneer didn't waver. "It's just peers protecting peers, which you should have learned long ago."

Fenwick said, "One thing I don't get, if peers are supposed to be protecting peers, why the fuck aren't they rushing to silent-up on our side? Why be on Carruthers side?"

"By saving the kid and Tasering Carruthers, you broke the Code of Silence."

Fenwick held out his wounded arm. "He didn't miss by much. It was only luck that kept me alive."

Smeek leaned forward and rapped his knuckles on the table top. "You guys are lucky you have your jobs. Your boss Molton will be losing his soon."

"All for a Code of Silence to protect what?" Fenwick demanded. "What are you all gaining by this bullshit?"

Smeek stood up. "Good to see you. Goodbye."

Saturday 5:17 P.M.

In the car, Turner said, "I hate arrogance."

Fenwick gave him a long look. "I'm usually the one who bitches."

"Maybe it's just the one who's driving. This is the first time I've done it in a while."

"Vehicular slander? No, that's not right. Vehicular defamation?"

Turner said, "Vehicular pissed off."

"Then you may be right, it could be the driving part of this, if that is the correct medical term."

Since they were close by, they stopped at the new cardinal's residence. They didn't get past the secretary who told them he'd be glad to make them an appointment for when the cardinal was back from Rome. Not catching people at home was one of the banes of their existence. Sometimes, they were lucky. Sometimes, they weren't.

Back in the car, Turner asked, "Next?"

"Ken Coscarelli, the guy in the department helping make Carruthers's cases disappear."

Their call was sent to voice mail.

"Now who?" Turner asked.

"Griffin."

"As the assistant Chief of Detectives, he'll know we've seen the Superintendent."

"How?"

"Would we have the nerve to show up if we didn't have high clearance?"

Fenwick asked, "Has he met me?"

"He'll know," Turner insisted. "And you have met him. Numerous times."

Fenwick grumbled, "Yeah, you're right."

By now, it was nearly five, but the traffic wasn't bad on a Saturday. The sky had completely clouded over. The wind still blew at gale force.

Griffin lived on the far north side in a house just short of a mansion in the flight path from O'Hare. His wife answered the door and led them to the back garden where Griffin was on his knees pulling weeds.

The assistant Chief of Detectives peered up at them and said, "This is the best time to do gardening, when the ground is damp. Weeds come right up by the roots."

He stuck a trowel into the ground, stood up, and brushed dirt off his knees. He wore a Chicago White Sox sleeveless t-shirt, a Chicago Bulls pair of long shorts, and flip flops. He took a long guzzle from a can of beer, put it down, wiped sweat from his forehead.

He did not offer them a seat or a beverage. He said, "If you had the nerve to come here, it means you've got Molton's support, and my guess is you've been off to tattle to the Superintendent as well."

Turner said, "He's been to the station."

"Good for him, paying his respects to his newest heroes."

Fenwick asked, "How did all the complaints against Carruthers disappear?"

Griffin said, "I'm not in charge of complaints."

"You're in charge of all the detectives in the CPD. Every complaint against us crosses your desk."

"I don't remember any against Carruthers."

Fenwick said, "We checked. He had more than any other detective who works under you."

"If they've all been erased, how could you check?" He gave a rollicking sneer.

"You think Area Ten doesn't keep records?"

"Molton did that?"

"We have duplicates of everything. In the station, 97 complaints. In his official file with the department, you're right, none. How long did you think you'd get away with that?"

"Someone obviously did. What's the date for your first complaint?"

Fenwick asked, "Why is that important? They've gotten away with this for years. You're disputing the Area Ten records?"

Griffin said, "I can just as easily dispute yours. You said somebody erased. I say somebody added."

"For years?" Turner asked. "Why bother making stuff up for that long a time?"

Griffin sneered. "Don't you think every one of your questions works both ways?"

Fenwick said, "Not in a reality-based world."

But Griffin would give them nothing further. He drank more beer, knelt to his weeding, and waved them goodbye.

Saturday 5:51 P.M.

They'd been rushing about the city all afternoon in a car that felt more like it was trying to move the humidity out of their way, like a snowplow in winter trying to plow through a drift. Even in the air-conditioned car, Fenwick sweated. The clouds in the west were continuing to darken. Weather radar showed a continuous line of storms forming along the Mississippi River and moving slowly east.

Fenwick banged his hand on the door handle. "Who did call about getting us assigned to the case?"

Turner pulled onto Lakeshore Drive. He glanced at his partner then back to the road. He said, "There was no such call."

Fenwick said, "Double fuck."

They each mused in silence for a moment. Fenwick thumped his door handle again. "You gotta be right."

"Simplest thing in the world. Why would Molton question the assistant Chief of Detectives? He'd just assign us like the good employee he is." Turner pulled around a van swaying because of the wind. "And if it is one vast conspiracy, why not then assume, when Carruthers misses us on the street, and they move onto another crazed notion."

Turner's phone binged with a text. He handed it to Fenwick who read it. "Fong says he's got one more thing. No details. Asks us to meet him," he paused and looked, "not in the station. Says there's a coffee shop at Harrison and Devon."

Turner nodded. "Yeah, Harriet's."

Sometimes, if Fong was in a secretive mood, or the thought he had something really incriminating or just a major oddity, he asked to meet off site. It was a quirk they mostly endured with equanimity. And he'd been a big help in this case and many others. They were quite willing to be as indulgent as they needed to be.

Turner headed over.

Wind buffeted the car. Turner wished the storm would get it over with.

Harriet's had a low ceiling and a long row of booths along one wall that stretched nearly half a block. Fong was in the last one, far back. Each booth had a sconce, some of which had light bulbs and a few of which were working. The one at Fong's booth was not.

His lap top was open and plugged into the wall. In the light from his monitor, he looked like the just beginning stage of a horror movie transformation from human to not-human. He shoulders were slumped. He seemed to sag in his seat.

"What's wrong?" Turner asked.

For an answer, Fong pressed a key on the computer and turned the monitor to them. A Chicago street scene in daylight began to unfold.

Turner and Fenwick watched. First, it showed DeShawn Jackson running by. Then it showed Carruthers shouting. Fong had the sound turned low so they had to lean close to hear. Carruthers wasn't waving his gun. He was alternately listening to his phone and then screaming. The rest of the video showed Carruthers moving a few feet away from his car. He bellowed at the kid. Then he brought up his gun.

Fenwick said, "So what? We know what he did."

Fong said, "This is the video from the missing dash cams. I've synced it with all the other dash cams and videos. Now watch." He pressed a few keys. Three images appeared on his monitor.

The same scene unrolled but now from several points of view. Fong put it on half speed. Again, it was a record from the moment DeShawn first ran past, to Carruthers beginning to fire. The last frame showed Carruthers taking his first shot. Fong froze it at that point and said, "You see it? He waited for you guys. He didn't raise his gun until you guys turned that corner. He wasn't going to shoot until you got there."

Turner said, "It couldn't be bad timing? Odd timing? Coincidence?" He shook his head. "None of us believes in coincidences."

Fenwick said, "The whole DeShawn thing was set up to kill us?"

They both sat back.

"Want to see it again?" Fong asked.

Fenwick said, "I want to learn about the slowest way to kill a person, and then I want to find a way to prolong that."

Fong said, "Torture doesn't work."

Fenwick said, "You misunderstand. I don't want to torture Carruthers for information. I want to torture him to inflict pain. Pain up to the point to just before he'd be dead. Then I want to leave him like that in some dark basement until he is starving and dying of thirst. Then I want to torture him again, and then send a million jolts of electricity through his body until it is fried into an unrecognizable pile of ashes."

They sat in silence for several moments.

Fenwick said, "Or a bus."

Turner sighed. He knew the reference. Fenwick loved stupid comedy movies. One of the scenes his partner loved most was when they included an illogical and gratuitous appearance of a bus running over a character. Fenwick thought the 'bus' bits in the movie "The Comebacks" were among the best humor moments in cinematic history. Turner could never figure out how much competition there really was for buses gratuitously running over characters. He didn't ask Fenwick. He feared his partner might know the answer. Sort of like Groucho Marx telling a character to, "Walk this way," in so many movies.

Instead of responding to the irrelevancy, Turner asked Fong, "How'd you put this together?"

"Barb Dams and I have been working the secretaries and techno people networks. I have friends. She has friends. Somebody was trying to suppress some of these."

"Who?" Fenwick asked. "They're next on my list after I'm done with Carruthers."

"Don't know that yet. I'm working on it."

Turner said, "He had no idea he was being filmed?"

Fong said, "He was crazy or desperate enough to take the risk. Or thought his clout was powerful enough to protect him from a murder charge."

Both detectives sat silent, their eyes going from the screen, frozen on Carruthers's first shot, to each other, to Fong, to the middle distance.

Fong said, "I've made copies. I've sent them to you, Dams, and Molton. I have people on the Net waiting for word from me or you guys to have them go viral."

Turner said, "We gotta think."

Fong yawned and shook his head.

Turner asked, "Have you slept?"

"I know I did once."

"You should head home."

"Yeah."

After another round of profuse thanks, they left.

They drove to the station.

Turner said, "Somebody knew these existed, had access to them, tried to hide them, didn't have enough savvy to keep them hidden."

"Any number of possibilities."

"We never talked to DeGroot today. Anybody else we missed?"

"The entire level of brass downtown?"

Turner nodded glumly. Raindrops splattered the windshield for a minute then stopped.

At the station, they trudged in silence up the stairs to their desks. To Turner, Fenwick looked like a bulldozer snarling at a starting line, waiting to be released upon the unsuspecting world. He felt the weight of the afternoon they'd spent listening to lies, evasions, half truths. Frustration and anger ate at his soul.

On the way to their desks, Turner stopped in the washroom as Fenwick continued on.

Turner heard the door open. He concentrated on his business at the urinal. Someone shoved him hard into the wall. Between getting himself put together, zipping up, and trying to keep his balance, he tipped and began to fall.

He heard a clink and was shoved around with a handcuff on one wrist and the other end attached to a silent and clammy pipe.

He got a look at his attacker.

Carruthers.

Saturday 6:30 P.M.

"Go ahead," Carruthers shrieked. "Call for help. I can kill you now or get a few things off my chest and kill you then. Your goddamn perfect kids and your goddamn shove-it-up-your-ass husband will all be sobbing because you're gone. They'll all be sobbing by morning."

Turner shook his head. "Why is making my kids and my husband miserable so important to you?"

"You've made me miserable."

"So why punish them?"

"I want to punish you and anything you've ever touched."

"But I'll be dead. How would I be punished?"

"Just content yourself with being dead."

Turner didn't bother to debate this bit of illogic. He said, "I'll do my best."

Carruthers said, "And your goddamn obese pig partner. I may kill him, too."

"You do know there is no possible way for you to get away with this?"

Carruthers chuckled then said, "I came to finish the job."

"What job?"

"We've wanted you dead for a very long time."

"Who is we?"

Turner edged his butt so his body was in a more comfortable sitting position.

Carruthers gave him a smile that revealed yellow teeth. Turner had never noticed them before. Had he ever seen Carruthers smile? At the moment, he wasn't sure, and he knew that he didn't care.

Carruthers reached over and turned the lock at the top of the restroom's aged door.

Someone would notice it was locked and get a janitor to open it. He hoped. Or Barb Dams had a key.

Carruthers said, "I know you don't think I have friends."

"Why does what I think matter?"

Carruthers snorted. "Fuck you."

"You couldn't have planned all this yourself."

"I'm too stupid, as you all have pointed out for years." He let go a grimace that showed just a small line of his yellow teeth. "You guys have been right about that, I suppose. No one would believe I'd planned all this. No, people far above me, who you will never be able to touch, took care of all this. They let me help." He shook his head. "I wasn't even very good at that. Once I failed that first time, I know they abandoned me."

"That first one wasn't well thought out."

"Sure, protestors around, a frightened kid running around, and you accidentally caught in the crossfire. It was perfect. I knew your every move. We knew your every move. It isn't only Fong that can do electronic shit. I got excited. I missed." He sighed. "They've abandoned me since then. All of them. It's hopeless."

Carruthers paced and waved his gun around then aimed it at Turner. Whether pacing or in the rare moments of stillness, the gun and the hand he held it with wobbled, trembled, and shook.

"If they break the door in, I'll shoot."

"I'm not sure anybody knows I'm missing yet."

"They'll figure it out."

"I thought you came to shoot me. If that's true, what difference does it make to you if the door is broken in. You didn't think you were going to be able to get away with murder inside a police station?"

Carruthers actually stopped pacing.

Turner said, "You've gotten away with everything else, so you thought you could get away with this?"

"Does getting away with anything matter anymore?"

Turner asked, "Why did you want to talk to me in the station after the shooting in the street?"

"I wanted to see how lost you were to the Code of Silence. How lost you were to doing right by your fellow cops." He gave his grating laugh. "I wanted to fuck with your mind."

"For what purpose?"

"Because I may be stupid and inept, but maybe I could do that."

Turner's hands gripped the pipe he was attached to. His eyes stayed on Carruthers's gun hand, but his mind whirled. Thoughts of his husband and his sons raced through his mind. Is this what people thought of as their lives flashing before them? He thought of the first time he'd held each of his sons after they were born. He shook his head to bring himself back to the present.

Carruthers leaned his body against the opposite wall and let himself slide to the floor.

Turner watched the slow motion plop.

Carruthers's hand with the gun landed on the floor with a slight click. For the first time, gun and hand didn't wobble. Carruthers looked down at it for a second.

Turner bunched his muscles for a lunge.

Carruthers raised the gun. His hand no longer trembled. He said, "My guess is if you tried lunging at me, you'd wind up about six inches short. And anyway, I can maneuver and you can't."

Turner leaned his back against the wall. It dripped from humidity. Water soaked into the back of his shirt.

Turner mused idly that he'd never seen the old dump from this angle. And despite Molton's strict orders on cleanliness, he could see bits of dirt in the grout that separated the yellowing tiles.

Carruthers said, "You know that kid you saved has a juvenile record."

Turner thought for a moment, "You couldn't have known that at the time of the shooting. How do you know it now?"

"They all do."

Turner didn't bother to ask, they who? Didn't matter. Just as long as you were a member of any group that Carruthers was prejudiced against, you were a 'they'.

Turner asked, "Why would it make a difference?"

"It makes me look like a good guy, trying to rid the city of one more piece of vermin."

"We've seen video of you not raising your gun until we came around that corner. You were waiting for us. You were planning murder."

"There is no such video."

Turner said, "Reality was never your strong suit."

"We've been planning to get you for a long time. Once you had that video showing I'd given solid information to the Catholic Church, we knew you had to go."

"But I only showed you after you shot Fenwick."

Carruthers's laugh came out more as a cackle. "What I knew and when I knew it, is of no concern to you."

Turner asked, "You planned murder?"

"I have friends."

"Randy, did you ever think that the scheme was awfully convoluted? That maybe they didn't care if you lived or died?

"You're the only one who ever calls me by my name, Randy."

Turner had never thought about that.

Turner asked, "What can I do to help?"

After the initial shriek at him, Carruthers's voice had returned to a normal level. He said, "Help? Are you mad? Unless you choose to die, there's nothing you can do to help."

"How'd you even get into the station?"

"I still have friends and supporters here."

"No, Randy, they are not your friends or supporters. A few people have a twisted notion of loyalty that somehow redounds to your benefit, but if I were you, I wouldn't make the mistake of calling them friends."

"You and your fat friend have always tried to make my life harder."

"Randy, we barely think about you, but your betrayal of us to the church went beyond all bounds."

"You were going to try and get me fired."

"Your sense of loyalty seems twisted."

"I'll be protected."

"Randy, you're going to get fired. You're going to lose your pension. It's all over. How is doing what you're doing now, and killing me going to get all that back for you?"

"I don't want it back. I want you dead. All these years, you've been the one, hiding behind your kindness and politeness. You were worse than the ones who actively worked against me."

"What does killing me gain you?"

"Satisfaction."

"Is there really that much satisfaction in seeing someone dead? We've found videos of you torturing people. They are on those dark web police sites. We spent the afternoon talking to your supposed friends. Have any of them called to report to you? Have any of them taken one of your calls in the past few days?"

Carruthers whispered, "No."

"Randy, they're cutting you loose. They're just going to try to save their own jobs and pensions. They no longer care that you exist."

Someone rattled the doorknob to the room. Turner heard a voice he didn't recognize say, "This fucking door is never locked."

Carruthers yelled, "Get away from the damn door."

"Who the hell is in there?"

Carruthers bellowed, "I'm going to kill him."

Silence from the other side of the door then rapid footsteps away and moments later the sound of many footsteps approaching.

Fenwick's voice bellowed, "Open the goddamn door."

Carruthers fired a shot into the ceiling. Bits of plaster hit the floor.

Silence now from outside the door.

Then Molton's voice came, "Randy, is that you?"

Carruthers screamed, "Fuck you all to hell." He raised the gun and placed the muzzle in his mouth. Before Turner could move or speak, he fired.

Turner remembered the next few seconds as small bits of eternity dripping by. He noted the silence. Even the distant noise of the city that leaked through the opaque window that looked out on the alley was absent. He smelled gunpowder from the two shots.

Spots and splatters of gray, maroon mush, remnants of Carruthers's brain were scattered on the wall behind his head.

As he watched, Carruthers's hand dropped to the floor. The gun skittered a few feet away from him. His body toppled to the right and flopped onto the floor.

Turner became aware of shouts and rumbles from the other side of the door.

In one titanic crash, all of Fenwick burst into the room. Molton and Dams followed.

Turner felt blood drip onto his hand.

He looked. Put his hand to his chin to a stinging sensation. When he drew his hand away, he saw blood.

"Did he!" Fenwick bellowed.

Turner pointed to the floor behind Fenwick. The hefty detective turned. He stopped and said, "Oh."

Saturday 7:17 P.M.

With no shirt on, Turner sat at his desk. His elbows were propped on the top of the paperwork. His head resting on his fists as he faced Fenwick. Molton, Dams, Rodriguez, Wilson, and Roosevelt, and half the staff clustered around.

He listened to their murmured assurances and good wishes. He'd washed off his own blood from the cuts he'd gotten when Carruthers had surprised him at the urinal and banged him around for a few seconds.

Fenwick's arm wound had reopened from his spectacular crash through the door. He had a few drops of blood on his arm. He ignored them.

Dams brought Turner her special hot chocolate normally saved for winter mornings. Turner found it comforting. Eventually, the rest of the staff moved away.

Fenwick said, "You want to go home?"

"Not yet. We've got a million things to do here, not the least of which is reporting this to everyone and sundry."

One of the things that took longest was getting Fong and camera equipment up to the washroom. Turner had to endure extra minutes of confinement as Molton insisted every inch of everything in the washroom be recorded. He was not going to let Carruthers's suicide be twisted into anything but what it was.

"Want to talk about it?" Fenwick asked.

Turner thought of the gray and red bits of Carruthers's brain and blood dripping down the wall. He shook his head, "This is going to take a while."

That sat in silence. Dams brought him another shirt. He put it on. It draped over his frame and hung nearly to his knees. She smiled, "I could only find one of Fenwick's. Sorry."

As he put it on, he said, "It's perfect." He didn't bother to button it up, but let it drape over his shoulders.

She left them. Turner heard the rumble of distant thunder.

Fenwick asked, "Did he come to commit suicide, kill you, kill both of us?"

"He made threats against you and me."

"Did he come at someone's behest to kill you or us?"

"A behesting?"

Fenwick said, "Need I remind you, even at such a time as this, that I am the failed humor guy in this relationship?"

"Often as possible, although it is impossible to forget that you think you're funny."

Fenwick said, "Somebody ordered him to come in here and kill?"

"Who would trust him with that knowledge? That person would be vulnerable to Carruthers's blabbing, at the very least be in Carruthers's power."

"Not a good place to be."

"We wouldn't trust him."

Fenwick said, "Unless he's expendable. Maybe whoever is behind all this wanted to get rid of him."

"Or maybe Carruthers was just fucking nuts and stupid. And desperate."

Fenwick said, "He couldn't have killed the two activists, so we still have that to solve."

Turner nodded. "Yeah."

Fenwick asked, "No hint on who was behind him?"

"I have no idea. Not specifically." Turner scratched the thick mat of hair on his chest.

Fenwick asked, "Who could push him to kill?"

Turner said, "Someone who had power over him. Someone who was protecting him. Someone close to him."

"His wife?"

"Why would she want me dead? I don't know her. Not in any significant way."

Fenwick said, "She was married to him. How can you marry something that stupid and not be just as stupid?"

"Maybe she loved him. Somebody must."

"His mother might have."

"I've heard that happens a lot."

"His clout?" Fenwick asked.

Turner said, "We spent the past few days with a few members of the upper echelons of the Chicago police department. If we were in front of the person who was behind all this, why didn't they kill us then? The obvious answer is if Carruthers kills me or us, that person has deniability. If Carruthers kills himself, before or after doing either of us in, that person may feel themselves home free."

"So, it's over with Carruthers being dead?" Fenwick asked.

"I guess. I suppose. I hope. Although that doesn't solve the murders of Shaitan and Bettencourt."

Fenwick yawned. "I'm trying hard to care."

Molton joined them at their desks. He pulled up a fan and a chair.

"Guys from downtown gone?" Fenwick asked.

"For now."

"You've done everything you could to protect us."

Molton said, "You guys should call it day. There's no more to be done now. Go home."

The detectives nodded.

As Turner got in his car, his phone buzzed. It was a text from Ian. It asked to meet him at Nick's Coffee Shop, the same place he'd met Mrs. Carruthers.

Turner sighed, mulled, and sent, "Yes."

Saturday 7:30 P.M.

It began to rain as Turner strode along the river walk to Nick's door. He got a hot chocolate, didn't see Ian, and walked to a booth in the back. A few customers dotted the interior. He checked his phone, but there were no new messages. He checked weather radar. Storms stretched from the city west to Iowa. The reds, oranges, and yellows indicating the strongest storms were still far to the west, training in a line aimed directly at the center of the city. He hoped to be home before the worst hit.

Five minutes later, Ian walked in. Turner watched Ian thwap his hat against this thigh to knock water off of it. He purchased a beverage, spotted Turner, and headed back.

Ian sat, said, "Hi."

Turner said, "So what's happened that we had to meet?"

"I haven't been idle. When I figured out during our talk this morning that the two cases were connected, I've been asking questions. I heard you were pursuing the DeShawn case. Is Carruthers really dead?"

"Really, really dead."

"Good. But you have bashed a hornet's nest. I caught a whiff of this a few hours ago. My sources, not solid yet, say each of the people you've talked to has sounded the alarm."

"We started with the Superintendent."

"My sources say he is not to be trusted."

"Who is your source and don't you dare try to hide behind the Constitution. You've screwed up. There's more payment still to be made for that."

"Someone in the assistant Chief of Detectives Griffin's office confirmed by a source in State's Attorney Smeek's office."

Turner asked, "You didn't think to ask these sources before this?"

"No. I was concentrating on the Shaitan and Bettencourt murders, so I was looking into the protesters. I wanted to find out who killed them before you did, so I'd be off the hook. Then this morning, I realized the focus changed or maybe the events overlapped. So I worked other sources, and I got this."

Turner said, "Who is to say that your sources aren't trying to protect their asses and deflect suspicion to the Superintendent?"

That stopped Ian.

Turner said, "So according to your information, the command structure is completely behind this."

Ian said, "I hate to add, but I can't confirm, Molton might be in on this, too."

Turner shook his head, "If Molton was with them, or they could trust him, they wouldn't need all these elaborate lies and deceptions."

Ian nodded agreement then said, "They plan to do everything they can starting Monday to destroy you and Fenwick."

"Well, hurray for them."

"Can you stop them?"

"I have no idea."

Before they stepped out into the downpour, Ian said, "I hope to have your forgiveness someday."

Turner said, "I hope to be able to give it to you."

In his car, he texted Fenwick who was stuck in traffic on the Kennedy. He'd moved a half mile in the past fifteen minutes. Turner gave him the news.

Fenwick said, "Double and triple and quadruple and forever

fuck."

Turner said, "Yeah."

Turner's phone beeped with a text. He asked Fenwick to hold on. The text was from Fong. It said, "Just left Harriet's. Gotta talk to u." Again no details. "At El station at Devon. Will wait." Turner knew Fong always took public transportation to and from work.

He switched back to Fenwick who said, "I'll come back. I'll call the station with all this while you get over to Fong."

Turner took Halsted up to Harrison turned left and headed over to Devon.

As he drove, the rain picked up. The wind howled. The one pedestrian he saw had an umbrella turn inside out. After a few seconds of struggle, the man was turned completely around. He abandoned the umbrella to the wind.

Thunder and lightning flashed and crashed.

Turner parked in the bus stop at the apex of the bridge. He took out his red Mars light from under the front seat, pushed the button to lower the window. Rain poured in and soaked his arm, the door, and the frame. He stuck the Mars light on the roof of the car, pulled his hand in, and pushed the button to raise the window.

He glanced out the windows. A few people huddled inside the glassed in station. He didn't see Fong.

Turner took in a deep breath and opened his door. It was blown back against him. He shoved at it, got it open, and dashed the few feet into the station.

None of the people in the immediate vicinity was Fong. Thoughts flitted through his mind. Why the hell did Fong call from here? Should he wait for back-up? He moved down the steps toward the platform.

At this point the El tracks ran down the center of the expressway with the stations at street level. He crept down the stairs. No one huddled under the overhang that stretched five El car lengths beyond the station. The overhang along with the station was newly renovated. The overhang gleamed in the cleansing rain. It was held up by foot-thick struts every ten feet. Between the struts were metallic placard holders for giant ads, sealed against the rain.

Traffic on the expressway inched by in both directions. He walked down two El car lengths. The overhang by this point would protect someone from falling rain, but not from the driving maelstrom that this storm was. He was about to turn back when he saw a body fall just behind the next strut.

Turner hurried forward. Ten feet away, he saw it was Fong. He hurried forward and knelt next to the tech.

Fong was breathing.

Thunder and lightning danced about them.

Turner looked up. Huddled against the strut on the side most out of the storm was the Superintendent of Police, Izzy Labato.

Saturday 8:47 P.M.

The first thing Labato did was toss a phone at Turner. The Superintendent's put his face close enough to Turner's so he didn't have to shout. "That's Fong's. I knew a message on it would get you here. You are such a fucking do-gooder."

Turner breathed deeply. "You."

Labato smiled, "All of us."

"All?"

"Anybody who has been down here since the Tasing incident has been in on it. We really did want you at a press conference. We thought your partner would be funnier than all hell and a perfect antidote to all that heroic bullshit. Brandon Smeek, Adam Edberg, Clayton Griffin, Daniel Currington, Frank Bortz, that dumb fuck Commander from the local district Palakowski, Ken Coscarelli, Chris Randall from the FBI.

"Not Carruthers's lawyer, Cannon?"

"A useless tool, but not one of us, and not all the members of the Police Board, just DeGroot. He was enough."

"All to do what?"

"Why to get you and Fenwick, but especially you."

Turner felt the rain plastering against his skin. He wondered if he'd live long enough to be dry again. Fong was completely soaked. Turner didn't dare try to jump the tracks to get to safety. He saw Labato's gun. A wild dash in dry weather was risky with the electrified third rail. In the rain while carrying Fong, a slip to death was far more likely than sure-footed safety.

Turner kept one hand on Fong's shoulder. He could feel him breathing. With the other, he wiped away the rain from his own face. The overhang kept some of the worst of the downpour off them, but the wind carried enough blasts of spray to drench them.

Why was Labato even talking to him? Unless there was a sniper waiting, and the poor visibility in the rain or Turner's current position was all that were keeping him alive. If he tried to run, he'd be an even bigger target.

Turner said, "The same sniper who killed the two activists is here now. You brought him with you to kill us this time, but you didn't count on the pouring rain."

"It'll let up."

"Not soon enough to save you." Turner asked, "Who is the sniper?"

"DeGroot. Besides police training, he was Special Forces in the Army."

Turner said, "Carruthers was supposed to kill us that night."

Labato said, "There's not supposed to be a Tased cop. You think the police brass cares about dead thugs, no matter what color?"

"Some do."

"Can't help that."

"Molton."

"We'll get rid of him, reassign him, force him to retire. He's as stubborn as you."

"You are really that much of a shit."

"There were enough of us who feel that way that we won an election."

"Wasn't leaving Carruthers to do the shooting kind of leaving things to random chance?"

"Or you'd kill him. That would work, too. Save us all our jobs."

"Kind of a dumb plan."

"Who the hell knew you'd do something heroic?"

"It was just instinct," Turner said.

"Not my fault you can do things that are lucky."

"You counted on Carruthers being a good shot? You counted on no one taking pictures?"

Labato said, "Pretty much worked."

Turner guessed he hadn't seen what Fong had uncovered.

"Why didn't you guys just kill Carruthers?"

"We thought of that. That's not how it works."

"That's more tons of bullshit than produced by all the bulls on the planet since the big bang."

Turner wondered where Fenwick was. Where the sniper was.

Labato asked, "Do you think we haven't had you in our sights for a long time? Did you think Carruthers was working with the Catholic Church without direction and guidance? What kind of hubris do you have that you didn't think what you were doing wasn't being noticed? Did you think the church was going to go quietly or take this lying down? You caused scandal to the faithful."

Turner could imagine Fenwick's snort. With his arm still on Fong, he felt the man still breathing. The wind still drove the rain onto them. He asked, "Why save Carruthers all these years?"

"You know the drill. Family, connections, clout."

"You condone incompetence?"

"Do you think that makes a difference?"

"Don't you?"

"And you're so fucking perfect?"

"You want us dead because we're competent?"

"Because you broke the code."

"Fuck you and your code."

"You sound like your partner."

"It's catching. Why didn't you have the sniper kill us?"

"Efficient in the short term, you're right, but there were some among us who objected to blatantly killing two detectives. A few were pushing to simply destroy your careers. That was untenable. And besides, if we had to, we wanted to blame your deaths on activists getting even with cops."

"Innocent people died."

"We could have killed two random people anywhere. Or one. Or a thousand. We didn't care. In this case, only two. It was fun to watch you two scramble around, basically watching you try to solve your own murders."

"And Carruthers shooting us?"

"Blamed on the kid for being a danger. Collateral damage. And we were willing to sacrifice Carruthers. He's hated you for so long. It was his idea. Couldn't plan it, of course, but the germ came from him. Collateral damage from a street killing."

"One of his few ideas ever," Turner said.

"Don't care how many he had."

The storm continued unabated. Labato was hunched nearly double. Their faces were barely a foot apart. Rain pounded on the metal roof. Being under the canopy continued to keep them from the worst of the drenching downpour, but the spray blown by the wind was as bad as ever.

Lightning struck at the top of the bridge over the Eisenhower Expressway a block behind them. The explosion of sound made Turner jump.

"You were never going to win," Labato said. "You cannot win. The forces of the world are arrayed against you."

Turner looked at the metal around them and said, "I think we should move from under here."

"You afraid for your immortal soul? You should be."

Turner put his arms under Fong's shoulders, and with him began to edge backwards toward the station. He wasn't sure he wanted to take the stairs and go higher up, but he felt exposed and vulnerable from the words, and the weather, and the sniper he was sure had to be nearby. He then realized he could barely see to the buildings on the far side of the surrounding streets. The sniper would have the same barrier to seeing him.

Behind Labato, lightning hit the juncture of the walkway where the metal canopy met the concrete walkway. Flashes of electricity surged toward them.

Turner threw himself on top of Fong.

Labato gave a triumphant snarl.

Turner looked up.

The flash rushing toward them must have hit some kind of transformer a few feet behind Labato. A cascade of sparks flew around him, illuminating him like a saint in a medieval painting. Labato fell to the ground.

Turner heard the sound of metal twisting and grinding against itself. It rose to a screech that almost drowned out the din of the storm.

Turner yanked and dragged the still unconscious Fong until he and the comatose man were at the next strut. It took only a few seconds. He turned to go back for the prone superintendent, but the lightning hit the far end of the overhang and travelled down it towards them. It hit the twisted break in the overhang, burst into a shower of sparks. The metal groaned louder than the thunder and crashed to the pavement crushing the Superintendent under it.

As Turner looked up, he saw the canopy come crashing down toward him. Electricity crackled for an instant around them, and it was gone.

Turner glanced back. The rain sluiced through the blood coming from the mush that was the Superintendent. Labato was crushed, the entire top half of his body smashed to pulp under the weight of the fallen canopy.

Turner scrambled back on hands and knees. The next canopy,

hanging by a few fragile strips of metal, swayed in the wind, creaked, and caught him a glancing blow as it fell.

Turner attempted to rise, but found that his leg was pinned by the wreckage. He looked back. Fenwick was dashing down the concrete stairs, then thrusting away debris, and hurtling toward him.

For a few seconds, he lost sight of him behind some debris, but then Fenwick emerged from the other side of the crumbled mass. He rushed forward. He stopped at Fong, rushed to Turner, "You okay?"

Turner nodded. He pointed at the Superintendent. "He was behind it all."

Fenwick glanced at the Superintendent. Fenwick said, "I hope it lasted long enough to hurt."

Saturday 10:05 P.M.

Minutes later, Fenwick had inched Turner and Fong toward the next still standing overhang. Turner's leg was still caught. Fenwick heaved at the metal strut but couldn't budge it.

Turner looked back at the quickly dissipating bloody gray rivulets of remnants of the Police Superintendent.

Turner saw two men running from the far end of the platform toward them. They passed the Superintendent. They carried guns in their outstretched hands. Fenwick began to reach for his weapon.

Turner stopped him.

Up close, they were two young men in their early twenties. They stopped at Turner and yelled, "You Paul?"

Turner nodded.

"You're okay?"

Turner nodded.

"You're safe." It wasn't a question.

Another nod.

Fenwick bellowed, "Who the hell are you guys?"

The youngest said, "Neighborhood watch. Your sniper is on top of that building." He pointed across the lines of barely moving traffic to a three-story building. "He's not going anywhere, but he's very wet." He put his gun away.

Fenwick shouted, "We gotta move this overhang off my partner."

The two newcomers and Fenwick heaved. With Turner pushing from underneath, they managed to raise it enough so he could scrabble away. They let it thunk to the ground.

Pain shot from his leg.

Fong stirred. On their knees, Fenwick, with as much help as the new guys could provide, got them just inside the first door of the station. Seeing they were inside and out of the storm, the two newcomers dashed off down the platform continuing to the farther doors, up the stairs, and away.

Turner sat up against the glass. He listened to the rain still slashing against the pane, an inch the other side of his ear. Once again, he was sodden. They had propped up Fong next to him. Fenwick was on his feet on his phone. Turner heard sirens in the distance. Through the downpour, he began to see rotating lights.

Fong stirred. Turner put a hand on his arm. Fenwick knelt on the other side. Fong made eye contact with Turner. Fong said, "I'm not dead. Good."

Turner asked, "What happened?"

"The Superintendent was on the platform. He asked to use my phone. I got bashed."

Turner said, "He confessed. None of it got recorded."

Fong smiled. "I've been wearing camera devices since all this started."

"Devices?" Fenwick asked.

"Backups to backups."

"It recorded while you were unconscious through this storm?"

Fong gasped and winced. "I think I broke some ribs." He gave a grin. "Of course it worked through all this. Am I an electronic genius? Yes. It's on the devices here. It was streamed live to my basement. Remember I offered to set up 360° recording for you guys? I set myself up that way. I'm no fool."

In the hospital, they were hooked up to a million things. Molton appeared.

Turner thought it was kind of amusing to watch Fenwick hover like a mother hen. A nurse at one point tried to shoo him out. That didn't work.

Although his leg throbbed, Turner thought it was being dry that most helped him feel better. The doctors quickly determined that his leg was not crushed or broken, but everything just short of that. They stitched him up and applied cold compresses.

Once he was treated, Fong set up a computer, and they watched his recording. Molton knew a friendly judge who was summoned. They watched again. The judge ordered arrests. Molton sent out his minions under the direction of Roosevelt and Wilson. However, he left to help effect the arrests of the highest up brass.

DeGroot was found half-drowned, but alive, tied next to a sniper rifle with his prints on it.

Saturday 11:15 P.M.

Much later, after Ben had sat with Paul until he was ready to be discharged from the hospital, they parked in their own driveway. Paul saw Mrs. Talucci on her porch. He said to Ben, "I'll be right in."

Paul climbed Mrs. Talucci's porch and leaned his butt against the railing. Despite the pain pills he'd been given, his leg still hurt, and he limped.

She put her knitting down but continued a gentle rocking. A few lingering showers were predicted, but the air was cooler. The front had finally passed.

He told her what happened.

He finished. "The guys who caught the sniper, the ones who joined Fenwick and me on the platform, said they were from the Neighborhood Watch. There is no Neighborhood Watch."

Mrs. Talucci smiled. "Fenwick called the station. He got Barb Dams. She called Molton, and all the cavalry she could think of, including me. She and I figured there had to be at least one sniper. I couldn't mount an assault. I am not all-powerful, despite my reputation, but I could do a little."

"You did a lot."

"Enough, I hope."

He hugged her.

She said, "The boys were never going to lose their father or Ben his husband. Not if I had anything to say about it." She ceased rocking. "I haven't seen the news. What will happen now?"

"Much of it has happened or is just finishing up. Fong was wired. He was lucky the lightning was not directly attracted to him, but we were under that overhang that saved us while it killed the bad guy. We've got enough to break this ring of silence." Turner smiled. "As far as I know, Fong may have posted it online, sent it to every media outlet on the planet. Although the key probably is that U.S. Attorney Whitaker is doing the investigating and taking a lot of it out of the hands of the corrupt local folks. He even said he got a lead on two detectives from Area One that the assistant Chief of Detectives put up to trying to impersonate us. Roosevelt and Johnson found that out and told us when they stopped by the hospital."

Mrs. Talucci said, "Hell of a nerve." She picked up her knitting. "I hear they've arrested nearly half the top brass in the city."

"Maybe not quite that many. Molton's going to hold a press conference tomorrow to answer questions about how Superintendent Labato, assistant Chief of Detectives Clayton Griffin, Commander Palakowski, Adam Edberg from the mayor's office, State's Attorney Brandon Smeek, and a few small fry conspired to protect Carruthers and kill me and Fenwick. I don't think he'll try and explain the intricacies of who did what. They'll sort out Fong's video. According to Molton the more of them who hear it, the more of them who are trying to make deals, on Carruthers, us, and the deaths of Shaitan and Bettencourt."

"So those last two died for nothing."

"The conspirators didn't care. Once Carruthers missed, that plot was set in motion. The rumors about the killings got on the news so fast because it was planted by the conspirators. We know the Superintendent was behind the whole thing."

Mrs. Talucci nodded. "Corruption in the department? Has to go to the top. How can it not?"

"At least it did here."

Fourth of July 4:31 P.M.

"So all that heroic bullshit that first day was to save our own butts? We weren't heroes?"

Madge stirred the coals. The two families were enjoying their Fourth of July holiday together in the Turner's backyard.

Madge said, "Bullshit? An heroic action doesn't become less heroic because of its motivation. The result was heroic."

Fenwick said, "I feel like a damn fool."

Madge said, "And this is new?"

"I don't like to feel like a damn fool and get shot."

"You saved DeShawn. He's out of the hospital, and he and his parents plan to be at the ceremony honoring you both, which you have been grumbling about continuously."

"And you've been nagging about my grumbling for just as long."

Madge took out her phone and checked the time. She said, "You have two minutes of free grumbling."

Fenwick looked at Ben and Paul. "She does this."

Madge said, "One minute fifty seconds."

"Fine." Fenwick gave it his best silent fume, shoulders hunched, lips pursed, gut sucked in.

Madge was immune.

Turner stopped setting out plates and utensils. Ben reentered the kitchen and moments later backed onto the porch. He was carrying a Fourth of July sheet cake with red, white, and blue icing in the shape of a flag.

They oohed and aahed.

Ben put the cake down then pulled several sparklers out of his back pocket. He placed one on each corner of the cake and lit them. They glistened in the afternoon light.

Fenwick said, "We were discussing heroism."

Brian said, "Are we for or against it?"

Fenwick said, "We lived through it."

Paul said, "That's about all you can expect, really."

Fenwick, "So they were a bunch of delusional fools? Or were we the delusional fools?"

Ben asked, "Are we talking about the protesters, the police brass, or both?"

Paul said, "All of the above?"

Fenwick said, "The cops all got their asses arrested. We've got too many recordings of too much for any of them to survive unscathed. I just wished I'd have been there to laugh in their faces as they got hauled off."

Madge said, "Probably not as helpful as anyone would have liked." She smiled, "But an eminently satisfying moment that you can fantasize about."

Ben cut the cake.

Fourth of July 11:04 P.M.

Jeff helped with the cleaning from the party late into the evening. Mostly, he tried to get out of chores. His luck had run thin in recent years, as the manipulations "I'm in a wheelchair," or "I'm on crutches," and "I'm smart and have too much homework," had long since ceased to get him surcease from familial responsibility.

Paul took the time with him putting away the last dishes as Jeff dried them. Paul could hear the murmur of Ben and Brian's voices from the swing on the front porch. All the doors and windows were open to catch the fresh breeze. A new storm system was expected, but with nothing as severe as the previous one.

Paul suspected Jeff's delaying and helping meant he was up to something, or he wanted to talk.

Last dish done and counter wiped, Jeff said, "Can you help me onto the back porch?"

Jeff didn't really need such help as the whole house was wheelchair accessible, but Jeff reached for his crutches, pulled himself out of the chair and toward the back door. Paul followed and was ready to help as Jeff needed.

Paul sat down on the swing next to him. Jeff kept his eyes focused on his empty lap. Paul looked out at the mist-enshrouded back yard. He let the silence stretch. The shadows of night gathered around them.

Jeff broke the new silence. "Are they still going to try to kill you?" The light from the kitchen drifted onto the porch and he could see the near-tears in his son's eyes.

Before Paul could answer, Jeff continued, "Don't lie to me. I'm not stupid. I know you solved all this. I know powerful people have fallen. I read the papers. I listen to you and Ben talk. It's what you don't say when we're around."

"Uh?"

"You leave out danger and foreboding completely. And yet when you go out, you always check everything."

"I always do. I'm a cop. We've discussed my job. What more can I say or do to help you?"

Jeff gave a gruff, "I'm not sure," in his newly discovered older-teen voice. He continued, "Sometimes bad guys win. Some of those guys might get away with what they did."

"Sometimes they do. But it's the kind of person I am that makes a difference. Not what I can get away with and lie about. For me, it doesn't matter how much money or power you have. The key is always kindness, rich or poor."

They sat next to each other in silence for another while. The noises of the neighborhood muttered and flowed around them.

Jeff said, "Good is something you do, not something you talk about. Some medals are pinned to your soul, not to your jacket. You know who said that?"

Paul shook his head.

"Gino Bartali, an Italian cycling champion who saved over eight hundred Jews in World War II. That's what you and Mr. Fenwick do. You always do right."

"As best we can."

"And Mr. Fenwick just doesn't want the publicity."

Paul felt his son snuggle slightly. He looked down at him. Jeff's eyes met his in that forthright way they'd had since he'd met his eyes the day he was born.

"Did you almost die?" Jeff asked.

"Yes."

"I was scared for you."

"I appreciate that. How did you know things were bad?"

"There's certain things to watch for around here. One is when Mrs. Talucci goes into full protection mode. She doesn't do that unless something is really wrong."

"That's pretty observant."

"And Ben was worried. You know how I try to let him be competitive when I play chess with him?"

"Yeah."

"He didn't even try. He was too distracted to finish. You guys really love each other."

"Yes, we do." He sighed. "We've talked about my job."

"Yeah, but this felt different. All the violence in all the papers. All the fear that's attached to being a cop, a detective, seemed worse this summer. Or I was more scared."

"I'm sorry you were scared. You know I take every precaution."

"Yeah, but that doesn't stop there being bad people in the world."

Paul said, "I don't think there's anything that can stop there being bad people in the world. We've been at this as a species for what, millions of years, and at what we call being civilized for thousands of years, and we still haven't figured out how to stop being mean to each other."

"I want it to stop."

"Me too."

"That's your job. To stop it."

"It's my job to do what I can. What's most important to me is being kind and loving to you boys and to Ben, and to myself if I can manage that, too. To teach you boys that's the best way to live. Even then, I don't always succeed, but I always try."

"You know dad, sometimes you do weird stuff."

They smiled at each other. "All parents do, I think," Paul said.

"But you believe what you say. And you try to live by those beliefs. Lots of people say stuff and don't mean it."

"I do my best."

"I know." They were silent several moments then Jeff whispered, "There's so much violence in the world."

Paul whispered back, "I know."

"Can anybody make it stop?"

"I don't know," Paul said.

They watched the darkness in silence a bit longer.

Distant lightning flashed far to the west. A very far rumble of thunder nuzzled their ears.

Jeff said, "Storms are some of my earliest memories. Brian used to run to wherever you were. He was always scared."

When Brian was small, this was true. He was far too superior to the elements by this point in his teenage life to admit such had ever happened.

"I remember that too." Paul said, "He'd stay close and watch television. You'd watch him with your little brother eyes."

Thunder rumbled.

Jeff said, "There's always going to be storms."

"Yes."

The boy nodded then said, "I still like storms especially when you're around."

About the Author

Mark Zubro is the author of thirty-five novels and five short stories. His book *A Simple Suburban Murder* won the Lambda Literary Award for Best Gay Men's mystery. He spends his time reading, writing, napping, and eating chocolate.

CPSIA information can be obtained
at www.ICGtesting.com
Printed in the USA
LVOW07s2132051217
558563LV00020B/4/P